OTHER BOOKS by KASSANDRA LAMB

The Kate Huntington Mysteries
Psychotherapist Kate Huntington helps others cope with trauma, but she has led a charmed life...until a killer rips it apart. (10 novels) ~ Plus the **Kate on Vacation Mysteries** (4 novellas)

The C.o.P. on the Scene Mysteries
Eight days into her new job as Chief of Police in a small Florida city, Judith Anderson finds herself one step behind a serial killer. (spinoff from the Kate Huntington series; 5 stories–more to come)

The Marcia Banks and Buddy Cozy Mysteries
Marcia Banks trains service dogs for veterans, and solves crimes on the side, with the help of her Black Lab, Buddy. (13 novels/novellas)

The Unintended Consequences Trilogy
writing as Jessica Dale ~ A sweet romance combined with three chilling mysteries, and a couple of ghosts. (3 stories)

Malignant Memories

a C.o.P. on the Scene Mystery
Kassandra Lamb

a mistero press publication

Published by *misterio press LLC*

Cover art by Melinda VanLone,Book Cover Corner; Photo credits: (woman) © Konstantin Kamenetskiy |Dreamstime.com; (motel) © Imageegami | Dreamstim e.com; (city skyline) © AlexGrichenko | Dreamstime.com (purchased right to use)

CHAPTER ONE

The woman seemed off.

Walking toward the elevators—something I did umpteen times a day—my steps slowed. I watched her out of my peripheral vision.

Then I stopped and pivoted, standing a few feet away, just in case...

The woman was waiting patiently in front of the watch desk for the sergeant to finish a phone call. She was young, early to mid-twenties, dark haired, and wore a cotton dress, high-necked and long-sleeved, a faded red with a muted flowery print.

Its skirt skimmed the middle of her bare calves. Sneakers, grayed with age adorned her feet. No socks.

A plain Jane at first glance—except her high cheekbones, doe-like brown eyes and plump lips would be quite beautiful with a touch of makeup.

And a bit more flesh on her bones. The dress hung loose on her too slender frame.

And there was definitely something odd about her, besides the outdated dress. Odd enough that I was wishing we had a proper police reception area, with the sergeant's desk behind bullet-proof glass. One of these days I'd talk the city council into giving my department its own building.

It was her expression—vague, almost dreamlike. Was she high on something?

Sergeant Armstrong hung up his phone and looked up, his expression carefully neutral. But his hand, under the edge of the desk, was poised near his holstered pistol.

He's noticed.

"Can I help you, ma'am?" he said.

"I don't know." Her voice was soft and as vague as her glassy eyes. She reached into a pocket in her skirt.

I tensed, bracing to lunge and restrain her if she pulled a weapon.

But she produced a thin strip of white cardstock. I quietly expelled air.

Armstrong's hand was now *on* his gun's butt, the holster unsnapped. He glanced over at me, hovering nearby, then back at the woman.

She held a business card up for him to read, without relinquishing it. "Is this me? Am I this person?" Her tone was now one part desperation, one part astonishment. "Am I Judith Anderson, the Chief of Police?"

Twenty minutes later, I was staring through the one-way mirror into the smaller of our two interview rooms. The woman sat at the table, a paper cup of water in front of her.

Despite the grimness of the situation, I suppressed a chuckle at the memory of Armstrong's reaction when she'd asked if she was me. His eyebrows had shot up to where his hairline would be, if he didn't shave his head.

I'd stepped up to the desk at that point. "What's your name, ma'am?"

She shook her head. "I don't know." I had to strain to hear her.

"Do you know where you are?"

"In a police station?"

I mean..." I waved a hand in the air, to indicate she should think beyond the building we were in.

"A city?" she said, a question mark still in her voice.

I gentled my own voice. "Do you know what city?"

She shook her head again. "I found the card in my pocket." She moved her hand vaguely toward her skirt.

And that's when I'd noticed that some of the flowers on her dress were not as muted as the others. They were a darker, brighter red, and round, more or less. Were they berries? *No... Shit!*

I'd spotted my young assistant, Officer Gloria Barnes coming my way. As usual, her uniform was meticulously pressed, her dark hair up in a neat bun, and her eyes eager for a new day.

I stifled a sigh. How long would it take for this job to snuff out that rookie eagerness?

I motioned her over. In a low voice, I said, "Get a large evidence bag and find that woman something else to wear, then put her in an interview room." I gestured with my chin toward the woman in front of the sarge's desk. "Bag her clothes and take them to Bert's lab for analysis."

"Why do you want her clothes analyzed?" Barnes asked.

"See those dark red berries on her dress?"

She'd nodded.

"They aren't berries," I'd said. "They're blood."

Lieutenant Bradley, my second in command, stuck his well-groomed head into the observation room, pulling me back to the here-and-now. "Chief, we just got a homicide call. Middle-aged white guy at the Beachview Inn."

"Drugs?" The Beachview wasn't exactly known for high-class patrons.

He shook his head. "Doesn't look that way. He was found naked in his room. Lots of blood, the uniform said."

Hmm... My mind flashed again to those dark red "berries" on our Jane Doe's dress.

And here I'd been thinking, just this morning, that things had been quiet for a whole month. I was even getting a little bored.

Now the week was off to an all too interesting start. And not the best timing, with one of my detectives tied up in a training in Jacksonville and another out sick.

I ran a hand through my short dark hair. *As Aunt Jean would say, watch what you put out into the universe.*

Barnes was not happy that she had to stay behind and deal with our mysterious visitor. I threw her a bone. "Chat her up. See what she has to say for herself."

"About what?" Barnes asked.

"Anything. Where she's from, what she's been doing recently? See if she can remember anything at all." I pulled my slim wallet from the back pocket of my black pantsuit's slacks and plucked out a twenty-dollar bill. "And see if she wants something to eat from the vending machines."

The woman had said a polite *no* earlier to coffee, tea or soda. *Who doesn't drink at least one of those beverages?*

Personally, I was useless until I'd had at least two cups of caffeine in the morning.

"But don't let her get away from us," I added, "not until we figure out what's going on."

Barnes nodded. "Can I arrest her if I have to?" she asked, a bit too eagerly.

"No, but you can officially detain her, if need be. Suspicion of assault."

CHAPTER TWO

Lieutenant Bradley—nattily dressed in a navy blazer, gray slacks and a light blue shirt that matched his eyes—drove us to the Beachview Inn in his police-issued sedan. It was one of two unmarked cars in our motor pool now. The previous chief had preferred having detectives use their own cars and submit mileage. But I'd crunched the numbers and discovered, surprisingly, that owning a small fleet of unmarked vehicles would ultimately be cheaper. I had two more in my budget request for next year.

The Beachview was only twenty minutes from the municipal building, which housed the police department as well as the city government. Indeed anything in my adopted town of Starling, Florida was no more than twenty minutes from anything else, barring traffic issues. It was not a big city.

The Beachview Inn was ancient and nowhere near a beach. It was in Starling's tiny red-light district on the northeastern edge of the city—a row of rooms with peeling pastel walls and a separate brick box of a building that housed the office.

"Pull in over there," I said to Bradley, pointing to the broad-shouldered man in a khaki uniform leaning against a Clover County Sheriff's Department cruiser.

I climbed out of the car. "Good morning, Sheriff."

Sheriff Sam Pierson nodded, a slightly impish smile on his face. "Mornin', Chief."

Neither of us were about to let on that we'd already seen each other this morning, when we woke up—in my bed—then had a quick cup of coffee and toast at my breakfast bar, before starting our official workdays.

I leaned against the fender of his cruiser, leaving a few inches between us.

Bradley, one of his classic half-smiles on his handsome, boyish face, stood by his car, giving us some privacy.

I am not a short woman, but I had to tilt my head to look up at Sam beside me. He had his beige wannabe-Stetson shoved back some, exposing short sandy-gray hair. Crow's feet bracketed his blue eyes, above tanned cheeks.

For a moment, the urge to stand on tiptoes and kiss those crow's feet was almost irresistible.

Down, girl, I told myself and said out loud, "Is this another one of those properties that straddles the city/county line?"

He shook his head. "No, but it's close to the line. The manager, Fred Murdock, he calls me when there's a big problem."

I gave him a confused look.

Sam sighed. "Previously, when he called the Starling police, they rarely arrived in anything resembling a timely manner. So, if the problem was a big one, he'd call me instead of 911."

"Previously, as in under the command of my predecessor." Said predecessor was awaiting trial on corruption charges for taking bribes from various local criminals. And some of those locals apparently conducted their nefarious business at this motel. I made a mental note to have the watch commanders beef up patrols here, especially at night.

Sam was nodding.

"Did you suspect Chief Black was being paid off to look the other way?" I asked.

"Not at the time. I just assumed his people were as lazy as he was." He sighed again. "And anything that happens at the Beachview that merits calling law enforcement, well it ain't gonna be pretty."

I scanned the area. The place was probably once quite festive looking, each unit painted in light shades of blue, pink, yellow or lavender. But the phrase "gone to seed" was inadequate to describe its current state. "Lemme guess, very few people who rent a room here actually stay all night."

"Sometimes the druggies do, if they pass out. Come on, I'll introduce you to Fred."

One sad, straggly palm tree adorned the dirt patch in front of the grimy glass door leading into the office. Sam had reached for the handle when a voice hailed us. "Chief, Lieu, over here."

The kid dressed up like a police officer seemed vaguely familiar. I glanced at his name tag as he jogged toward us. *Thompson.* Ah, yes, the rookie who'd pulled protection detail last fall when an innocent child was the focus of unknown criminals.

The officer had been standing next to an older couple before coming over to us. He tilted his head back toward the pair. "Wife found the body."

Bradley and I nodded in unison. "I'll be along in a minute," I said, gesturing for Bradley to follow the rookie back to the witnesses.

Sam gave me a small smile. "We'll make this quick." He knew me well. I was itching to be in on the interview with the older couple.

A balding, jowly white man stood behind the fake wood counter in the motel's office. Sam gestured toward him, then at me. "Fred Murdock, meet the new Chief of Police of Starling. Chief, this is the Beachview's manager."

I offered my hand. The man seemed startled, but quickly recovered. He wiped his palm on his tee shirt's front and shook my proffered hand. The shirt, dark gray, was rumpled, but it looked clean.

Still... I glanced around the office, a visible layer of dust covering just about every surface. I planned to wash my hands at the first opportunity.

I pulled out one of my cards. "I understand you've had problems in the past with our officers not showing up promptly. Call me if you have any such issues in the future." I did not write my private line number on the back of the card as I often did. I was hoping the man didn't call, but I needed to mend fences here, restore faith in our department.

"I'll fill Fred in on the details of the change of management at SPD," Sam said. "Go on to your crime scene."

I nodded. "Nice meeting you, Mr. Murdock." I turned and headed for the door before he could respond.

Officer Thompson was standing near the older couple outside the fourth unit down. He came to attention as I approached, stopping just short of saluting. "Chief Anderson, these are the Blanchards, Ellie and Hank, from Pensicola."

"At ease, Officer," I muttered for his ears only, while I quickly studied the witnesses.

Hank was a big lumberjack of a man, with a thatch of steely gray hair and only a small paunch pushing against his belt. He wore jeans and a green plaid flannel shirt. His white skin was tanned to a dangerous level, with age spots sprinkled on the backs of big hands. I doubted he used sunscreen.

Ellie was short and plump with hardly any wrinkles on her fair face. Her blondish-gray hair was cut in a shoulder-length bob and topped with a wide-brimmed straw hat. She wore a brightly colored muumuu, with a black sweater draped over her shoulders, and a big smile.

Thompson glanced down at his notepad. "Mrs. Blanchard saw the door was–"

The woman and I held up a hand each. "Ellie," she said.

The rookie's cheeks pinked, and he opened his mouth.

I saved him from either having to awkwardly use her first name or ignore her request. "I'd rather hear it from *Ellie* myself."

"Hank and me," she said, "we're here 'cause of our fiftieth anniversary, retracin' the steps of our honeymoon. Only this place was a lot nicer back then."

They had to have married fairly young, as they didn't look much older than late sixties.

"We got in late, after ten. This mornin', I was walkin' past that room." Ellie gestured toward the open doorway of the next unit over, which was adorned with half a roll of crime scene tape. "And I saw the door sittin' ajar, so I poked it a little farther open, callin' out, 'Hello, y'all okay in there?'"

"Curiosity killed the cat," Hank muttered, but he had a faint, indulgent smile on his face.

"Meow," Ellie said with a small grin. It had the feel of a well-used exchange.

Then her grin faded. "There was so much bl-blood," she stuttered.

"Did you go in?" I asked.

"No, I high-tailed it down to the office and told the young man behind the desk someone had been hurt. He didn't seem all that interested, so I pulled out my cell and called 911."

Hank leaned his head down slightly, used to talking to someone much shorter. He had a good six inches on my own five-seven, and even more on his short wife. "We pushed the door open far enough to see..." He paused, cleared his throat. "The man wasn't breathin' and he was naked, so we stayed out here, guardin' the door 'til this young fellow arrived." He gestured toward Thompson.

The *young fellow* turned to me. "I went in to check for a pulse, otherwise I didn't disturb anything. Ambulance is on the way."

As if on cue, an ambulance turned into the parking lot, its lights flashing and siren screaming. It stopped, the siren ending abruptly with a sickly squawk, and two white-clad paramedics jumped out.

I held up a hand and called over. "Just one of you for now, with me."

They both froze in the act of pulling equipment from compartments on the side of the vehicle. The older of the two trotted over to me.

"You think he's deceased?" he asked.

I nodded. "Go check, but try not to disturb anything you don't have to."

The guy frowned. "This ain't my first rodeo."

I gave him a half smile by way of apology. I'd only been in this job for seven months now and had barely gotten to know my own officers, much less the Starling Fire Department's personnel.

"Thompson, get rid of some of this tape here." I pointed to the doorway. "And expand the scene to include all the rooms on this side and the parking lot."

I refrained from pointing out in front of civilians that you start by taping off a larger exterior perimeter. You can always pull it in later if warranted.

Hadn't his training officer taught him that? But then again, this might be his first major crime scene. We didn't have all that many homicides in Starling, not since we'd caught that serial killer last fall.

The paramedic had paused at the now liberated motel room doorway. He donned disposable booties over his shoes, gave me a nod, and ducked under the one remaining, chest-high piece of crime scene tape.

Bradley was on his phone. "I'm calling Bert and Ernie."

Thompson, his hands full of crumpled tape, snickered.

I glared at him, and his white pimply face paled even further. Yes, our crime scene techs carried the names of the Sesame Street characters—and they even looked the parts—which gave us all moments of amusement. But not in front of civilians.

I glanced at Ellie and Hank, who were watching us intently, then met Thompson's gaze again.

He swallowed hard and nodded slightly. Message received.

I turned on my heel, donned my own fashionable blue paper booties, and followed the paramedic into the motel room.

Ellie was right. There was a *lot* of blood. Spatter on the walls and even the ceiling, and one side of the bed—under the naked, overweight victim—was soaked with it.

The heat was on in the room, even though the March day was quickly heading toward eighty. The hot stuffy air, permeated with the coppery smell of blood and the stench of released bowels, made my stomach heave. It threatened to give back my breakfast toast.

I swallowed hard and opened my mouth to breathe through it, rather than through my nose. That helped some.

"I can't officially pronounce him, but he's long gone," the paramedic said from the bedside. "Skin is cool to the touch."

I nodded, and he stepped around me and toward the door. "I'll check that the ME's people are on the way."

"Thanks."

My hands in my jacket pockets, I turned in a slow circle, taking in the other furniture. A low dresser with three drawers, a small table and a straight-back chair, facing out toward the room, as if someone had sat there recently.

But the items on top of the table and dresser were the most interesting parts of the scene. A camera tripod was set up on the dresser and a portable row of bright lights, still on, was on the table, with cardboard covered in aluminum foil propped behind it to direct the light toward the bed. But no camera.

"Making porn," Bradley said from the doorway, mimicking me with his hands in his pockets.

"Looks that way." I retraced my own steps back to the door, and Bradley and I moved out into the fresh air.

I gratefully filled my lungs with it.

Within twenty minutes the parking lot was crowded with vehicles, including a couple of cruisers, Bert and Ernie's van, and a car with *Medical Examiner* on the door.

The latter had produced a young pathologist, Sandy Krone, who had geared up in protective clothing, goggles and such. She was now examining the body inside the room.

Bert and Ernie, also looking like spacemen in their protective gear, were in there as well, trying to stay out of Sandy's way as they collected evidence.

Bert came to the open doorway. "Chief, lemme show you something."

I donned blue nitrile gloves, and again the shoe coverings, and followed him.

"The place is wiped clean of fingerprints," he said over his shoulder.

"Say what?" That was more than a little unusual. There should be dozens, even hundreds of prints in the room.

"Only a couple of partials," he said. "Under the handles in the bathtub, probably from somebody turning the water on or off."

Then he pointed to the straight-back chair facing out into the room. "I think there were three people here."

"Why do you say that?"

"Look closer."

Slightly annoyed, I leaned over some and studied the chair. There were specks of blood on the edges of the chair's back and on the legs, but the area in the middle of the back and the front rungs between the legs were clean. "Someone was sitting here when the guy was being stabbed."

"Could be," Bert said. "Ernie's getting something from our van to wrap the chair. We're taking the whole thing to the lab."

"Anything else interesting?"

"Yep. Blood and a few hairs in the drain in the bathtub. Some long blond, one short and dark." He frowned. "No hair follicles, though."

Which meant DNA extraction would be unlikely.

"Dark one could've come from the victim," Bert added.

"Nope," Sandy said from behind us. "This guy hasn't showered anytime recently."

I turned to her. "How do you stand the smells?"

She shrugged, her protective coverall rustling. "You get used to them."

I glanced toward Bert, tall and thin, with wispy dark hair—currently under a hairnet—and serious eyes. I hid a smile. He really did look like his Muppet namesake.

He rolled his eyes. "I never have."

Sandy gave him a lopsided grin. "You get to grab your evidence and run. I spend much more time with the corpse."

"Any ID on the victim?" I asked.

Both Sandy and Bert shook there heads.

"Anything else?"

Bert nodded. "I did a quick blood-typing on some of the fresher smears on the walls. AB positive, same as the victim's."

I glanced at Sandy. She was doing something I didn't really want to think about to the body. But she gave a slight nod, indicating she had typed his blood for Bert.

Again, I swallowed hard. Despite all my years as a homicide cop in Baltimore, I'd never become totally used to the sight and smell of blood. I was beginning to think it was hereditary. My Aunt Jean fainted at the sight of blood, as had my grandfather.

"But there are other bloodstains here." Bert was waving a hand toward the dark green wall above the old-fashioned wooden headboard. Was it painted that color on purpose to disguise the bodily fluids the occupants left behind?

My stomach flip-flopped again.

"The fresher blood is over top of some of them," Bert continued. "We're gonna have to cut out a portion of the wall and take it to the lab to analyze all of them. Plus the bed frame."

I grimaced. *Fred Murdock's gonna love that.*

"You're thinking more than one person has been cut in this room?" I asked.

He nodded. "The question is...how long ago?"

CHAPTER THREE

My assistant had been quite industrious while we were gone.

I was once again in the observation booth, watching our Jane Doe in the interview room next door. She now wore navy sweats Barnes had pulled from her own locker—the pants too short and the top barely coming down to the woman's waist. And yet both pieces of clothing were too wide for the waif.

The sweatshirt slipped off one pale, thin shoulder. She didn't seem to notice, just continued to stare into space.

Barnes had gotten little out of her via direct conversation, only that she thought she might be in her early twenties, and she didn't think she was from Florida. So Barnes had run the woman's prints.

No hits.

Then, with the woman's permission, Barnes had recorded her voice and gotten every uniform and detective she could find to listen to it. One of the uniforms, who was from neighboring Georgia, said she could be from his home state.

Barnes had checked recent missing person reports in that state, as well as Florida. No one who even vaguely resembled this woman.

Now Bert was analyzing the blood on her dress, before starting on the contents of the motel room. I'd asked him to make the dress a priority. I needed to know if this woman was somehow involved in that homicide.

If not, I wasn't sure that having tiny drops of blood on her dress was enough grounds to hold her. I might have to turn her over to the social workers soon.

Barnes stuck her head into the observation room, yanking me out of my reverie. "Your friend from Maryland is here."

Damn! Of all the days for this to happen, when I was supposed to go to lunch with Kate Huntington, who was in the area visiting her parents.

But then again, maybe this was a good thing. If anyone could figure out what was going on with this woman...

I walked back to my office and greeted the middle-aged woman sitting in my most comfortable visitor's chair.

Kate jumped up and threw her arms around me, squeezing hard.

I stiffened, then instructed my body to relax. It kind of complied.

Kate got the hint and let go. "Sorry. I'm a hugger. I forget sometimes that not everyone is."

Meeting her gaze—at the same level as mine—I gave her a genuine smile. "Damn, it's good to see you." And it was.

Her mop of dark curls had a fair amount of gray in it now. And she had some extra padding around her middle, hidden under a bright turquoise tunic over her jeans. But otherwise she was the same old Kate. Her sky-blue eyes shone with intelligence and...

And what?

Enthusiasm for life? Yes, that was it. And it was one of many reasons why I liked her. No matter how many times life knocked her down—and it had done so way too often—she got back up and somehow regained her enthusiasm.

"I hope you remembered your sunscreen," I said as I went around my desk and sat in my chair. "Even in March, the Florida sun will fry that fair skin of yours to a crisp."

Kate chuckled and settled again in front of my desk. "Already a seasoned Floridian, after, what? Seven months."

"So, how's the family?" I asked, even though I wasn't sure I cared, but it was the polite thing to say.

"They're good. The kids are being teenagers—enough said. And Skip says hi, as do Rose and Mac."

Skip Canfield, Kate's sometimes annoying private detective husband, and Rose Hernandez, his business partner and former Baltimore County cop.

I had a lot of respect for Rose, a short, compact woman who was as no-nonsense as they come, and a damned good investigator. Barnes reminded me a little of Rose, although my assistant was less serious...and a bit more girly-girl. She even wore pink at times when off duty. Rose, despite her name, wouldn't be caught dead in that color.

And Mac Reilly, another detective in their agency, a former Green Beret, and Rose's husband. He had my respect as well.

"Tell them hi back for me," I said, smiling again. Then my mood sobered. "I'm afraid I can't go out today after all–"

"Lemme guess, big case," Kate said with a grin.

"Yeah, two of them actually, and brand new. And there's a part of it that you may be able to help with. Do you mind if we order sandwiches from the deli across the street? Their tuna salad is great."

Kate was leaning forward, literally on the edge of her seat. "That's fine. Tell me about the cases."

I filled her in, first about the mystery woman, and then the call to the motel and the bloody homicide scene we'd found there. "We don't know if the two cases are related, but it's a bit of a coincidence that she shows up with blood on her dress on the same day. We haven't been able to get anything out of her, other than she doesn't drink caffeine, although she can't remember why not, and she guesses she's early twenties, which we'd already figured out, based on her appearance. Oh, and she doesn't think she's from Florida."

Kate's brow furrowed. "Do you want me to talk to her?"

"Would you?" I told her the woman was in an interview room. "You'll have to tell her up front that she's being record-ed and observed."

"It might be better in a more private space."

I gave that a moment's thought. "We can move you two to a conference room if she won't talk this way, but I'd like to try to get whatever she says recorded. With that blood on her, she could be..."

"A criminal," Kate finished my sentence. "Okay, we'll try it."

I led the way to the interview rooms.

When I introduced Kate as a psychotherapist, the young woman's eyes lit up and she leaned forward. But just as quick-ly, her gaze turned wary.

I excused myself and left it to Kate to introduce the idea that they were being recorded. In the observation room, I found myself holding my breath as Kate did so.

The woman nodded, and I blew out air. First obstacle over-come, I turned on the equipment.

"What would you like me to call you?" Kate was asking.

The woman shrugged.

"What's your favorite name?"

The woman thought for a moment. "Chrissy, but I don't think that's *my* name."

"Would it be okay if we called you that for now?"

The woman squirmed a little in her chair, tugged at the gap-ing neckline of the too wide sweatshirt, but then she nodded.

"Chrissy," Kate said, "do you remember coming to the po-lice station this morning?"

The young woman nodded again.

"Good, and what's happened since then?"

"They brought some water, and these clothes to wear." She looked down at herself as if she were examining someone else's clothing, which she was. "And some food."

"Was the food okay? Would you like anything else?"

She shrugged. "It was from a vending machine, but I'm okay now. I'm not hungry anymore." She began patting the pockets of her borrowed sweat pants, her expression becoming agitated. "I should pay that officer back, who brought the sandwich. But I don't have any money."

Kate gave her a warm smile. "It's okay. Don't worry about it."

"But it's not right to take something that isn't yours, or to be beholden." She shook her head. "No charity."

Kate nodded. "Who taught you that?" Her voice was gentle.

The girl gave her a blank stare.

"It's okay," Kate repeated. "You're our guest. It's okay to accept refreshments when you're someone's guest, right?"

Our *guest* hesitated, then nodded slightly and visibly relaxed.

"What else can you remember about today?" Kate asked. "Maybe something that happened before you came to the police station."

The young woman stared at the ceiling for a moment. "I was standing on a sidewalk, and I found a card in my pocket."

"A business card?"

She nodded but said nothing more.

"Can you close your eyes," Kate said, "and imagine you're standing on that sidewalk again. What do you see around you?"

"Buildings. Tall buildings. My feet hurt. I think I've been walking for a while."

"Was anyone with you earlier?" Kate asked.

She opened her eyes and shook her head, perhaps a little too vehemently.

Or maybe you're reading into that, Anderson, I told myself.

Kate asked her a few more questions, with nothing worthwhile coming from the answers. My mind was wandering when she said, "Tell me about your childhood."

The woman gave her a blank look. "I don't know."

"Do you have any brothers or sisters?"

She thought for a beat. "I don't think so. Maybe."

I expected Kate to follow up and ask if maybe she had a sister or maybe a brother.

But she didn't. "What was your favorite thing to do when you were a kid?"

Ah, I get it. Kate was trying to get her to remember something easy, to begin to nudge the door of her memory open.

The woman began to shake her head, then froze. She glanced around the sparse interview room, her expression panicky. "Woods," she said, a note of fear in her voice.

Hmm, not so easy after all.

"You're in the woods?" Kate dropped her voice almost to a whisper.

The woman nodded, her gaze still darting around the room.

"Did you like being in the woods, or not?"

"No," she said emphatically, then seemed to collapse in on herself. "I mean, we used to..." she trailed off, now huddled in her chair, staring at her hands in her lap.

And that was all Kate could get out of her. After that, her answer to every question was, "I don't know."

We sat on either side of my desk, fat tuna salad sandwiches in front of us. I opened a bag of chips and put it in the middle of the desk, then unwrapped the large dill pickle that Mr. B, the deli's owner, always threw into the bag when he knew the sandwich was for me.

This one was conveniently sliced down the middle to share. I smiled. Mr. B took good care of me, saying it was the least he could do after saving his granddaughter from becoming the hostage of "Nazi pigs" last month. There was more to the story than that, but that was the important part as far as he was concerned.

I placed half of the pickle on the wrappings from Kate's sandwich. She had already bitten into the sandwich and was rolling her eyes with pleasure. "That's great," she said after chewing and swallowing.

"He puts a little bit of pickle relish in it. Gives it that zing." I took a bite of my own sandwich. Once I'd swallowed, I asked, "So, what do you think?"

Kate was chewing again, but she nodded her head. Quickly swallowing, she said, "It's definitely a case of dissociative fugue, which is very rare. It's a type of psychogenic amnesia."

"Have you ever had a case of it?"

"Not in a client, but a student of mine disappeared in the middle of the fall semester last year, then reappeared near the end. After she came back, her mother called me and told me she'd done this before, twice—just took off. And when she returned, she never knew where she'd been. The mom wanted to know if there was any way she could make up the classwork she'd missed."

"Did you let her?" My stomach rumbled, protesting how slowly I was eating. I chomped off another bite of sandwich.

She shook her head slowly. "I wanted to, but she'd missed too much. I arranged for her to get a medical withdrawal so the grades for the semester wouldn't hurt her GPA, but she lost a semester of time and tuition."

"Did you find out where she'd been, or what set it off?"

"No, but she'd had a glassy look in her eyes the last time she was in my class, and I remember thinking that something we were discussing had maybe triggered her."

"Is that what happens, something triggers some dormant...whatever in their subconscious?"

Kate shook her head again. "It's such a rare disorder that there's very little research on it. But dissociation in general is often caused by a traumatic event, or something reminds the person of a past trauma that is unresolved."

I sat back in my chair, dropping the remnants of the first half of my sandwich onto its wrapper. "So maybe our girl is dissociating because of the trauma of killing someone?"

"Or fighting him off," she said, "as he tried to kill her."

"There were, um, *stains* on the walls of the room..." I'd almost said *blood spatter*, then remembered that Kate was not law enforcement and perhaps would not wish to discuss blood and guts while eating. "They might be from more than one person. But our gal doesn't have any wounds on her, that we can see at least. And she doesn't act like she's in pain."

"You might want to ask her if she'd be willing to do a rape kit," Kate suggested.

I nodded.

"There's also the possibility," Kate said, "that something happened this morning or last night that triggered an old trauma. Maybe something that happened in those woods she seems to be afraid of."

I nodded again and picked up the second half of my sandwich. "It doesn't help that we're down two detectives this week. One's out sick and Agent Wellbourne...I've mentioned her to you before, right?"

"The one who's on loan from that state agency, the FLE?"

"FDLE, the Florida Department of Law Enforcement. She's at a training workshop in Jacksonville." I made a scoffing noise. "Learning some new de-escalation techniques."

Kate's eyebrows went up as she swallowed a bite of her sandwich. "You don't approve?"

"No, it's not that. De-escalation of tense situations is important. But I'm already short-staffed. Every time I get close to a full contingency, I discover that yet another of my people was in Chief Black's pocket."

So far, I'd lost two detectives, one sergeant and two patrol officers to Black's corruption.

Kate nodded, took another bite of her sandwich.

"I've been trying to think of a diplomatic way to steal Wellbourne," I said. "She's green, but she'll make a great cop with a bit more experience under her belt. She's in over her head at FDLE, though. I think she's happier here. But I don't want to piss off the agency's director."

Kate snorted softly. "You realize that only a *female* police chief would worry about whether or not her people were happy."

I froze, my sandwich halfway to my mouth. I'd never really thought of myself as a *female* anything. Oh, I *am* female—Sam can attest to that. But...

Am I getting soft?

"I can see I struck some kind of nerve," Kate said, her intense blue eyes boring into mine.

I shook my head and dropped the remainder of my sandwich on my desk. "Let's go see if we can convince our Jane Doe to do a rape kit."

―――――⚬―――――

"Chrissy" said she hadn't been raped, at least not that she could remember. But she did agree to go to the hospital. We were now at Shands-Starling, the city's only hospital, waiting for a nurse trained in doing rape kits to arrive.

Kate said she'd stay with the young woman, so I could go back to the office if I wanted. "Can you send someone to get me later?" We'd left her rental car in the municipal building's parking lot.

I nodded, then took her aside to speak privately. "I'm not sure what I should do with her after this. I can't just let her go, not until we have some explanation for the blood on her dress."

Kate chewed on her lower lip, her blue eyes more gray now. I'd noticed in the past that her eyes shifted color like that, when she was worried or stressed.

"I'm sorry," I said. "This isn't exactly what you had in mind for a vacation, I'm sure."

Kate shook her head. "Not a problem. I feel bad for the girl. We should probably get her admitted here, for evaluation. Do they have a psychiatric ward?"

I nodded. "It's small, but the psychiatrist in charge of it, Dr. Moody, is a good guy. I've dealt with him once before."

Kate chuckled. "Dr. Moody—what a great name for a psychiatrist."

I smiled, then thought for a moment. "I think I'm going to officially get her Baker-acted. And I'll put a guard on her room, until we know more."

"Baker-acted?" she asked, her eyebrows raised.

"The Baker Act. It's the law that allows for involuntary hospitalization for psychological evaluation." I shook my head slightly. "Floridians use it like a verb."

It hadn't been too difficult to convince Shands-Starling's Chief of Psychiatry to commit our Jane Doe. He'd never seen dissociative fugue "in the flesh before." His fascination with the case struck me as a bit inappropriate.

"I'll read up on it tonight and do a more thorough evaluation tomorrow," Dr. Moody said. "For now, myself and another doctor will talk to her and then Baker-act her, if she won't admit herself voluntarily."

I tensed. "I'd rather you Baker-acted her, so she can't check herself out. Otherwise, I'll have to arrest her, or at least take her into protective custody. She had blood on her dress, remember?"

He frowned. "It's protocol to try to get the patient to commit themselves voluntarily."

"Doctor," I said, "I don't think she really quite understands what's going on. The whole voluntary/involuntary thing may go right over her head."

He nodded, his expression now a bit grim. "If she's not capable of giving voluntary consent, we'll have to Baker-act her."

He balked, though, at the idea of a police officer at her door. "That might upset some of our other patients. If we've Baker-acted her, she'll be on a locked ward, and I'll note on her chart that she isn't allowed any visitors except you or your people."

"No, *only me*," I emphasized. "Not my people. Anyone could come in here saying they were from our department. How would you know otherwise?" I wasn't about to admit to him that I didn't trust all of those who really were "my people."

When I'd accepted the job of Chief of Police here, I hadn't realized I was taking over a corrupt department, thanks to my predecessor, John Black. Although several bad cops had been exposed, I wasn't sure they were the last of the rotten apples.

And if "Chrissy" hadn't committed a crime, she could end up a victim. She might have witnessed something.

And someone might come looking for her to silence her.

CHAPTER FOUR

As the afternoon wore on, I was getting more and more antsy, waiting for someone to get back to me with *something*.

The nurse who'd done the rape kit exam had given us her verbal report. It wasn't all that helpful though. There were no wounds on the woman's body, so the blood wasn't hers. And the nurse was relatively certain she hadn't been raped, although there were signs of rough sex in the past. And she'd had dried blood under her fingernails on her right hand. The nurse had clipped the nails into an evidence bag.

Kate had returned to her parents' place in St. Augustine. Once there, she'd texted me to call her if I needed any more help with the case. I'd texted back, thanking her again for today's assistance.

But I had no intention of disrupting her vacation further.

Instead, I texted our janitor, who was on the verge of receiving his masters' degree in social work. Bill Walker was planning to become a mediator for couples with domestic violence issues, a topic he knew intimately as a reformed wife batterer himself. But his masters program required him to become well versed in all the tasks a social worker might be expected to perform. Currently, he was doing a field practicum in the hospital's psychiatric ward.

Hey Bill, I texted, *are you doing any counseling with patients on the locked ward?*

Some. I'm at the hospital now, about to finish my shift.

Can you keep an eye on a Jane Doe who was just admitted? Maybe talk to her and see if she'll tell you anything about who she is or where she came from?

I can try, but anything she tells me is confidential.

If she tells you anything that might be useful, can you ask her if you can tell me?

Sure, I can ask.

Thanks.

I put my phone down and skimmed a new email from Bradley, updating me on the progress, or rather lack there of, with the homicide case. He had Cruthers, our sole present and healthy detective, and some of the uniforms canvassing the area near the Beachview Inn. But so far, it was a futile effort. That was a section of town where folks rarely talked to the police unless they absolutely had to.

My phone pinged. A text from Bert Deming. *Are you in your office, Chief?*

Yes, I texted back.

Be right there.

In less than three minutes, he was standing in my open doorway, Barnes hovering behind him.

I motioned for them to both come in, then for Barnes to close the door.

Bert perched on the edge of one of my visitors' chairs. Barnes leaned her butt against the door, notepad in hand. It was her usual spot when "sitting in" on interviews or briefings, even though she wasn't technically sitting.

"We were able to type some of the other blood stains on the wall and the bed's headboard," Bert said. "But the bad news...it's O positive, the most common blood type in the U.S." He cleared his throat. "The blood on our Jane Doe's dress is also O positive."

"So, not the victim's blood from that motel room," I said.

He nodded. "The cases may not be related."

I blew out air, not sure if I was disappointed or relieved. "Anything else?"

"The blood on the chair is also O positive."

"Old stains then," I said, my stomach clenching with frustration.

"Hard to tell. They were tiny droplets. But I'm leaning toward saying they were fairly fresh."

"So someone could've sat in that chair recently, while yet another person was cut in that room?"

Bert shrugged.

"Any sign of the knife?" I asked.

"Nope. Sandy said it was probably decent sized, more like a hunting knife than a pen knife."

"Those partial fingerprints?" I asked.

He shook his head. "No matches in the system."

Which meant whoever left them had never been arrested. I swallowed a sigh. "Thanks."

"We've still got a lot of trace evidence to analyze." Bert rose from his chair. "I'll let you know if we find anything."

I nodded, as my desk phone rang—my private line, Bradley's name on caller ID.

I grabbed up the receiver. "Tell me you got something."

"Maybe," he said. "I've been talking to the motel's clerk. I'm bringing him in."

"Fred Murdock?"

"No, the night clerk. He's the young man that the Blanchards initially reported the body to. He didn't call 911, but he did call Murdock. Then he went home."

Damn, I'd missed that. I'd assumed the Blanchards had meant Fred Murdock when they said "young man," even though he was middle-aged. But he'd likely seem young to them.

"This kid's being somewhat reticent about answering my questions," Bradley said. "I figured a trip to the station might loosen his lips."

"You think he knows anything useful?"

"He might know more about the victim. He's the one who rented the room to him."

Fifteen minutes later, I was shrugging into the jacket of my black pantsuit while exiting my office. In response to a text from Bradley, I was headed to the interview rooms to observe, and maybe sit in on, the interrogation of the night clerk.

But a meticulously dressed woman was blocking my way, standing next to Barnes's desk. Her tailored skirt suit said she was somebody important, or at least *she* believed she was important. Silver streaks in the black hair she had pulled back in a chignon said she was middle aged. But the smoothness of her medium brown skin belied that, making it hard to guess her age. Somewhere between forty and sixty was the best I could do.

She broke off whatever she was saying to Barnes and turned to me. Offering a hand, she said, "Chief Anderson, let me congratulate you on being Starling's first female chief of police." She was smiling, but it didn't quite reach her brown eyes.

I narrowed my own eyes, thinking she must be a politician, or a reporter. I wasn't sure which was worse.

"Do I know you?" I blurted out.

"Sorry, I'm Anita Wells-Olson."

As I belatedly and hesitantly shook her hand, she added, "I've been remiss. I really should've come downstairs and welcomed you personally awhile ago."

"From the fifth floor?"

"Oh, sorry again. The fourth floor. I'm, um, the city comptroller." She raised her eyebrows in an expression that said she was surprised I didn't know who she was. "We met, briefly, at the reception Mayor Daniels held for you when you came on board."

"Ah," I said, recognition finally dawning. She was one of the dozen city department heads in the reception line that evening.

She gestured toward my office. "I wish this were only a social call, but I need to talk to you about something."

I nodded, still a little off-balanced. She walked ahead of me into the office. I turned to Barnes. "Let Bradley know I've been delayed, to start without me if he's ready."

I hated to miss seeing the clerk's body language as Bradley questioned him, but choosing just the right time to begin an interview was sometimes key to getting the interviewee's cooperation. Making him cool his heels for too long might make him less responsive.

I tugged on the hem of my suit jacket as I rounded my desk. Ms. Comptroller had already settled herself in my sole comfortable visitor's chair. The other two were chrome and leather contraptions that had people squirming in less than five minutes.

As I sat down behind my desk, she gave me another smile, this one more genuine. "I see why you invested in a third chair. Those things…" She gestured toward the other chairs and rolled her eyes.

Note to self: don't forget that she knows every expenditure the department has made.

That thought made me wary, but I returned her smile. "I inherited those from Chief Black. I'm pretty sure he picked them *because* they're uncomfortable. Discourages unwanted guests from lingering."

I didn't tell her that—if she'd given me the chance—I would've directed *her* to one of the "torture chairs," as I'd come to think of them.

"So, Ms. Wells-Olson, what can I do for you?"

Her mouth quirked up on one end. "Actually, it's doctor. I have a PhD. But I'll answer to just about anything, as long as it's not rude."

I chuckled. I was getting used to the abundance of PhDs in the area. With two of the state's universities in the region, the University of Florida and the University of North Florida, we had an inordinate number of "doctors."

"Speaking of rude," I said. "If I seemed a bit off a minute ago, it's because my first assumption was that you were a politician. I, of all people, should know better than to go by stereotypes."

Her eyes went wide in her face, and she did something funny with her mouth, something halfway between an O and a moue. Then her face relaxed and she burst out laughing.

It was a big belly laugh. She even placed a brown hand on her slightly rounded belly, covered in the cream-colored silk of her skirt.

"I'm sorry." She flicked a finger under each eye, before the tears of laughter could run down her face and spoil her perfect makeup. "I'm not used to being judged by *that* particular stereotype."

"What do you mean?" I said, wary again.

She gave me an indulgent smile. "People of color are most often judged by stereotypes associated with their color."

"Oh," I sat back in my chair, "I didn't even think of that."

Her smile grew broader. "And that says something about you."

"Something good or bad?"

"Good." She nodded, still smiling.

Then her expression abruptly sobered. "Damn, we're having such a good time here, getting to know each other. But I'm afraid I'm the bearer of bad news."

The smile that was forming on my own face quickly faded. "About what?"

"The mileage vouchers your detectives submit."

I held up a hand. "I know that's rather unorthodox, and I'm working to get unmarked vehicles for all of them to drive—department-owned vehicles. But I also inherited that mess from the previous chi–"

"I know," she interrupted. "That's why I'm giving you a heads up before I open a formal investigation."

"Whoa! Formal investigation? What's to investigate?"

"The vouchers are padded."

"What?" I half shouted.

Barnes popped into my doorway. "Chief?"

I shook my head. "Close the door."

She tilted her head with a questioning look, but she did as she'd been instructed, with herself on the outside of that closed door.

My stomach churning, I turned back to the bean counter in front of my desk. "How do you know they're padded?"

She sat back in her chair and blew out a sigh. "Let me start from the beginning. I too was brought in fairly recently, just a couple of months before you came on board. My instructions were to discreetly audit each department, searching for waste." She paused. "But also for anything that looked off."

One hand reached up to smooth her already well-behaved hair. "I've done several departments already. It's slow going. I'm doing it all myself, because of that word *discreet* in my orders."

She expelled another sigh. "I started on the police department a few weeks ago. When I got to the mileage vouchers and began crunching numbers, I realized two things. One, a lot of money was being paid out there, and–"

I jumped in. "I noticed that too, when *I* crunched the numbers. Buying department-owned vehicles would actually be cheaper in the long run. I'm putting two a year in my budget request."

She held up her hand to stop me. "The second thing I found..." She paused again, took a breath. "The detectives would have to work fifty-hour weeks, *every* week, and be on the road *all* of those hours in order to drive that many miles. And this past month, your Detective Cruthers drove even more miles than usual."

I felt like someone had kicked me in the stomach. *Cruthers?* He was the detective I trusted the most after Bradley.

Then I remembered and blurted out, "He was in a workshop last month, over in Jacksonville." The same one that Wellbourne was taking this week. The FDLE was offering it twice a month, encouraging all the law enforcement personnel in the area to take it.

I narrowed my eyes at the woman across my desk from me. She was right. I had been enjoying getting to know her, but now I was wishing she'd sink through my floor.

Her eyebrows were in the air. "Chief, he submitted for nine-thousand miles."

"Oh... Is that... How much..." My heart pounding, I trailed off, not even sure how to formulate a question at this point.

"Assuming an average of forty miles per hour over the course of the month, he would've been on the road, *on police business*, for over two-hundred hours. In other words, every hour of every workday, assuming an average of nine hours per day. And keep in mind, last month was February, a short month."

My mind was swimming from all the numbers. "What have the detectives normally been submitting per month?" I asked, stalling, trying to gather my thoughts.

"Between four and seven-thousand miles per month."

I did my own quick math in my head. "That's crazy. They'd have to replace their cars every two years."

I paused, thinking about who drove what. None of my detectives had a car that was more than three years old.

I told the comptroller that, then added, "Lieutenant Bradley's is the newest car. It's a 2021 Honda CRV."

"He submitted a voucher for last month for seven-thousand miles."

My heart rate skyrocketed. I smacked my desktop. "That's impossible!"

Doctor Wells-Olson had jumped in her chair when my hand hit the desk. Now she was glaring at me. "I can show you the paperwork."

"Please do." I glared back. "Bradley has been using a police-issue sedan for the last two months."

She cocked her head to one side. "He has?"

"Yes, and I trust him with my life. Indeed, he has saved my life already, in the few months we've been working together."

"Being a good cop and being honest with his paperwork are not necessarily the same thing. Can I speak with him?"

"Not right now. He's interviewing a witness."

Dr. Wells-Olson rose from her chair. She laid a business card on my desk. "That has my private line on it. Please be discreet in your communications, with me and with your people, until we get to the bottom of this."

I took a deep breath, trying to calm down.

"This is not personal," she added. "Against you or any of your people. I just want to find out what's going on."

I nodded, took one of my own cards from my desk and wrote my private line number on the back. I handed it to her as I rose. "Thank you, Dr. Wells-Olson, for bringing this to my attention."

She sighed and gave me a small smile. "You might as well call me Anita. This could be a long investigation."

I attempted a smile back. I probably failed, but I didn't totally care.

Nope, not a long investigation. Not if I have anything to do with it.

CHAPTER FIVE

On my way past Barnes's desk, I said, "Can you make me a list of anyone you've ever seen me give my card to?" The exchange of business cards with the comptroller had reminded me about the card our Jane Doe had shown the sarge this morning.

I planned to make my own list of card recipients, but Barnes might think of some people I'd forget. She was incredibly observant.

By the time I got to the interview rooms, Bradley was seeing the motel's night clerk out the door. He handed the kid one of his cards, with the usual "call if you think of anything" spiel.

Crap! Would I ever be able to think of everyone I'd done that routine with in the last seven months?

"What'd he have to say for himself?" I asked.

Bradley gave me his signature half smile, one end of his mouth quirked up. It reminded me of Ms. Comptroller, which made me frown.

Excuse me, Doctor *Comptroller.*

Bradley's face sobered. "You okay, Chief?"

"Yeah. I need to talk to you about something else, privately, so let's walk toward my office as you fill me in."

I pivoted and he fell into step beside me. "Kid asked, no, *begged* me not to tell Murdock about the set-up. He had a deal with our victim, who told him his name was Jack Smith. Not his real name, which is John Bartholomew Spencer. The deal was Smith/Spencer would not be interrupted while using the room, no matter what, nor would the clerk tell anyone in authority that he had ever been there."

"So," I said, "that's why he didn't know what to do when Mrs. Blanchard reported a dead man in that room."

"Exactly. The 'no matter what' specifically included anyone in a nearby room reporting screams or other suspicious sounds. The clerk figured he was making porn because attractive women often came and went when Smith was in residence."

"Which fits with the camera tripod we found."

Bradley nodded. "Smith checked in last night around eight. He had one woman in the car with him. She stayed in the room and he, Smith, went out again. Came back half an hour later with white paper bags that the clerk assumed were fast food. He didn't see anybody come or go after that."

"But there was no woman in the room this morning."

Another half smile. "I pointed that out. He said he might have fallen asleep at the front desk a couple of times. And before you ask, Smith's car was gone this morning as well."

Bradley ran a hand through his wavy brown hair. "He said Smith always parked it next to the office, so he, the kid, could keep an eye on it. It was, quote, 'kinda fancy' for that neighborhood and Smith didn't want anyone messing with it."

"So, either the woman took the car," I said, "or somebody 'messed with it' during one of the kid's naps."

Bradley nodded again. "And the kid never took down the license plate number. He did say it was a BMW, dark navy.'"

"Research that car," I said.

"That was my plan," Bradley said.

"Description of the woman?"

"Nope," Bradley said as we entered my office. "He didn't get a good look at her, just a shadowy head inside the car."

Barnes began to follow us. I shook my head.

She stopped abruptly and gave me her questioning look again. I almost always let her sit in on briefings from Bradley. It was part of our deal when I'd yanked her out of the rookie pool and made her my assistant, shortly after I'd started as chief.

John Black had stripped the departmental clerk's billet—among many other things—from the PD's budget, right before he'd retired. I had no doubt whatsoever that it was an act of sabotage, to cause me to fall on my face.

I had not obliged. Instead, I'd used several work-arounds, including the deal with Barnes, to compensate. She would learn how to be a detective at my elbow in return for taking care of the huge amount of administrative minutia involved in running the department.

Now she backed slowly out of the office, drawing the door closed behind her.

I gestured toward the comfy visitor's chair and sat down in my own behind the desk. "You can't say *anything* to *anybody* regarding what I'm about to ask you." I tilted my head toward the closed door. "Not even your sister."

He and Barnes were half-siblings, but they both knew when to keep their own counsel.

Bradley raised an eyebrow in the air. "Okaaay." He dragged the word out some.

I gave him a hard look. "Did you submit a mileage voucher for February?"

Both eyebrows shot up. "Last year?"

"No, *this* year. Last month."

"No. Why would I, now that I have my unmarked?"

I nodded. "Before you got the police-issue car, how many miles did you normally submit per month?"

"Most months, around a thousand. Sometimes as much as twelve hundred if I had to drive to Jacksonville a lot."

I paused to do the math. That was a rough average of thirty-three miles per workday. The City of Starling was approximately thirty-five square miles. So he would've traversed the city a few times a week, plus, as mentioned, several trips outside the city per month. A thousand to twelve-hundred miles was about right—but a long way from the seven thousand miles the comptroller said he'd submitted.

"Hmm, at fifty cents a mile," I said, "you got around five-hundred to six-hundred dollars a month?"

"Correct. I put it aside in a separate savings account, and then paid cash for a new car every three or four years." He sighed. "I guess I'll have to take out a car loan now, like everybody else. But..." he held up a finger, his expression brightening. "I won't have to replace my car nearly as often."

I studied his face. Was he telling the truth? I was pretty sure that he was. But cops learn how to lie, and to do so with a straight face. We lie to suspects all the time, about certain things—like whether or not their cohorts have ratted them out.

"One more question," I said. "Who did you submit your vouchers to in accounting?"

"Clara something. I can't remember her last name. Not sure I ever knew it. Young, red hair."

I nodded. "Thanks. That's all."

His eyebrows went up again. "You're not going to tell me what this is about?"

"Not yet. And it's not that I don't trust you." I paused, fighting the temptation to fill him in. I never kept *anything* from Bradley. "And like I said, tell no one."

"Okay." He stood, gave me a small salute along with a half smile, and left my office.

I felt equally weird about blowing Barnes off when she sent me a questioning look. "Once you've got a start on that list," I said, "go on home. That's where I'm headed."

Which wasn't quite accurate. I was going to my cousin Paul's apartment. He was hosting dinner for me and Sam tonight, to celebrate his new dispatcher's job and his new abode.

But I was careful not to mention our family connection at the office, not wanting to be accused of nepotism. Indeed, Paul hadn't even told me he was moving to Starling. He'd just shown up one day last month, the move and the new job a *fait accompli*.

———◇———

I stopped home long enough for a quick shower, a change of clothes, and to grab the bottle of Chardonnay I'd bought for the occasion.

He'd insisted on no house-warming gifts, which wasn't like Paul. He adored gifts.

But I figured wine was appropriate whenever one was a guest for dinner.

I found the building without difficulty—it was in a decent part of town. At his apartment's door, I rang the bell as I mentally cleared the decks, attempting to purge all thoughts of our current cases. I plastered on a smile.

It became more genuine when I saw the apron wrapped around my cousin's slender body. It read *Don't Kiss the Chef. He's easily distracted.*

I started to thrust the wine bottle in his direction.

"You're late," he snapped.

I twisted my wrist so I could see my man-sized watch. "Only by seven minutes, which is early for me."

Indeed, police cases so often kept me at the office late, it was unusual for me to make it to social events at all.

He harumphed, gave me a sour look and turned away. Striding toward the kitchen, he called over his shoulder. "Put that in the fridge. No doubt you didn't chill it yet."

"Actually, I did," I said as I complied, wondering what had him in such a foul mood.

"Where's the sheriff?" he grumbled while stirring something on the stove.

"He's on his way." I stepped over to him. "That smells good."

I wrapped an arm around his shoulders for a sideways hug—my favorite kind since it was short and minimal contact. But he shrugged me off.

What the hell? I opened my mouth to ask him what was wrong.

The doorbell rang.

"Get that, would you?" he said, eyes on whatever was in the pot.

It was Sam, of course, also wielding a bottle of wine, this one red—our favorite.

In jeans and a green sweatshirt, his blue eyes sparkled as he stepped over the threshold. "Do hugs in your cousin's apartment count as PDAs?" We had a strict rule about no public displays of affection.

"No but," I jerked my head in the direction of the kitchen, "he's in a mood, for some reason."

Sam pecked me on the lips instead. "I'll save the hug for later," he whispered.

I smiled. Hugs from Sam were in another whole category.

Paul greeted Sam and pointed at the refrigerator. "Put that in the fridge as well. Put a slight chill on it."

I opened my mouth to say we preferred room temperature, then thought better of it.

We stood around the kitchen for a few minutes, making lame small talk and feeling awkward. Finally, Paul picked up a soup plate, filled it with his specialty, chicken and sausage gumbo, and handed it to me. He tilted his head toward a small dining area.

Sam took charge of the wine and when we were all seated, he raised his glass. "To Paul's new apartment and job."

"Hear, hear," I said and raised my glass.

Paul's smile was feeble.

We ate in silence for a few minutes, me debating if I should ask him what was wrong in front of Sam.

Yes, damn it. He'd invited us over, he could at least explain his foul mood.

I opened my mouth, then shut it again. *The date, of course. Damn!*

It was March fourteenth, the anniversary of his sister's abduction.

———◆———

At nine-fifteen the next morning, I rode the elevator to the fourth floor of the municipal building.

I was trying to ignore thoughts of last night. Or at least of the first part of the evening.

Paul, Sam and I had somehow gotten through the meal. Then I'd claimed a headache, and Sam and I had left.

Paul seemed relieved that we were leaving early. At the door, he'd leaned down and whispered in my ear. "Sorry. I didn't realize the date when I set this up, only that I was off work today so I could cook. I..." His voice caught a little. "I thought I would be okay, but..."

I'd nodded and impulsively kissed his cheek—surprising both of us. "I love you," I whispered back.

He'd ducked his head and mumbled, "Love you too."

Once in the apartment building's parking lot, I'd stepped into Sam's arms and squeezed him tightly.

He held me slightly away from him. "What's that about?"

I looked up at him, opened my mouth. But my throat closed. I couldn't talk about it.

It dawned on me that I'd never talked about it—with anyone. Not in the thirty-one years since it happened. And not
even with my mother, with whom I'd been close, until my
father left us and she'd spiraled downward.

No one in the family *ever* talked about that day, when
Meredith....

My chest tightened now, like it had last night. I blinked hard.

It was as if she'd evaporated into thin air.

"I'll tell you another time," I'd said to Sam last night.

"Is this related to his mood?" His voice was gentle, his expression concerned, as he'd cocked his head toward the building we had just left.

I'd nodded. "Come on, let's go back to my place."

Sam had given me a small grin. "I brought a fresh uniform,
hoping you would ask."

My memories of the rest of the evening were much more
pleasant, but I shook them off when the elevator dinged and
the doors opened.

I'd only been on the municipal building's fourth floor a
couple of times, and that had been to visit Human Resources
regarding jobs that needed filling.

HR shared the floor with the city's accounting office. I wandered around that area, glancing at name plates on desks. No
Clara anywhere.

A few people asked if they could help me. One even recognized me, calling me *Chief*. I smiled politely, shook my head,
but kept walking.

Finally in a back corner, I found a desk piled high with
papers, and a cute twenty-something redhead valiantly pulling
papers off of stacks, skimming over them, and stamping something on them.

"Clara?" I guessed.

Her head popped up. "Yes?" Her voice was soft, almost
timid.

"What happened to your nameplate?" I couldn't think of anything else to ask her, and I wasn't about to ask her what I really wanted to know, not here at least.

She stood up and leaned over the piles of papers. "Damn. It fell off again." Her cheeks pinked and she ducked her head.

Then she plopped back into her chair and disappeared under her desk. She came up with the plastic nameplate, in a metal holder.

It read *Clara Hopkins*.

"Can I help you with something?" she asked me.

I shook my head. "Nope. I'm new. Trying to get to know people's names."

She nodded and gave me a shy smile. "Okay. Well, welcome aboard."

Obviously, she hadn't recognized me. I smiled back and quickly walked away before she did.

I was barely back in my office when my private line rang, *Comptroller's Office* appearing on caller ID.

Shit! I picked up the receiver. "Hello?"

"Chief, Anita Wells-Olson here. Were you just up here?"

"Uh, yeah," I said, going for a casual tone. "I realized I'd never really explored the whole building, so I did a bit of a walk-around."

"Okaaay." She dragged the word out.

"Was there anything else?" I asked, again the casual tone.

"Um, yes, I was about to send you a scanned copy of that mileage voucher and realized I didn't have your email address."

I gave it to her.

"Thanks. I'll be in touch." She disconnected.

I held the phone receiver out in front of me. "I'll bet you will."

"Chief?" Barnes said from the doorway.

I hung up the phone and turned, gave her a pleasant smile. "Yes?"

"I finished the list of people I know of that you've given business cards to. I emailed it to you."

"Great. Thanks."

She went back to her desk, and I downloaded the Word doc she had sent. Three names down, the person she'd listed prompted an addition to the list. A couple of additions, actually.

Barnes had written *Mary Striker, the woman at the shelter for prostitutes.*

To be more precise, they had been prostitutes who wanted out of the life, and some hadn't been in that life willingly. They had been trafficked.

I had personally interviewed two of those women after we'd busted the local trafficking ring last fall. I'd given each of them my card.

I changed the font color to red and typed on the next line, *black woman, something Tate, daughter Sherrell,* and on the line under that, *Misty something.*

I'd have to pull the case file and get their full names and any contact info we had.

I opened my mouth to call for Barnes and she popped into the doorway, startling me.

Dear lord, is she now reading my mind before I even call her name?

"A Dr. Moody is on the line," she said.

I blew out air. "Oh, okay. Put him through."

"Hey, Doctor–"

"Chief, I'm so sorry. The Jane Doe, she's gone."

CHAPTER SIX

"Gone? What the hell do you mean?" I snapped into the phone.

"She got away from us," Moody said. "Claimed she felt ill. She even threw up in her room. An intern was taking her to the infirmary. She sucker-punched him and took his badge."

I jumped up from my chair. "Barnes!"

She popped into my doorway again.

"Our Jane Doe got away from the hospital. Tell Sarge to get a BOLO out and we need every available officer for a search party."

Barnes nodded and disappeared.

Into the phone, I said, " How long ago?"

"The charge nurse said they left for the infirmary twenty minutes ago. The intern went back to the ward after he came to and reported she'd gotten away from him. She called me right away, and I called you."

I ground my teeth. "Can you have as many of your staff as possible search the building and grounds for her?"

"Already happening. But, um..." he stopped talking.

"But what?"

"The intern said his car keys are missing."

So much for her never stealing!

I clamped my mouth shut to keep the curse words swirling in my brain from getting out. "I want to talk to that intern. I'll be right over."

I ran out of my office and toward the fire stairs. No time for the elevator.

The intern was on the short side and slender—a hundred-thirty pounds at most. And he couldn't have been more than twenty years old, so not a graduate student, as I'd first assumed.

He'd explained that he was a junior at the University of North Florida in Jacksonville, majoring in psychology. And he'd seemed quite nervous as he'd stuttered his way through that explanation.

As he should be. Losing a patient wasn't a good thing. Although he'd suffered a bloody nose for his efforts to hang on to her.

"We were in the hallway," he said, from across one of the tables in the employee break room. "She pulled loose from me and started running. I caught up with her, grabbed her arm, and she hauled off and gave me this." He pointed to his red nose, with a bit of dry blood crusted under the nostrils.

My stomach a little queasy, I tried not to look at it, focused instead on the young man's eyes.

"I don't think it's broken." He was gingerly touching his nose. "And she stole my badge, as well as my car keys."

I'd already gotten the plate number, make and model of the car from Dr. Moody—who'd had the foresight to get the info from HR. I'd called the watch sergeant to add it to the BOLO.

My stomach churned some more. Taking the badge and keys implied much more malice of forethought than just a desperate attempt to get away.

"You want to press charges?" I asked.

He began to shake his head. "Not if I get my car back in–"

"You *do* plan to press charges, don't you?" I interrupted. I wanted our Jane Doe back in police custody. If she did a runner, who knew what would happen to her?

And I'd never find out what that bloody dress is about. I hated loose ends like that.

"Um, I guess." His tone was tentative.

"You said you were knocked unconscious. How long were you out?"

He rubbed a goose-egg bump poking through his buzz cut on the side of his head. "Yeah, when I hit the floor–"

My phone pinged. I glanced down at it on the tabletop. *Sam,* the screen read. I ignored it.

"I was only out a few minutes, though," the young man said.

I opened my mouth, and the phone pinged again. "Excuse me. I need to check this text." I tapped on the message.

Found her but it's not good. She's standing on the railing of the riverwalk. The sheriff is trying to talk her down.

What? The sheriff? This was Sam's phone. What was going on?

I texted back, *Who is this?*

Barnes. I lost my phone. Long story.

Where on the riverwalk?

At NE 59th Avenue.

I looked up at the intern. "Give me your address and phone number and go home. I'll contact you later to finish this."

Looking more than a little green around the gills, he rattled off his info.

I plugged it into my notes on my phone. "Better still, you should go to the hospital and get checked out. You've probably got a concussion."

I remembered Kate saying that anytime someone was knocked unconscious, they had a concussion, and it could be a serious one.

"We're in the hospital," the intern pointed out.

"Oh, yeah, well go down to the ER. I'll contact you later."

Out in the hallway, a tall, lanky young man in a short-sleeved dress shirt and tie fell into step with me.

It took me a second to recognize my thirty-something janitor. I'd rarely seen him in anything but gray overalls.

Bill Walker shoved too-long dark hair off his forehead. "I heard what happened. I can help search for her."

"They've found her, by the riverwalk, but Barnes says it's not good. She's on the railing, threatening to jump in the river."

"I might be able to talk her down."

"Sheriff Pierson's working on that," I huffed out as I power-walked toward the double glass doors of the hospital's exit. "Did you get a chance to talk to her yesterday afternoon?"

"Briefly," Bill said, easily keeping up with my pace. "But I kept it light, just trying to build rapport. I'll follow you, in case I can help."

I nodded as we hit the doors, then split to go to our respective cars.

———◆———

Barnes was right. It wasn't good.

The Jane Doe—or Chrissy as Kate had been calling her—was perched precariously on the top of the metal railing along the riverwalk. She held onto a lamp post with one arm, but she was swaying on her feet.

Sam was about ten feet away from her, sitting on the top of the railing and quietly talking to her.

I sidled up next to Barnes, who was watching them intently, her mouth slightly open.

"What's happening?" I whispered.

She jumped.

"Sorry." But I hid a grin. I wasn't at all sorry. She did that to me all the time, appeared out of nowhere and startled me.

"He was standing up, so he was on her level," she whispered back. "But he almost fell in. This isn't a good spot on the river. It's shallow near the shore here and the bottom is rocky."

My insides clenched and a lump formed in my throat. *Dear God, Sam....*

Movement in my peripheral vision. I glanced over. Officer Thompson stood with a couple of other uniforms. A small crowd of looky-loos was forming beyond them. Thompson had already handed off his duty belt to one of the others and had nudged off his shoes.

My muscles relaxed a little, and I made a mental note to praise him later for his forethought, even if he didn't end up going for a swim.

"You said you were looking for Jake," Sam said in a soothing voice. "Who's Jake?"

"Chrissy" cocked her head to one side. "I don't know. I think maybe he's my uncle."

"What's his last name?" Sam edged toward her.

She shook her head. "I don't know." Her voice was sliding toward whiny.

And I was losing patience. I hadn't had much to begin with, not since she'd cold-cocked that intern. She wasn't the inno-cent woman-child she pretended to be.

"How'd she end up on the railing?" I whispered out of the side of my mouth.

"Thompson and Dulles were chasing her." Barnes also kept her voice low. "I wasn't far behind them. It looked like they had her cornered, but then she climbed up there and threatened to jump."

I nodded and caught sight of something on the riverwalk beyond the woman. I carefully kept my gaze on Sam so as not to alert "Chrissy" that Bill Walker was creeping up behind her.

He too was shoeless and he'd ditched his tie. Beyond him, two more uniforms were keeping pedestrians at bay.

I glanced over at Thompson and the others. They were all studiously keeping their eyes glued on Sam.

Good job, guys!

Sam had almost made it to the lamp post. "Now Chrissy, I'm gonna stand–"

"No!" She jumped back. "Don't call me that!" But she'd kept a hand on the pole. Good thing because one of her feet almost slipped off the railing.

She wobbled, and I held my breath.

"Okay, okay," Sam said, "I was just going to stand up so we could talk face to face."

"No! Stay back!"

Sam raised a hand in a placating gesture, and suddenly the woman's feet were in the air, arms and legs flailing.

My heart stuttered. *She's falling...*

But she flew backward, a muscular arm wrapped around her waist.

She struggled and screamed like a banshee, but a couple of uniforms helped Bill Walker get her on the ground. One of them was Thompson.

He glanced up at me, as Barnes and I trotted up. "Arrest her," I said, my voice harsh in my own ears.

"Yes, ma'am," Thompson said. "Uh, for what?"

"Assault and theft. She slugged an intern at the hospital and stole his badge. And his car keys. One of you, see if you can find that car."

"And keep an eye out for my phone," Barnes added. "It slipped out of my hand when we were chasing her."

———◦———

Sam lounged in my visitor's chair.

"Thanks for rescuing our Jane Doe," I said.

He shrugged. "Walker helped."

"Yes, but his part wasn't dangerous." I wasn't about to admit how scared I'd been that he would end up in the river, his head bashed against a rock.

"Happy to help." He gave me one of his easygoing smiles. "Where was the intern's car?"

"In a shopping center parking lot, not far from the hospital. It seems she just, quote, 'borrowed' it to get far enough away from the hospital to feel safe. Then she took off on foot. Officer Dulles said it was easy to spot, it was parked crosswise of three parking spaces."

"Not the world's best driver apparently," Sam said.

A faint ringing sound. At first I wasn't sure where it was coming from. I opened my bottom desk drawer. The ringing got louder. My personal cell phone, stashed inside my laptop case in the drawer.

I pulled it out, glanced at caller ID and answered right before it could go to voicemail. "Hey, Kate."

"Hey, Judith. Just touching base. How's the case going?"

"Hmm, seems our Jane Doe isn't quite as innocent as she seemed." I filled her in on her escape from the hospital and the rescue at the riverwalk.

"You want me to come talk to her again?" Kate asked.

That would be great, but... "I hate to keep interrupting your vacation."

"Oh, that's okay." Her tone was downright enthusiastic.

It dawned on me that she was as fascinated by this unusual case as Dr. Moody was, but she was hiding it better.

"It could be very helpful if you had another go at her," I said. "Frankly, I'm not totally sure what to do with her now. Technically, she's under arrest..."

"You're not going to put her in jail, are you?"

No, but maybe our holding cell overnight, to get across to her that she needs to cooperate?"

"Let me talk to her first before you decide anything. I'll be there in forty minutes."

"Okay." But I was already talking to dead air.

I chuckled softly. Yes, Kate was more than a little eager to investigate this unusual case some more.

Barnes appeared in my open doorway as I hung up the phone receiver. "Sarge has a Mr. and Mrs. Blanchard at his desk. They're asking to speak to you."

"They already gave their statements. I thought they were on their way to their next stop on their honeymoon remake."

Barnes shrugged. "Shall I go get them?"

I nodded.

She handed me a slip of paper. "I've got a disposable phone for now. Here's the number."

"How'd you get one so quick?"

She opened her mouth, but I waved my hand in the air, indicating there was no need to answer. She probably had a box of them in her trunk. She must've been a hell of a Girl Scout. She took their motto, *Be prepared*, to a whole new level.

While we waited, I told Sam about the Blanchards reliving their honeymoon for their fiftieth anniversary, beginning with the Beachview Inn.

He snorted. "I'll bet it wasn't quite so sleazy back then."

Ellie Blanchard appeared in my doorway. "Come on in," I said.

Sam jumped up and offered her the comfy chair. Hank started for one of the others.

"Fair warning," Sam said, "those other two are torture instruments, designed to discourage unwanted visitors from lingering." He perched on the corner of my desk.

Hank chuckled. "I'll stand, I think."

But he didn't have to. Barnes rolled her own desk chair into my office for Hank, then took up her usual post, leaning against the doorjamb with pad and pen in hand.

"Chief," Ellie said, her face troubled, "we was on our way to Daytona Beach when I remembered somethin'."

"You could've called," I said gently.

She shook her head slightly. "I think I heard somethin, in the middle of the night last night. At first, I thought I'd dreamt it. It was a hard knock on the wall, and the words, kinda faint, 'help me.'"

"Our victim?" I said, more statement than question.

"No, it was a female voice." She shifted in her chair. "Ya know how sometimes ya wake up sudden like, and you're not sure if the noise you thought woke you up was real or in a dream? It was like that. I lay there and listened real hard, but I didn't hear no more noises."

She paused and her cheeks turned pink. "Well, no more different noises. We'd been hearin' gruntin' and groanin'..." she glanced at her husband.

He was trying to hide a grin, but wasn't completely successful.

"...kinda off and on," Ellie stumbled to a conclusion.

Hank's face sobered. "And I recalled another thing, too. I heard some sobbin' and somebody cussin' on the other side of the wall, when we first got there. I dismissed it at the time, thought the neighbors was watchin' a movie."

All of that fit with our belief that a porn video—perhaps one that included violence—was being recorded in that room. But how much of what the Blanchards had heard was make-believe for the camera, and how much of it was an actual conflict? Because, based on the blood and the dead guy, at some point the fantasy they were acting out had become reality.

"And you didn't see anyone coming or going from that room," I asked, "or hear any names mentioned?"

They both shook their heads.

That jived with what they had told Thompson earlier.

"Okay," I said. "Thanks for coming in." I resisted the urge to point out again that they could've called. Apparently the mental health professionals weren't the only ones fascinated by the inner workings of our cases. "Barnes, could you type all that up real fast, so the Blanchards can sign it as an addendum to their statements?"

My private line rang. *Shands-Starling Hospital* came up on the caller ID.

"Excuse me, folks. I need to take this."

Sam lifted his butt off my desk and herded the Blanchards out. "I'll call you later," he mouthed in my direction.

I picked up my phone. "Chief Anderson."

"Why haven't you brought my patient back?" Dr. Moody's voice, impatient.

I froze for a second. He had to be kidding. "You mean the young woman charged with assault?"

"That intern never should've pressed charges. Patients hit the staff all the time. They know it goes with the territory."

"Doctor, the kid was knocked out for several moments. This wasn't just a little smack while she was struggling to get away. She slugged him, quite intentionally."

"Still, she belongs here, not in jail."

"I'm not sure where she belongs at this point. I have our psychological consultant on her way to talk to the *prisoner* again."

"*I* haven't even talked to her yet. I was going to have a session with her this morning, after she'd gotten settled in."

I paused, debating. Did I really want to make an enemy of this man?

"Why don't you come over to 3MB and observe as Kate talks to her. She—Kate, that is—has already developed some rapport with the woman. She's a specialist in trauma recovery, and an expert on dissociative disorders." I wasn't at all sure Kate would agree with that last part, but she was more of an expert than this guy likely was, considering the population she had treated.

I also wasn't sure how she would feel about having a larger audience, but one step at a time.

———◦———

Kate agreed to have Dr. Moody observe, if Jane Doe was okay with it. She joined the prisoner in our interview room, but kept the microphone off until she'd talked to the woman a few minutes.

Then she sat back, clicked on the sound, and identified herself. "I am interviewing a young woman who seems to be suffering from a dissociative fugue. For lack of a better name, she has agreed to have us call her Jane. She has also agreed to allow Dr. Alexander Moody of Shands-Starling Hospital and Chief of Police Judith Anderson to observe this interview. Is that correct, Jane?"

"Yes," the young woman said in a soft voice.

I was wondering what had happened to the name *Chrissy*, when Kate addressed that very issue.

"Jane, you objected to Sheriff Pierson calling you *Chrissy* this afternoon. Do you know why that name bothered you?"

She shook her head. "I guess I was upset. Jake hates it when I get like that."

"You seemed to be looking for Jake when the sheriff found you? Who is he?"

Jane's eyes went wide. "I don't know."

Kate sat quietly for a moment.

"I just had this urge to find him," Jane said. "I was afraid he'd be angry."

Kate nodded. "Let's try something. Can you close your eyes for a moment and let an image of Jake come into your mind's eye."

Jane hesitated, but then closed her eyes.

"Tell me what Jake looks like," Kate said.

"Um, he's tall...and handsome." Jane smiled a little. "He has dark hair with some gray at his temples. *She* calls it distinguished." She came down hard on the word *she*.

"Who is *she*?" Kate's voice was soft and low.

Jane's eyes popped open. "I don't know, I... Um, I'm not sure I like her." Tears pooled as she lowered her gaze. One broke loose and trickled down her cheek.

Kate ignored it. "You said you were afraid that he would be angry?"

Jane shook her head slightly. Her eyes had drifted closed again. "No, he's never angry with me, only disappointed sometimes."

"Can you tell me about one of those times when he was disappointed?"

I gritted my teeth, trying to rein in my impatience. Jake obviously wasn't our murder victim from this morning. That guy was only five-nine and roly-poly. Hardly tall and handsome. And he was almost completely bald.

"Um, mostly if the teacher sends a note home," Jane was saying. "I have trouble sometimes paying attention in class."

What the hell? Now she was talking about her childhood. I raised a hand to knock on the glass, but caught myself.

"She has to tug on whatever thread she's offered," Dr. Moody said from beside me in the observation room. "She's doing fine."

I swallowed a groan.

"Were there other times when he was disappointed?" Kate asked.

Her eyelids still at half mast, Jane's face clouded. "What are you doing, Daddy?" Her hands flew to her mouth. "No, Daddy, no," she screamed.

CHAPTER SEVEN

Kate didn't react.

Across the table from her, Jane rocked in her chair, sobbing into her hands. "Daddy, why did you do that? Why did you hurt Chrissy?"

Inside the observation room, Moody and I both jerked. *Chrissy?*

But again, Kate did not visibly react. "How did he hurt her?" she asked, her voice so soft I could barely hear it.

"He hit her, and now she isn't moving. He says we have to hide her."

"Where is he going to hide her?"

"In the woods. We have to clean her up first, and take her deep into the woods." Jane had stopped crying, but her voice was a little garbled as it came from behind her hands.

"Did you do that?"

Jane nodded, her hands still over her face. "I have to promise never to tell *her*, or anyone else. I can never tell anybody, ever. *I have to forget.*" The last sentence was said in an emphatic voice.

"How old is Chrissy?" Kate asked, her voice soft.

Jane's hands fell away. Her eyes were still closed. "She's fifteen. Her birthday was last month, and mine was yesterday. I'm a month younger than her."

Jane paused, her face twisting. "*She* baked me a cake, with fifteen candles." Then her mouth relaxed into a small smile. "I blew them all out at once."

Kate leaned forward some. "I'm going to count to five in a minute. And when I get to five, you can open your eyes. And you will remember only what it's safe to remember, okay?"

No response from Jane. She sat there, eyes closed, face slack, while Kate counted slowly. At five, Jane opened her eyes.

"How do you feel?" Kate asked.

"Okay. Are we going to talk now?"

"Uh, maybe we'll talk some more later," Kate said. "You seem kinda tired."

Jane's shoulders slumped. "I am, a little."

"Would you like to go back to the hospital and get some rest?"

Jane nodded.

I should've been annoyed that Kate assumed she was going to the hospital again, but my brain was too busy trying to process what had just happened.

If anything, I was mostly annoyed that she'd told Jane to only remember what was safe. *Why the hell did she do that?*

———— ⋅◦⋅ ————

"Jane" was on her way back to the psychiatric wing of our local hospital, this time with an escort/guard in tow. Dr. Moody had balked again, until I'd told him the alternative was I locked her up in a holding cell.

I'd assigned Officer Peters, in plain clothes. She was to sit outside Jane's room on the locked ward, with only pepper spray as a weapon.

A compromise with Moody, who'd wanted no weapons. "She has to have a way of defending herself," I'd insisted. I understood that we didn't want a gun on a psychiatric ward, but I'd lobbied for a baton as well. The doctor had stood firm.

I hoped Peters, who was one of our most promising young officers, didn't resign after a night in the loony bin.

Now, Kate and I were filling our stomachs with Chinese carryout. Brought by Sam, who'd intended it to be dinner, but we'd never had lunch.

He had chatted with Kate briefly. Then he discreetly withdrew from my office, after I gave him our signal, a hard stare followed by two blinks.

"Is everything okay between you and Sam?" Kate asked.

Apparently, she'd caught the hard look and thought I was angry with him.

I was angry, but not at Sam.

"Yeah, we're fine," I said. "So, what did you make of what Jane was saying?"

"Don't you have a national database of some kind for crimes?"

I narrowed my eyes at her. Why was she answering my question with a question?

"Yes, ViCAP. Stands for Violent Criminal Apprehension Program. It's through the FBI."

"Does it include missing persons?"

"Yes."

"Can you search it for a fifteen-year-old female victim, missing or found injured or dead in woods, with a time parameter of four to ten years ago?"

I stared at her for half a beat, my anger dissipating.

I shoved my sweet and sour chicken aside and pulled my keyboard over in front of me. "We'll get a whole lot of hits on *missing*. I'll try dead or injured in woods first."

I typed out an email to our computer tech, otherwise known as Derek the Geek. He was our designated contact with the national system. I gave him the keywords Kate had listed minus *missing*, marked the email urgent and then sat back in my chair.

"Does this ViCAP keep cases on file even if they are solved?" Kate asked.

"Usually, in case other similar crimes pop up that might be by the same perpetrator."

I pulled my dinner back over and took a bite, more to make my next questions seem like just conversation. "Why'd you end the interview when you did?" I'd intended to stop with that, but blurted out, "And why'd you tell her to only remember what was safe?"

Kate stared at me, then cleared her throat. "I could've probed for more info, but that would have been risky. I figured we had enough to find out who Jane is."

"Risky how?" I said, my chest constricting again with irritation.

"She might've shut down. I figured it was best to end on the pleasant note of her birthday celebration." Kate leaned forward some. "The *she* that Jane kept referring to, I think that's her mother."

"I caught that. Sounds like no love lost there."

Kate shrugged. "Oh, they probably loved each other. The relationship between mothers and teenage girls is tricky."

You should know, I thought. Kate's own daughter was around fifteen, if I remembered correctly.

"You didn't answer my second question. Why tell her to only remember what was safe?" I hoped I'd succeeded in keeping the irritation out of my voice.

Something flashed in Kate's eyes. "I have an obligation to not destabilize her further." Her tone was a bit sharp.

"She's not your client. As you remind her at the beginning of each interview, you work for the police department and nothing she says is confidential."

Kate pursed her lips. "Have you ever heard of the Hippocratic Oath? It applies to *mental* health professionals as well."

"First, do no harm," I muttered. I took a deep breath. "Okay, let me rephrase the question. What led you to believe that remembering more would be *unsafe*?"

"She might have been threatened with dire consequences if she didn't keep the secret. You have to take this process slowly."

"What process?"

"Uncovering a delayed memory."

"A repressed memory..."

Kate shook her head. "We haven't used that term, *repressed*, in years. They are technically dissociated memories, or delayed memories."

I sighed. "Still, I wish you hadn't told her that."

"You'd rather have her go catatonic on us," Kate snapped.

Apparently, I wasn't the only one who was feeling irritated. I tried for a conciliatory tone. "You really think that could happen?"

Kate huffed out air. "Maybe."

That reason made sense, but I identified another source of my disquiet. "I wish you'd told me you were going to use hypnosis. That might compromise the case if it ends up in court."

"I didn't 'use hypnosis.'" She made air quotes. "She slipped into an altered state on her own. That can happen with people prone to dissociation. I just took advantage of it."

"But it'll look like hypnosis to a judge." Belatedly, I realized my irritation was more frustration about this whole Jane Doe case.

And the fact that it was distracting me from the homicide case that should be my first priority.

I shook my head, trying to clear it. "What do you think happened?"

"I have some ideas, but I don't want to speculate. Not yet, with so little information."

I nodded. I suspected we were both thinking the same thing. Daddy was molesting his daughter and decided to expand his interests to her best friend. When said friend resisted, he'd killed her, either accidentally while trying to restrain/silence her or on purpose.

But all that had apparently happened years ago. Why was it bubbling to the surface now, and while "Jane" had amnesia for recent events and even her own identity?

My police issue cell phone rang. The screen read *Derek*.

I snatched it up off my desk, hit the button for speaker, and answered.

"Hey Chief, we've got over two hundred hits. Can you narrow things down for me?"

"Maybe try Christine as the first name of the victim?" Kate suggested.

"Can I narrow the time parameters?" he asked.

"No," I said, as Kate shook her head. "But try variations of names with the nickname of Chrissy. And whatever you get from that, see if any of them involved a witness who was the girl's friend."

"Okay, I'll see what we get." He disconnected.

Bradley appeared in my open doorway. Kate and I both jumped a little. We were definitely on edge.

"Sorry," he said, "am I interrupting something?"

"No." I gestured for him to come in.

But since the comfy chair was taken, he leaned a shoulder against the door jamb. "I dug deeper into our homicide victim's arrest history. He's been a very naughty boy."

Bradley waved a hand toward my computer monitor. "Don't know if you've gotten a chance to read my report yet."

No! I thought, *Thanks to our Jane Doe.* But I wasn't about to admit that out loud.

After a beat, Bradley filled the silence. "Well, he's been arrested six times in the last fifteen years. Four were for distribution of porn, in three different states, including twice in Jacksonville. Once he got caught in a sweep in Jax, arrested for soliciting prostitutes. Sixth time was just last year, also in

Jax. He was charged with assault for roughing up a prostitute while they were making a porn movie, but she later dropped the charges."

"Hmm," I said, "maybe the hooker turned on him this time."

"Could be," Bradley said. "I put in a request with Jax's vice unit to send me any of his cinematic endeavors they have on file."

"And see if you can find that prostitute."

He gave me a two-fingered salute and disappeared from my doorway.

I turned back to my food.

After a few minutes, Kate shoved hers aside. "I think I've lost my appetite. All those years of hearing my client's horror stories *had* thickened my skin..."

"But," I finished for her, "you've been wrapped in the cocoon of academia for the last few years."

"Yeah." She sighed and began to push herself up from her chair. "I guess I'd better get back–"

My phone rang again, with *Derek* on the screen.

I grabbed it and put him on speaker.

"Chief, twelve hits on Christine," his excited voice came from the phone, "but none of them involved a friend. Then I tried Kristen."

Silence. "And?" I said.

"Sorry, I was sending you the case report. A fifteen-year-old named Kristen Ashton went missing in Deweyville, Alabama in 2016. She was supposed to be at a sleepover at her best friend's house. Her body was found ten days later, in the woods near the town."

CHAPTER EIGHT

Sam had returned. He'd been hanging out with Cruthers in the bullpen, while eating his own dinner. "You guys done with all the confidential stuff?"

"Yes," I said, distracted. I was reading the ViCAP report.

"We may have found our Jane Doe," Kate said. She'd settled back into her chair.

"Oh?" Sam perched on the edge of one of the uncomfortable chairs.

I summarized the report for him and Kate. "When the best friend was interviewed she said that *Krissy*," I came down hard on the name, "got mad at her over a boy they both liked and insisted on climbing out the window and going home."

"But she never made it," Kate whispered.

I shook my head. "After a three-day search, the sheriff's department shifted it over to missing persons, assuming she'd run away. A hiker stumbled over her body ten days after she went missing."

"Who was the best friend?" Kate asked.

"Cecilia Brown. She ran away a month later. Left a note saying she couldn't face her friend's family anymore, that she had to get out of town." I shifted my gaze from my computer screen to Sam and Kate. "She hasn't been seen or heard from since."

I picked up my desk phone's receiver and called information, seeking the number of the Deweyville, Alabama sheriff's department.

But I didn't get much farther than that. The woman who answered the phone refused to contact the sheriff, who'd left a bit early to go fishing. "He won't like it if I call him, 'less it's an emergency."

"I have some information that may be relevant to an old case of his."

"An *old* case. So not ex-act-ly," she dragged out the word, "an emergency, ma'am."

I ground my teeth, before admitting to myself that she was right. I reined in my impatience and left a message.

At eight-forty the next morning, I was sucking down my third cup of caffeine and staring at the list Barnes had compiled. It contained all the names that either of us could recall of folks to whom I had given my business card.

Now that we were possibly about to receive confirmation of Jane Doe's identity from an Alabama sheriff's department, did we really need to pursue this avenue?

But even after we identified her, Jane would still have no clue where she got my card. And that piece of info could help us figure out the story behind the blood on her dress.

I was reluctant, though, to call the first of the four names with asterisks next to them—the ones I'd told Barnes I would call myself. I hated that I would be stirring up bad memories.

Instead of reaching for the phone, I let my mind wander back to last night. Sam had bid us goodnight shortly after my unsuccessful call to the Alabama sheriff. "See ya later," he'd said as he gave me a quick wink.

The line had seemed like a simple goodbye, but he'd meant it literally. He would go home, shower and change his clothes and meet me back at my apartment later.

"I'm out of here soon too," I'd said. "There's nothing more I can do tonight."

Kate had risen from her chair. "And I'd better get back to my folks' place. See you tomorrow at the hospital, Judith?" Her tone sounded perfectly normal.

"Yup," I'd said, striving to keep my voice casual, despite the anxious butterflies in my chest. I couldn't help wondering if our argument earlier had caused harm to our friendship.

No I was more than wondering; I was worrying, and I hated the feeling.

I shook my head to clear it and focused on the first starred name. Charlotte Tate had been one of the women we'd liberated from a sex trafficking ring last fall. She had said she and her daughter were going back to her hometown in eastern Tennessee and stay with her mother for a while, to regroup.

I had checked the time zones and that part of the state was also Eastern time, so it was almost nine there as well. I picked up my desk phone and dialed the number Charlotte had given us.

An older woman answered, and I asked for Charlotte. "Hold on." The sound of the receiver being set down on a hard surface.

"Hello, this is Charlotte."

Feeling awkward, I identified myself and asked how she and her daughter were doing. Social graces have never been my strength.

But I found myself relaxing, smiling even, as Charlotte described her new routine—her night job stocking shelves at the local grocery store, sleeping during the day while Sherrell was in school, then evenings as a family with her mother.

"It's a good thing we came home when we did," she said, in a lowered voice. "Mama's gettin' forgetful."

"It sounds like you all are..." I trailed off, struggling for the best word, "thriving. Um, I have a question for you...I mean, I wish this were only a social call to see how you are doing, but..."

Damn! I could interview hardened criminals but making smooth transitions in normal conversations sometimes seemed beyond me.

"Yes, Chief?"

"Do you remember that I gave you my business card?"

"Of course. I still have it."

"You're sure?"

"Yes, ma'am. Just pulled it outta my pocket and I'm lookin' right at it. I, uh, carry it around with me." A pause. "I guess it's become sort of a good luck charm. It reminds me there are still kind, carin' people in the world."

Heat rose in my cheeks even as my chest filled with a different kind of warmth. I didn't know what to say.

Then I realized I should say exactly that. "Charlotte, I'm speechless, and that doesn't happen often."

"Well, there ain't enough words in the English language to thank you for what you done. You gave me and Sherrell our lives back."

"Um, yeah, uh, you're welcome. I'm glad you're doing so well."

We signed off and I sat back in my chair, blew out air. I felt like I'd just run a marathon, exhausted but also pleased with my accomplishment.

Sometimes this job is actually worth it.

I glanced at the time on my computer monitor. Two minutes of nine.

Anxiety returned. But it might still be too soon to expect a call from that sheriff. It was only eight in his time zone. He might not even be in his office yet.

I called the next number on my list, that of Melissa Tracy, aka Misty Storm, but this call wasn't nearly as successful as the first.

Two rings and a click. "Hi, sugar," Misty's high-pitched voice, with a purr in it. "I'm so sorry I missed your call. If y'all leave your number I'll call ya back, and don't worry I'll be discreet."

I left a message and disconnected. I had a bad feeling the "I'll be discreet" comment meant she was hooking again.

By nine-thirty, I'd reached the other two people I'd wanted to call personally—both still had my card—and the sheriff of Deweyville, Alabama still hadn't called back. I'd called and was told again that he wasn't in, but would be shortly. I'd left a second message, this time with my cell number.

Then I headed for the hospital to meet Kate.

Barnes stayed behind. She was on her phone as I was leaving, plowing through the rest of the names on the business card list.

———⋅◦⋅———

The hospital's psych ward had an observation booth off of a therapy room that was far more basic than ours. Only simple recording equipment and a one-way mirror.

The cushioned armchairs in the therapy room were facing each other, a low coffee table in between, and they were positioned so that the observer behind the mirror saw both parties in profile.

Not ideal for determining if Jane was telling the truth—I'd have to rely on Kate's assessment of that—but it made sense for the hospital's purposes. I'd been told the room existed so that supervisors could observe the interns' counseling skills.

I perched on an uncomfortable stool and strained to make out the staticky conversation coming through a small speaker. Kate had already run through the initial disclaimers, reminding Jane that this was not a confidential session but rather an interview to assist the police in finding out who she was.

And it sounded like Kate's fears had been well founded—Jane was starting to shut down, giving mostly monosyllabic answers.

"You said you don't like the woods now," Kate said, shifting away from more direct questions.

Jane closed her eyes and shuddered. "No."

"But there was a time when you liked playing in the woods?"

"Yeah, before..."

I thought Kate's next question would be "before what?" But it wasn't.

"Tell me about playing in the woods," Kate said.

Jane's face slowly relaxed, and brightened even, as she described running semi-wild in the woods with her best friend.

"What else did you and Krissy like to do?" Kate asked. "Were you into boys?"

Jane shook her head. "Krissy likes them, but I'm not allowed to date."

Interesting. The young woman had switched to present tense. And she was keeping her eyes closed most of the time. Had she spontaneously regressed to that earlier age?

"Do your parents feel you're not old enough?"

Jane shook her head again. "Daddy says I don't need anybody but him."

Kate's eyes shifted my way. It was the briefest of glances, but full of foreboding. Her normally sky-blue irises were a cloudy gray and her lips were set in a grim line.

But she didn't pursue that line of questioning. "So Krissy likes boys. Any particular boy?"

Another head shake. "She liked this one boy, but his family moved away."

So much for them arguing over a boy. If this was the Krissy and friend from the Alabama case.

"Did Krissy dislike the woods later as well?" Kate asked.

Jane stiffened. Her eyelids fluttered halfway open. "I don't know," she whispered. "I, um, haven't seen her in a long time." A pause. "She ran away."

"Oh?" Kate said. "Did she tell you where she was going?"

Jane's head shake was vehement this time, and her eyes were wide open now. "No. I, uh...um, think maybe she was mad at me."

"Because of what Jake did?"

Jane looked confused. "No, Jake was later."

"Because of what your father did?" Kate amended the question.

"Maybe. I don't know."

Hmm, Jake is definitely not her father then, I thought, as my phone vibrated in my pocket. I pulled it out and glanced at the screen.

Damn, now the sheriff calls me back.

The phone purred and shook in my hand.

"So who is Jake?" Kate was asking.

I debated, then answered before the call could go to voicemail.

"Sheriff, thanks for calling me—" I stopped abruptly. Jane was staring at the mirror, a deer-in-the-headlights look on her face.

Damn! Apparently my earlier concern was valid—the reason I'd muted my phone to begin with—the wall between the rooms was not totally soundproofed.

<hr />

"Sheriff Taylor of Deweyville, Alabama was not very happy with his receptionist," I told Kate. "I got the impression she sees her job as protecting him from being bothered."

We were sitting in my car in the hospital parking lot, comparing notes. It was an unusually warm day for March, even for northern Florida. The temperature, at ten-fifty in the morning, was already eighty-three. I had the engine running and the AC on.

"Well, you didn't miss much after you left the observation booth," Kate said. "She reverted back to 'I don't know' for most of her answers."

I made a harumph sound. "The sheriff had the friend's fingerprints in the file, for elimination purposes. Only her prints, and some trace evidence, skin cells and a couple of hairs—also the friend's—were on Kristen's body. He's sending me the prints and the DNA profile."

"So we may know Jane's identity today," Kate said, her voice faintly excited.

"Will that help to get her to open up?" I asked.

She sighed. "Maybe. The name may trigger her memories."

"The sheriff said the friend, Cecilia—went by Cissy—she never returned to school that year, after Krissy's body was found. Her mother called the school and told them she was too upset, that she was home-schooling her for now. A few weeks later, the parents reported her missing."

"Cissy and Krissy," Kate said. "I'll bet the bullies at their school had fun with that."

I shook my head. "Sometimes I think you're even more cynical than I am."

"What do you mean?"

"You always look for how people might've been traumatized."

Kate shrugged. "I guess I do. Occupational hazard."

"Um, Kate." My stomach twisted as I braced myself to apologize. "About last night?"

She gave me a blank look. "What about it?"

"I didn't mean to give you a hard time."

"Hard time about what?"

"Um, how you ended the interview. You really don't remember that?"

"Of course I remember it, but I'm not sure why you are apologizing." She shoved silver-threaded dark curls out of her face.

"Well, I thought you might be, um..." I stumbled, searching for the right words, my body tense. "Uh, upset with me. We had a disagreement—"

"Why would I be upset? People disagree about things all the time."

My mind flashed to the woman sprawled on the floor, the empty pill bottle just beyond the reach of her cold, still fingers.

I shook my head to clear it. What did my mother's suicide have to do with a minor disagreement with Kate?

"Well, anyway," I said, my insides relaxing some. "I'm glad you weren't offended."

"Not in the least," Kate gave me a big smile. "Hey, ya wanna get an early lunch before we go back to your office?"

I returned her smile, relief washing through me. "Your parents are going to hate me."

She glanced at her watch. I was glad to see I wasn't the only person who still wore one, although hers was far daintier than my man-sized one.

"I'm supposed to go shopping with Mom at one-thirty, but I'm good until then."

Feeling a little light-headed, I said, "Let's do it," as I put the car in gear.

I entered the bullpen a few minutes before one, and Bradley popped out of his office. He fell into step with me as I strode across the large room.

"What have you been up to this morning?" I cheerfully asked, feeling the afterglow of a long, pleasant lunch with Kate—the kind of lunch we were supposed to have had two days ago.

"Watching porn," Bradley said.

I froze, a foot in the air, and whirled around. "Say what?"

His blue eyes twinkled. But before he could explain himself, Barnes called out, "Chief, Dr. Wells-Olson is in your office."

"Shit," I muttered under my breath, and the remnants of my good mood dissipated quickly.

"Follow me," I said to Bradley.

Anita Wells-Olson was sitting in my comfy visitor's chair, a smile on her face. She popped out of it, her smile fading, when she saw who was trailing behind me into the office.

I closed the door and nodded my head toward one of the uncomfortable chairs. Bradley perched on the edge of it.

I hoped he didn't think I was punishing him—those chairs were usually reserved for people I didn't like—but I could hardly evict the city comptroller from her chair.

Anita's forehead furrowed as she resumed her seat and I settled behind my desk. "I need to talk to you privately," she said.

I shook my head. "Lieutenant Bradley will be lead detective on this case."

Her frown deepened. "What case?"

"The fraud case." I turned to Bradley. "Someone has been submitting fraudulent mileage reports and debunking the city of thousands of dollars."

Bradley blinked once at the word *fraudulent* but otherwise showed no surprise at the turn of events.

"Tell her what you usually submitted in the past," I ordered.

He repeated to Anita the average number of miles he'd submitted per month, concluding with, "And my last voucher was filed in November of last year, right after the new unmarked sedans came in."

"And you can substantiate that?" Anita said.

Bradley shrugged. "I have copies of my vouchers but I can't prove that I submitted nothing for the last few months."

She scowled at him. "Copies don't mean much. You could have made those, then altered what you actually submitted."

I cleared my throat. She looked my way and I gave her my fiercest glare. "I trust the lieutenant. He is telling the truth."

I turned my head toward him again. "No one else is to know about this...yet."

He nodded.

"Start with a warrant request to look at the finances of Clara Hopkins," I said.

He blinked again, once. "*Before* we interview her?"

"Yes. We might not have enough probable cause to satisfy a judge, but give it a try."

Anita opened her mouth, but I held up a hand and added, "Keep Dr. Wells-Olson apprised of the investigation's progress. But otherwise, mum's the word, until we know who is involved and who has been innocently used, like yourself."

"What do you mean?" Bradley asked.

"Tell him," I said.

Anita's frown hadn't completely disappeared but she complied. "The vouchers we have on file for you are for two to three times that number of miles."

His jaw dropped.

"How are the vouchers paid?" I asked.

"By check," Anita said. "Made out to the, quote, 'Police Department Mileage Reimbursement Fund.' I assume you disperse the funds from there?"

Crap, I thought, *I need to involve Barnes then.*

"Get your sister," I told Bradley.

Anita's eyebrows went up at the word *sister*.

I considered trying to explain that it was a small city and an even smaller police force, so of course, some members would be related to each other. There was no nepotism involved.

I opted not to go there. Let her think what she wanted. She wasn't Human Resources.

Bradley stood and opened the door, gestured for Barnes to come in.

She did so, closed the door again, and leaned against it, notepad in hand.

"No notes," I said. "Do you disburse the money to the detectives for their mileage?"

"Yes," Barnes said. "I keep a spreadsheet."

"Show me."

She held up a finger and left the office.

She was back after thirty seconds of awkward silence among the remaining people in my office. "I just emailed it to you."

I woke up my computer and opened my email, clicked on the attachment. A spreadsheet appeared on my screen.

I rotated my monitor so the comptroller could see it.

She pulled reading glasses out of her suit jacket pocket and perched them on her nose. After staring at the screen for a good minute or two, she nodded. "All that seems legit. But the amounts are much lower than what was sent out by accounting." She looked at me over her glasses. "So where's the rest of the money going?"

"How do you get the checks and how do you deposit them?" I asked Barnes.

"They are physical checks," she said. "Which I've always thought was kind of old-fashioned. They come in the interoffice mail, and I take a photo of them with my phone and deposit them through an app."

"Can you show us one of those photos?" I asked.

She took out her phone and fiddled with it, turned it toward me.

I glanced at it. Looked like a photo of a check to me. I tilted my head toward Anita.

Barnes turned the phone in her direction. Anita looked it over, started to nod, then gasped. "Wait a minute. That's not our bank."

She took the phone from Barnes and turned it toward me again. "The city does its banking with Florida Credit Union. This check is drawn on an account at Cirrus Bank."

Bradley pushed himself to a stand. "Lemme see what they'll tell me there, but they'll probably want a warrant to cover their asses."

I nodded.

"Do you think Chief Black is behind all this?" Barnes blurted out.

I winced inside, barely maintaining a neutral external expression. "Maybe."

To Anita, I said, "We'll get this investigation rolling and keep you in the loop."

I meant it as a dismissal but she didn't move. Her sour expression said she wasn't at all happy.

I leaned forward. "Look, Barnes is most likely right. Chief Black has been implicated in several instances of fraud and bribery, and is currently awaiting trial. The previous mayor managed to keep all that out of the press, which of course we'll no longer be able to manage, once Black goes to trial."

Her expression had relaxed a little but that was all that had shifted.

"Bradley was not part of Chief Black's inner circle-"

He snorted. "He barely tolerated me, but he knew if he fired me he'd have a lawsuit on his hands."

Anita's expression morphed to confused.

"Bradley's gay," I pointed out.

She made an O with her mouth, then said, "And Chief Black was a consummate bigot, on many levels."

"Exactly," I said. "Barnes was only a rookie, a parole officer, when Black was here. I made her my assistant."

Anita nodded. Did that mean she now got it why I trusted them?

She rose from her chair. "Thanks, Chief. I'm more than happy to turn this over to you. Let me know if I can help."

"Just keep it all under your hat for now."

She nodded again and headed for the door. Barnes opened it and Bradley stepped back to let her pass.

I gestured for him to sit down again, in the comfy chair this time, and for Barnes to close the door.

Then I raised my eyebrows and said, "Porn?"

CHAPTER NINE

Bradley chuckled. "I spent most of this morning looking through the videos that Jacksonville's Vice Unit confiscated from our victim, John Spencer, the last time they arrested him. He has several aliases, by the way."

"Confiscated," I said, "as in physical copies, not digitized?"

"Yes and no. He put the videos on flash drives and physically delivered them or used kids as couriers. One of those kids turned out to be the son of a beat cop. Instead of delivering the drive to its intended recipient, the kid gave it to his father. Spencer was subsequently arrested and his stock was confiscated."

Bradley paused. "No sign of that prostitute he roughed up, by the way. She must've left town."

"Did you find anything interesting on the videos?" I asked.

He grimaced. "Several of the older ones featured a teenage girl who might be our Jane Doe."

Adrenaline surged, kicking my heart rate up a notch.

"Yes!" Barnes exclaimed and pumped her fist in the air.

I frowned at her, even though part of me felt like celebrating too. But fist pumps, even in my closed office, weren't very professional—especially in response to the news that a teen had been sexually trafficked.

She tried for an apologetic look but couldn't quite wipe the smirk off her face.

"So," I said, "maybe a solid connection between our cases."

"Yeah, if we can get a pic of Jane as a teen," Bradley said.

I turned to my computer and pulled up my email. Aha, a message from the Deweyville sheriff. Attached were the fingerprints and DNA profile of his missing girl, the friend of the murder victim.

We didn't have the DNA back yet on the blood from Jane's dress, but Bert could work on the fingerprints. I forwarded the email to him with those instructions.

"Fingerprints are in the works, but he didn't send a photo," I told Bradley.

I stared at the email. The sheriff's sign-off line was a little odd. *See you soon.*

I hit reply and asked for a picture of Cecilia Brown at age fifteen.

I turned back to Bradley. "Photo requested. Anything else?"

"Nope," he said. "I'm off to prepare the warrant request for Clara Hopkins's financials."

He left my office.

Barnes and I ate lunch at my desk—sandwiches from the deli—while dealing with various administrative tasks. I kept a watchful eye out for another email from Deweyville's sheriff.

"Contact HR," I said, "and get the job description for the department clerk who worked for Chief Black."

Barnes's pencil made a note on her pad, but her gaze was on me.

I held up a hand. "Don't worry. I'm not replacing you, at least not exactly."

She cocked her head to one side, her eyes still worried.

"We have the money for a clerk in the budget again."

Thanks to Mayor Hayes, I added inside my head. Black may have intended to sabotage me by stripping the departmental budget down to the bone, but Mark Hayes—who was the chair of the city council at the time—had pushed through an emergency budget increase shortly after I'd come on board. I'd been chasing a serial killer at the time, and fear had motivated the council to cooperate.

"I want to hire someone," I continued, "to take the clerical stuff off your plate, but you'll remain as my assistant and continue to go with me to crime scenes and such."

Barnes broke out a smile. "Thanks, Chief."

"Any luck with the list of people I've given my business card to?" I asked.

She shook her head. "I haven't caught up with a couple of them yet, but those I have reached either said they'd lost it or they still had it."

Which reminded me, I hadn't caught up with Misty yet myself.

"So somebody could've found one of those lost cards somewhere," I said.

Barnes got a funny look on her face. "Um, I suspect most of the people who said they lost it really pitched it in the trash."

I rolled my eyes, then nodded a dismissal

She gathered her pad and pen and headed for the door.

"Close that on your way out." I didn't particularly want my cops listening to me chatting with a hooker.

But I had no luck. I got Misty's voicemail again and left another message.

An hour later, I was finishing up reviewing the morning's incident reports, when Bradley appeared in my office doorway. "Any pic yet from that sheriff?"

"Nope, no email yet," I said, not bothering to keep the frustration out of my tone.

A throat clearing behind the lieutenant. "I've got one with me."

Bradley jerked around, revealing a tall, handsome middle-aged man in a khaki uniform.

———◇———

I did a double-take. This guy's uniform looked a lot like Sam's. Although, with my second glance, I realized his had two breast pockets on his long-sleeved khaki shirt while Sam's had only one. And even in what passed as winter in northern Florida, Sam wore mostly short sleeves.

Duh, that's why they're called uniforms, Anderson. They look similar.

The Deweyville sheriff's thick belt secured a leather holster to his hip. That and the badge on one of his pockets were the only things that identified him as law enforcement. His rugged face was capped by a thick thatch of salt and pepper hair.

He didn't waste any time. After a brusque round of introductions, he asked to see "the girl."

I picked up my phone to call the hospital, as Bradley said, "You have a photo?"

The sheriff nodded and fished his wallet out of a back pocket. Strange that he hadn't brought the case file with him. He extracted a photo from the wallet and handed it over.

Bradley stared at it, and an eyebrow went up.

At that point, I was distracted by the argument I was having with the nurse on the psych ward. She was resisting having her patient disturbed again today.

Bradley asked if he could keep the photo.

"No," the sheriff replied, his voice gruff.

Bradley switched eyebrows, but he set the photo down on the corner of my desk and whipped out his phone. The sheriff was reaching for the photo as Bradley clicked a picture of it.

I gave up on the nurse and pulled out Dr. Moody's card, with his cell phone number on the back. A call to him, and we were in.

"You can ride with us," I said, as I rose from my desk chair.

"I'll follow in my car," the sheriff said. "Come on." He turned to walk away.

Hmm, he might be handsome but he's not long on social graces.

At Shands-Starling, the good doctor told Sheriff Taylor to wait outside the ward. "We need to tell her first that someone from her hometown is here," Moody said, "and gauge her reaction."

The sheriff's frown expressed his displeasure at this announcement. He tried to insist but the doctor was adamant.

The doc used the plastic badge dangling from a lanyard around his neck to unlock the ward's entrance. The skinny intern from the other day was right on the other side and caught the door. His nose was no longer red, but it was still a bit lumpy. He'd seemed to be on his way out, but he loitered in the doorway, watching as we approached Jane's room.

I told Officer Peters that she could take a break. She shot me a grateful look and dashed for a nearby ladies' room.

The nurse had apparently told Jane that she had visitors coming. The two women came out of her room and into the hallway as we drew near.

Dr. Moody explained to Jane that we might have tracked down her identity. "Does the name Cecilia mean anything to you?" he asked.

I was watching her face carefully. Something shifted in her eyes, but she shook her head.

"Well," Doc Moody said, "there's someone here from Cecilia's town to talk to you. He's the sheriff there."

The young woman's eyes registered increasing wariness as he talked.

"And he may be able," the doc continued, "to tell us if you are the Cecilia who used to–"

Jane suddenly pulled loose from the nurse's gentle hand on her arm and ran for the ward's door.

Too late, the intern realized what was happening. He tried to close the door, but she grabbed the handle, yanked it wider and ran out.

I was close on her heels, having been the only one in our little group who'd anticipated she might run. Shouts and pounding footsteps from behind me, which I ignored.

I caught up with Jane just as she collided with the Deweyville sheriff.

He took her by the shoulders, looked down at her, and smiled for the first time since his arrival.

That smile gave me the creeps.

"Hello, Cissy," he said.

The girl burst into tears and crumpled to the floor.

A heated verbal tussle was in progress. The Deweyville sheriff insisted on taking "Cissy" home to her family. The doctor was resisting releasing her, saying she was in a fragile mental state and needed to remain in the hospital for now.

Meanwhile, Bill Walker had turned up and had hustled the young woman down the hall to a therapy room. Officer Peters had followed and stood outside that door.

Reassured that Jane/Cissy was secured for now, I stepped between the sheriff and doctor and held up my hand. "Sheriff, I'm not willing to let her leave yet either."

I glanced at the intern, still standing near the ward exit watching the drama.

"For reasons I cannot currently disclose, it's possible that she witnessed and/or participated in a crime." I paused.

The sheriff was frowning but he didn't object.

"Give me a moment with the doc and I'll lead the way back to the station." He had followed me to the hospital in what

I assumed was his personal vehicle, since it had no lights or decals on it.

"I'll tell you as much as I can," I promised, "once we get back there." I was actually willing to tell the sheriff most of it, but not in front of the nosy intern.

I led the doctor aside. "Dr. Moody, I'd like to have my consultant..." Movement caught my eye. The sheriff was headed for the ward's exit. The intern looked as if he might unlock the door for him.

Where the hell is Taylor going? I caught the intern's eye and shook my head.

Turning back to the doc, I continued, "I'd like to have Kate Huntington talk to the girl again. As a specialist in trauma recovery and dissociative disorders, she's probably the best equipped to help her reconnect with her identity, if indeed she is this Cissy."

Moody's expression was stubborn, but then it morphed into something more like concern. He sighed and nodded. "That's most likely what's best for her."

I gave him a small smile and headed for the door.

The sheriff was arguing with the intern, looming over him and gesturing toward the reader where the staff inserted their badges.

Why's he so anxious to get out of here?

Once at the door, I nodded at the intern. With a relieved look, he let us out.

The sheriff was quiet as we walked through the hospital corridors and out to the parking lot. "Follow me," I said again.

But once out on the main road in front of the hospital, the sheriff's car peeled off in the opposite direction.

That was weird. Where was he going?

Well, he was my guest, not my prisoner. I had no control over whether or not he followed me.

Maybe he was going to find a hotel, or get something to eat.

I shrugged and went back to 3MB.

Once there, I scanned the bullpen for Bradley as I walked toward my office. I didn't see him or Barnes.

I opened my office door and startled a little. The room was quite crowded, with both Barnes and Bradley standing.

And ensconced in the comfortable visitor's chair was a rotund man, rather jowly with thick lips. He wore a khaki uniform.

"Chief, I was about to call you." Bradley's mouth was twisted into a weird frown. He gestured toward the stranger. "Meet Sheriff Taylor of Deweyville, Alabama."

My stomach hollowed out.

CHAPTER TEN

"Caucasian," I said. "Tall, medium build, brown and black, with some gray mixed in. Rugged face."

I was responding to the sheriff's request for a description of the imposter.

Bradley had confirmed that he'd checked the Deweyville Sheriff Department's website and found a photo there of the sheriff. We were dealing with the real one this time.

Who now grunted. "Sounds a lot like Cissy's dad, Joe Brown. Uh, her stepdad actually, although he adopted the girls." He removed his khaki-colored brimmed cap and scratched his head through thinning hair. "But why the devil is he impersonatin' me?"

"Good question," I said from behind my desk. I gestured for Barnes to close the door.

Once the room was secure, I told him about Kate's session with our Jane Doe in which she revealed that her father had done something to her friend, then had hidden her in the woods.

"That's how we found your case," I concluded. "We searched ViCAP for an injured or deceased fifteen-year-old girl found in woods."

Taylor's face was now sagging. Maybe it was my imagination, but it seemed like he'd aged a year or two as I was speaking.

"The sheriff at the time, my predecessor, suspected Joe in Krissy's murder." Taylor paused. "But there wasn't enough concrete evidence."

"Why was he a suspect?" Bradley asked.

The sheriff sighed. "He was the one who found the body, and he tried to revive her, even though she'd been in that grave for days at that point. He said he just got carried away."

"Great way to cover himself," Bradley said, "in case there was trace evidence on her body."

"Or in the grave," Taylor said in a grim voice. "And there was a couple of his hairs in there."

"I thought a hiker found her," I said.

"Uh, yeah, him and his dog. The dog started diggin' and uncovered a hand. At which point, the hiker pulled the dog back and ran out of the woods, then called 911. But by the time we got there, Joe had come along, saw the hand, and dug her up."

Very convenient. I'll bet Mr. Brown has a police scanner.

Out loud, I asked, "So how did Mr. Brown know that we had a woman here who might be Cecilia?" I wasn't admitting yet that she was, not until we had more proof.

Taylor's ruddy cheeks turned a deeper shade of red. "I'm afraid that's on me. I wanted to prepare him for what might be coming. His wife tends to be a bit hysterical."

I stared at him, my mouth agape. "You gave him a heads up when you suspected him?"

He shook his head. "Not me. I was only a deputy then. And other than him findin' the body—which could've been legit, he's a hunter and the woods are near his place—it was mostly the sheriff's hunch that he had somethin' to do with it. And we didn't have any reason to think that Cecilia was involved in what happened to Krissy. She'd said they'd had an argument and Krissy had left to go home."

I nodded, acknowledging that they had lacked sufficient evidence at the time. But still, *this* sheriff gave a potential perp a heads up? Were they buddies?

Barnes coughing into her elbow distracted me. I gave her a sharp look. She seemed a little pale. Was she coming down with something? Maybe what Collins had. He'd tested negative for Covid but... The last thing I needed was an outbreak of something—Covid or anything else—in our small department.

I opened my mouth to say something to her, but Bradley was showing the sheriff a photo of our adult Jane Doe. "This Brown chap called her Cissy," Bradley said, "but I'm not sure we can take his word as solid proof of her identity."

The sheriff studied the photo. He shook his head slightly. "Certainly it could be her, but I can't be sure. There's a big difference between a fifteen-year-old and a twenty-one-year-old."

Barnes coughed again, and again I opened my mouth to suggest she go home. But this time I was interrupted by a knock on my office door.

Barnes opened it to reveal Bert Deming. I introduced the crime scene tech to Sheriff Taylor, then asked, "What have you got?"

"She could be Cecilia Brown." Bert's words echoed the sheriff's. "But the fingerprints are not an exact match."

Taylor scowled. "Whada ya mean, son?"

Bert held up a printout. "These are our Jane Doe's prints. She has several scars, most likely from cuts, on her fingertips. Maybe she worked in a meat packing plant or something?" He raised his eyebrows in the sheriff's direction.

"Not while she was livin' in Deweyville, she didn't," he said.

I pursed my lips. "It's also possible that someone intentionally obscured her prints."

"That could be why nothing came up when I ran them," Barnes said. "Maybe this Jake guy she mentioned did it."

It was the sheriff's turn to raise his eyebrows in a silent question mark.

But I didn't enlighten him about Jake. Instead, I picked up my phone and called Kate.

After I filled her in regarding our Jane's possible identity, she said, "I can come over tomorrow morning and talk to her again."

Then I described the earlier scene at the hospital in more detail. She audibly blew out air on the other end of the line. "Maybe I should come over now. It sounds like she's pretty upset."

Guilt and expediency did battle inside my head. I'd called Bill Walker from my car. He'd said he was able to calm the young woman down but she wouldn't talk to him about anything substantial. So she was no longer upset *per se*, but...

Expediency won. She might say more to Kate. "I'd appreciate it," I said out loud.

Forty-five minutes later, we were set to go. Kate was in the hospital's interview room with the young woman, and she was reminding her again that this would not be a confidential session.

The Deweyville sheriff had tagged along, so it was a bit crowded in the observation area. Bradley was there also, although I had convinced Barnes to go home. And Dr. Moody had joined us this time.

Bill Walker had seemed torn. But he only had a few hours to catch some sleep before his night duty as the PD's janitor. "Will I see you later?" he'd asked, giving me a meaningful stare. He was subtly asking if I was likely to pull an all-nighter because of this case.

I'd shrugged. "Not sure."

"Can you let me know what you find out?"

I'd nodded, and he'd left, glancing back over his shoulder before turning a corner in the hallway.

The hospital's recording equipment was not as good as ours, but it was better than nothing. Kate had pointed out that we wanted the session recorded so any defense attorneys involved later wouldn't be able to claim that she intentionally used hypnosis.

"But there's a real good chance she will slip into an altered state," Kate had added, "like she did before."

Sheriff Taylor had looked a bit confused but he'd remained quiet during this exchange.

Now Kate began with, "I understand you had a visitor today, someone who seemed to know you."

Jane shook her head, her hair falling forward and obscuring our view of her face.

I ground my teeth but forced myself to stay still.

"Did he look familiar?" Kate's voice was so soft, I could barely hear her.

Jane froze for a second, then shook her head again, the slightest of movements.

Why do I think you're lying, girl? My heart rate kicked up a notch.

"He wasn't the sheriff of your town?" Kate asked.

Another slight head shake.

"Was he your father?"

A more vehement head shake.

"Sweetheart," Kate said, "you're not in any trouble here. It's okay for you to answer truthfully."

Jane was still.

"He said your name may be Cecilia, or Cissy. Do either of those names mean anything to you?"

The young woman's body stiffened, but she didn't otherwise respond.

"Okay," Kate said, "let's go back and talk a bit more about the last time you saw your friend Krissy. Can you tell me what was going on right before she got hurt?"

Jane's head started swinging slowly back and forth. "No," came out of her mouth, but it sounded almost like a moan. "No, no, no. I can't remember!"

Dr. Moody rustled beside me. I shot him a sideways glare.

Kate reached out and patted Jane's hand. "Shh-shh. You're okay. It's safe here."

Jane stopped the slow-motion head shaking and leaned forward, as if she were seeking the comfort. But then she slowly drew her hand out from under Kate's.

"Sweetheart," Kate said, again in a soft, gentle voice, "is it that you can't remember, or that you don't *want* to remember?" She paused. "Or maybe you're not *supposed* to remember?"

"I can't remember; I can't remember," Jane repeated. Her voice broke on a sob.

Dr. Moody took a step toward the door. I put a hand on his arm to stop him.

"It's not allowed," Jane whispered.

Moody froze, I suspected more in response to Jane's words than my hand.

"What do you think would happen if you remembered?" Kate asked.

Jane looked up at her, made eye contact for the first time. "Daddy would get in trouble."

"How would he get in trouble?"

I was a bit surprised by Kate's choice of words, not *why* but *how*.

"He'd go to jail," Jane said.

"Why do you think that?" Kate asked.

"He told me he would, that people are ignorant. They don't understand."

I swallowed hard. I had a strong suspicion where this was going and it made my stomach roil.

"What don't they understand?"

"How daddies are supposed to love their daughters."

———◦———

Kate had been able to get a few more tidbits out of Jane, before she shut down.

The abuse had begun around age ten, shortly after the girls' biological father, who was in prison, had given up his parental rights and the stepfather had adopted the girls. Brown had said that now he was officially her father, and this was the way that fathers loved their daughters.

I'd stifled the urge to gag.

Brown had also worked hard to get Cissy and her younger sister to hate their mother and only trust him.

That made my chest ache.

At one point, Sheriff Taylor had mumbled, "I don't believe a word of this."

I'd shot him a sharp look. Perhaps not the most diplomatic way to interact with a colleague, but I didn't want him saying more and maybe the young woman would hear him.

Most of the time, she was answering Kate in short, monotone sentences, her head hanging down some, like she'd just been caught with her hand in the cookie jar.

"Cecilia," Kate said at one point, in a somewhat sharper voice.

The girl's head jerked up.

Aha, so you are *definitely Cecilia*, I thought.

"Sweetheart, you're not in trouble," Kate said yet again. "Chief Anderson will protect you, keep you safe."

I winced, wishing Kate hadn't said that.

Because there was still the matter of the blood on her dress.

CHAPTER ELEVEN

"How do we know she ain't makin' it all up?" Sheriff Taylor protested. "I mean, Joe...he loves them girls like his own."

I scowled at him from behind my desk, but Kate had more patience than I did. "Confabulation is rare," she said in a calm voice, from her perch on the edge of her chair. "And especially in this case where there was amnesia involved. And she was so reluctant to tell us even after she remembered."

Taylor was staring at her, a funny look on his face.

"*Lying*," I said. "*Lying* is rare."

He turned slightly in his chair—we'd given him the comfy one, which I was now regretting, especially since poor Bradley was in his sister's usual position, butt leaning against my closed door. The sheriff snapped, "I know what the hell con-fab-u-lation means." He spread the word out, emphasizing each syllable.

"It's not really lying," Kate said to me, "because the person doesn't realize their brain is making stuff up, to fill in the gaps." She shook her head. "It's not intentional. And it's not what's happening here, in my professional opinion."

"Well, I think maybe it is, and maybe it's intentional," Taylor said. "What better way to divert attention from whatever she's been up to than by accusin' her daddy."

I scowled at him again. I'm not the most patient person to begin with, and it was now after eight. Fatigue was starting to slow my brain and weigh down my limbs.

"Of course, that is possible," Kate said, now sounding like it was more of an effort to remain calm. "But I think you all need to proceed on the assumption that she is telling the truth, until you have evidence to the contrary."

"What about innocent until proven guilty," Taylor said.

"I meant as you *investigate*." There was definitely a sharp edge to Kate's tone now. She adjusted her position in the uncomfortable vinyl and chrome chair.

"And there's the note Cissy left," the sheriff said, "'bout how she was runnin' away 'cause she couldn't face Krissy's family no more. It didn't say nothin' about her stepdaddy hurtin' anybody—her or Krissy."

"Did you have the handwriting analyzed?" Kate asked. "To make sure it was Cecilia's."

The sheriff spluttered some, but then admitted the note was on her laptop.

"So it could've been written by anyone," Kate said.

Tired of the argument. I changed the subject. "Okay, we've got two major pieces to sort out still. The blood on her dress. And who the hell is Jake? That's not her father's name."

Taylor shook his head. "There's a couple a Jakes in Deweyville, but best I know neither of them normally rub elbows with the Browns."

"Did either of them disappear," I asked, "around the same time as Jane, I mean Cecilia did? Or maybe they started going away for periods of time?"

Taylor seemed to ponder that for a moment. "Can't say that either has been absent for any length of time. Well, exceptin' Jake Darnell. He's a long-distance truck driver."

"The perfect cover for a trafficker," I said.

Taylor frowned again. "Nah, he's a good family man, goes to church regular and all."

"Traffickers and abusers," Kate's low, gentle voice was at odds with her words, "can be very good at *appearing* to be good people."

Taylor looked at her, then sighed.

Bradley pushed away from where he'd been leaning against the door. "I could run a check on him. Might be more discreet than you trying to do it, Sheriff, with your people maybe noticing what you're up to."

Kudos to Bradley for diplomacy. Of course, we would have run our own check on the man anyway, but he made it sound like we were doing the sheriff a favor.

The latter narrowed his eyes at my second in command, as if to say what kind of dumb hick do you take me for. But his thick lips said, "Sure. Forward me your results."

"Did you bring the photo we requested?" Bradley asked.

"What photo?"

"Of Cecilia when she was fifteen," I said.

"When'd you request that?"

"We emailed around two-thirty," Bradley said.

"I was on the road already. Why do ya need to know what she looked like back then?"

And why are you being so evasive? I thought. If the roles were reversed, I would've long since sent him everything I had on the case.

Bradley and I exchanged a glance. I nodded slightly.

"We found some videos." He paused. "Porn. She might be the young girl in them."

The sheriff stared at him for a beat. Then he closed his eyes and his face sagged.

"You can't see who the male is," I added. "Could have been her father or this Jake person."

The sheriff shook his head slowly, back and forth. He opened his eyes and his generous lips became a thick firm line.

"I'll send ya the whole file, when I get home. I don't have time to let you make a copy of it now."

Hmm, so you had the file with you the whole time, you cagey bastard!

He paused, sighed. "I was gonna stay over. But now, I think I need to get back to Deweyville tonight, and be there when Joe Brown gets home."

If *Joe Brown goes home,* I thought, but I kept that to myself.

Bradley had walked Kate and the sheriff to their cars. At the latter, Taylor had paused long enough to show Bradley the pic of Cecilia from his file. Again, the lieutenant had taken a photo of the photo.

Now we stood at my desk, staring at the phone in his hand. He used his finger to move one photo over. "This is the one from the fake sheriff."

I sucked in air. The girl could be a younger version of our Jane, but the expression... It was a come-hither look that had no business being on a fifteen-year-old's face.

The photo had obviously been cut off at the neck. The bottom edge was crooked. Only one shoulder showed.

It was bare.

My stomach churned. "That son-of-a-bitch. We should've shown this to the real Taylor."

"I wanted to get your opinion first." Bradley flipped back to the photo from the case file.

I stared at that teen's smiling face for a moment. "It could be the same girl, but the different expressions make it hard to tell for sure."

"That's what I thought." Bradley pulled the phone away and scrolled to something else. He turned it toward me again. "Here's a still from one of the videos."

The girl in this one had a glazed expression. *Dissociated, Kate would call it.*

"Again, could be the same person," I said. "In the morning, have Derek use facial scanning to confirm."

Our facial recognition software was a recent purchase. Derek would be thrilled to take it for a test drive.

Bradley's face brightened. "Good idea."

It was almost ten by the time I got home. During the short drive, I'd instructed my Bluetooth to send Bill Walker a text.

Kate got a little more out of her. Likely she was sexually abused by her stepfather.

Shit! was Bill's response.

Then, *not surprised though.*

I sighed. *We'll talk tomorrow.*

Pipsqueak greeted me just inside my apartment door with a loud meow, protesting the delay in her dinner service.

I reached down and scratched behind her ears. "I know, life is hard, little one." I straightened. "And no Sam tonight to spoil both of us."

He had an early staff meeting tomorrow at the county jail. There had been a major shakeup there recently, after Sam had discovered that a couple of his corrections officers were on someone else's payroll besides his.

He was currently holding weekly staff meetings there, both to keep a closer eye on the jail's operations and to reassure his remaining people that he was on top of things.

"I don't know what you're complaining about," I said to the cat, as I dished up her canned dinner. "You've got kibble available all day long in that automatic feeder thingy Barnes bought you."

Pipsqueak ignored me as she tucked into her kitty paté.

I found two slices of cold pizza in the fridge. Nothing was growing on them so I ate them, then washed them down with a glass of red wine. A quick shower and I was in bed by eleven, and asleep within seconds.

The dead woman rose from the kitchen floor. Her back was to me.

I held my breath, waiting for her to turn around.

Usually it was my mother's face, but sometimes it was something more gruesome, like a black hole where her face should be.

I realized this must be another of those dreams where I knew I was dreaming. Lucid dreaming, *Kate had told me it was called.*

The woman slowly turned. It wasn't Mom. It was my Aunt Jean's face, with tears streaming down her cheeks.

"Find her, Judith." Her voice echoed in a surreal way. "Find your cousin."

I jolted upright, gasping for air, my own cheeks wet. Impatiently, I swiped at them with the back of my hand and struggled to suck air into my constricted lungs.

I turned to Sam, but of course his side of the bed was empty.

An odd mix of loneliness and relief washed through me, leaving my stomach hollow and my muscles limp. At least there was no witness to my tears, and to the nightmare that had caused them.

There was enough ambient light—from the lights of the city filtering around my drapes—to make out Pipsqueak curled up at the foot of the bed on Sam's side. She opened her big blue eyes and stared at me, as if asking if I intended to continue interrupting her sleep.

I shook my head slightly. She yawned, exposing tiny teeth and a pink tongue, and closed her eyes again.

"Great. You're a lot of help," I muttered.

One white furry ear twitched.

I sank back into my pillow, now wide awake. I hadn't thought about that horrible summer day in years.

I was at my Aunt Jean's—my mom was at the doctor's or something—and we were playing hide and seek in her backyard. Me, age six, Paul, age eight, and his older sister, Meredith, age ten.

The latter was "it," and Paulie and I ran to hide. I found the perfect spot, under the giant lilac bush at the corner of the house.

I'd heard the phone ringing inside, and then the slam of the screen door as Aunt Jean went in to answer it.

Minutes ticked by. I remembered stifling a giggle. This was such a great hiding place. The leaves were so thick I couldn't see out, which meant Meredith couldn't see in.

More time passed. It was probably only another minute or two, but to a six-year-old it was beginning to feel like forever.

I was about to peek out when I heard Aunt Jean calling our names. "Meredith, Paulie, Judith. Where are you?"

We're hiding, of course, I'd thought. But why couldn't she see Meredith?

Aunt Jean called our names again and I crawled out from under the bush.

The rest of that day was a blur of a six-year-old's impressions. My Aunt Jean crying, men in dark blue uniforms traipsing around the backyard, Paul looking dazed. Then my mother was there too, and she and Aunt Jean were clinging to each other and sobbing.

As a child, I'd had only a vague idea of what was going on, but now my stomach clenched.

There had been no trace of my cousin Meredith, then or since.

CHAPTER TWELVE

I never did get back to sleep.

And after my morning calisthenics and a long shower, I was still groggy. For a few seconds, the thought of calling out sick had some appeal. But I was too damned responsible for that, and there was too much to do today.

At 3MB, Barnes was at her desk. "I tested for Covid," she quickly said. "Twice, negative both times. It's only a cold." She held up a brown medicine bottle. "And I've got the cough under control now."

"Good," I said. "You up for a field trip?"

She jumped up out of her chair. "Sure. Where?"

"To visit our old friend Misty, who is not returning my calls."

"I found a current address for her."

I smiled. Barnes redefined the word *efficient*.

We exited the building into a beautiful March day. The sun was shining, low humidity, about seventy degrees. The fragrance of spring flowers on a warm breeze wafted over us.

"You want me to drive?" Barnes asked.

"Any codeine in that cough medicine?"

"I'm not sure. It's what my doc called in."

"Best if I drive then. Can't have the chief's assistant getting stopped for a DUI."

We climbed into my car and Barnes held her phone up. "Got the address programmed into Google Maps. Turn right."

Fifteen minutes later, we were rapping on Misty's apartment door.

Seconds ticked by. I rapped again.

More seconds turned into two full minutes.

"Maybe she's not home," Barnes said.

"This early, she's home." But I knew she was probably sleeping. I didn't care. After being ignored for two days, I was kind of liking the idea of rousting her out of bed.

Finally a bleary-eyed, thirty-something man opened the door a crack. He hid all but his head behind the door. "What the hell?"

I held up my badge. "Sorry to disturb you, sir. We need to talk to Melissa Tracy."

His eyes cleared, then morphed to wary. "Um, I'm not sure she's here."

Barnes, beside me, shifted her weight. I was pretty sure she'd just stuck her sturdy black oxford in the path of the door.

"She's not in trouble, sir," I said. "Unless she keeps ignoring my attempts to contact her."

Rustling and something gauzy moved behind him. Looking relieved, the man's head disappeared.

And Misty was standing in the doorway, wearing a chiffon contraption that no doubt was meant to be a robe. But one could make out the outline of her body through it.

"May we come in?" I asked.

Her expression said she really wanted to say *no*. But she plastered on a fake smile and pivoted aside, gesturing with her arm. "Sure, by all means."

We stepped over the threshold and I caught sight of the man—skinny, in nothing but boxers—scurrying through a doorway down a hall off the living room.

The apartment was nicely furnished, with tasteful touches like vases and colorful throw pillows.

I nodded. "Looks like you've landed on your feet, Misty."

This time, her smile was more genuine. "You remember my client Joey?"

"The one whose last name you wouldn't give us?"

"Yeah. His wife figured out he was using that escort service and she divorced him. He lives with me now and is my protector."

I tilted my head toward the hallway. "Boxer shorts guy?"

She nodded, a softer smile on her face now. "What can I do for you, Chief?"

"I need to know what happened to the business card I gave you?"

She gave me a strange look. "That's kinda weird."

"My asking about it or what happened to it, which is weird?"

"Both." She gestured toward a white leather sofa. I sat and she settled across from me on a matching armchair. She glanced sideways at Barnes, who had taken out her pad and pencil.

I looked up, made eye contact with Barnes, then lowered my gaze to the sofa cushion beside me.

She took the hint and sat, her hands relaxing in her lap, although she still held pad and pen.

"I have this friend," Misty said. "She's independent, like me, but she doesn't have a protector. Some pimp has been pressuring her to join his stable, so I gave her your card. I figured she might need it more than me."

"Does this friend have a name?" I asked.

"Um, she goes by Sara. I don't know if that's real or not. One doesn't ask too many questions." The words *in this business* were left unsaid.

She gave me a fake sweet smile, then her expression morphed into one of genuine concern. "Is she in trouble?"

"No, I don't think so," I said. "Have you seen the report in the paper, about a young woman with amnesia?" I'd been pissed at the Starling Sun when that article had come out on Wednesday. But now, as Misty nodded, I could at least appreciate that it was saving us some time.

"We're trying to figure out who she is," I added. A fib, since we were already pretty sure of her identity. But I wanted to know where Cissy got my card. It might give us some of the pieces that were missing in her memories. "Can you describe Sara?"

"Hmm, she's a little on the short side, and a tad plump, but a lot of guys like curves, especially older men. Blonde hair. Blue eyes. Nice complexion. She takes care of herself."

"You have a last name for her, and/or an address?"

Misty shook her head. "And I don't think she was ever arrested. She aims for a bit classier clientele. I can give you her cell phone number, but the last couple of times I've called her, it went right to voicemail."

She rattled off a number and Barnes wrote it down.

"When was the last time you saw her?" I asked.

Misty stared at the ceiling for a moment. "I think it was about ten days ago. We had brunch together, at the deli. She had a black eye, but it was fading. She said someone that pimp had sent around had given it to her. I encouraged her to report him to the police, but she was afraid to."

"Did she say anything else?"

"Yes, that she might just get on a bus and head west, although that sounded more like wishful thinking than a true plan. She has a fair number of regulars here." Misty's eyes went wide. "Wait, she insisted on paying for our meal, and she used a credit card. I only caught a glimpse of it, but I think her last name was something short, started with an S. Sessions or Samuels or something like that."

Barnes was scribbling again.

"That's really, really helpful," I said. I held out a picture we had taken of Cissy when she'd first shown up at the police station. "Have you ever seen this woman?"

Misty studied it, before shaking her head.

I rose from the sofa. Barnes followed suit. "Thanks for your time, and sorry for waking you so early."

Misty rose as well. "Wait, is that the woman with amnesia?" She gestured toward the photo still in my hand. "And what's she got to do with Sara?"

I hesitated, stared at her for a moment. "Can I trust you to keep something confidential?"

She nodded.

I wasn't sure I believed her, but I was about to make it worth her while. "A piece that we kept back from the press was that this Jane Doe had my business card in her possession, so we've been trying to track any folks I've given cards to. If you can locate Sara and/or find out what she did with my card, it's worth a couple of hundred to me."

I figured any less than that would not be enough for Misty to bother with. She was a high-end call girl, not a streetwalker.

She nodded.

"*But*," I said, "if I hear about the business card angle on the street or in the news, I'll know where it came from."

Misty made a cross over her heart with an index finger, then put it to her lips.

Once outside her apartment building, Barnes said, "Aren't you going to do something about her hooking?"

"What hooking?" I said. "She lives with a guy, and they have an open relationship."

"So no harm, no foul?" Her eyebrows were halfway up her forehead. "Haven't I heard you say that there's no such thing as a victimless crime?"

"Yeah, I probably said that before, but this one comes close. And I'm thinking I will cultivate Misty as a confidential informant." It was standard practice to overlook mild to moderate crimes committed by COs, a tradeoff for the information they provided.

Barnes gave me another sideways glance, but then she nodded. "Next stop, the deli?"

"Yup."

Sam was waiting his turn in front of the counter at the deli.

"I seem to be tripping over men in khaki uniforms everywhere these days," I muttered.

He turned and smiled at us. "What was that?"

"Nothing. I'll tell you later."

"Did you get any breakfast?" he asked.

My stomach growled by way of an answer.

Sam chuckled. "Two egg white and cheese sandwiches," he said to Mr. B behind the counter. "Bacon on hers." He poked his thumb in my direction. "You want anything, Gloria?"

Barnes's face brightened. "A chocolate milkshake. I'll pay you back."

Sam waved her off and ordered her milkshake. Mr. B stepped away to give our order to the gangly kid manning the grill.

"I thought you had a breakfast meeting at the jail today," I said to Sam.

He grimaced. "The jail administrator's idea of breakfast is donuts and coffee."

"Works for me."

"Says the woman who eats more cholesterol in a day than I do in a week."

"Are you gonna tell me you did *not* have a donut?"

His cheeks pinked, but then he grinned. "Yes, I had one, but I don't consider it breakfast."

I grinned back at him.

Mr. B returned and looked past us, about to take the next person's order. I raised a finger in the air. "Can I speak to you for a moment, Mr. B, about a police matter?"

Worry clouded Maurice Bernstein's brown eyes. "Something wrong, Chief?" He ran gnarled hands down the front of his white bib apron.

"No, no." I gestured for him to move to the end of the counter, out of earshot of the people waiting in line. "I need you to go through your credit card receipts," I said in a low voice, "for the last two weeks. I'm looking for a thirtyish woman, blonde, a little plump, who was in here having brunch with another woman–"

"Oh, yes. Misty's friend."

I was a bit surprised that he was so familiar with the local call girls, but maybe he only knew them as regular customers. "Her first name is Sara, last name starts with an S."

Mr. B glanced toward the counter, where three people now stood in line. "I'm shorthanded this morning. Can I do it later, after my granddaughter comes in?"

I paused. There really was no great urgency, now that we were pretty sure of Cecilia's identity. I was pursuing the business card angle only because Sara might know something relevant—something that might fill in some of the huge gaps remaining in Cissy's memory.

If the card Cissy had was even the same one that Misty had given to Sara.

"That's fine, Mr. B. I appreciate the help."

"No problem." He patted my arm and then bustled off to take the next person's order.

Sam walked up to me, a grease-stained white paper bag in his hand. "You wanna take these back to your office?" He handed Barnes her milkshake.

"Thanks," she said and eagerly slurped some down. "Oh, that feels good on my throat."

We exited the deli. Sam and I fell into step side-by-side as we crossed at the corner and headed down the sidewalk, Barnes trailing behind. There weren't many pedestrians now—most folks had apparently settled into their places of employment to begin their workday.

"So, why the comment about men in khaki uniforms earlier?" Sam asked.

As we entered the building and went up in the elevator, I filled him in on the events of the previous evening, including the preponderance of sheriffs.

Sam scratched his head. "You're assuming the fake sheriff was the girl's stepfather?"

"Yes." We exited the elevator on the third floor. "That's what the real sheriff thought, after I'd described him. He was wearing a khaki uniform, only long-sleeved and slightly darker than yours."

"What does the stepfather do for a living?" he asked.

I paused, recalling the background check Bradley had done on the man. He'd texted me this morning with the gist of the results. Details of his life were sketchy before Joseph Brown met and married Audrey Carmichael, and then adopted her two daughters. Around the time of that marriage, he'd started a home improvement company.

"Contractor, home improvements," I said.

Sam handed me the bag of sandwiches and pulled out his phone. He poked at its screen as we traversed the bullpen.

From behind us came the gurgling sound of Barnes's straw hitting the bottom of her milkshake. "Ahh," she said, and settled behind her desk.

Sam turned the phone toward me. "Like this?"

On the screen were the words, *Dickie's Work Uniforms*. Under them was a picture of a male model wearing dark khaki pants and shirt.

"Well," I said, "that solves that little mystery. I wonder where he got the badge?"

"Online, probably," Sam said.

"Probably," I said, heat rising in my cheeks. "I didn't look at it all that carefully. I should've."

Sam shrugged. "Hindsight is twenty-twenty." We entered my office.

Bradley had walked up and came in after us, then stopped just inside the doorway. "Uh, did you two want to be alone?" he said in a teasing tone.

I gave him a mock glare as Sam and I settled on either side of my desk, wrapped sandwiches in front of us. "Anything on the BOLO on Cissy's stepdad?" I asked Bradley.

Bradley shook his head. "No sign of him in northern Florida, so far."

I sighed. "I'm not sure if that's good or bad."

"Also," Bradley said, "that guy, Jacob Darnell in Deweyville, he checks out. No priors, good credit, nothing hinky that I can find."

"As Kate would say, that doesn't mean he's not a child abuser. It only means he's never been caught." I unwrapped my sandwich and took a bite. My stomach rumbled in happy anticipation.

Bradley nodded. "Next, I'm gonna dig deeper into Joseph Brown. Do you think it's worth sending someone up to Alabama to see what's going on in that town? The sheriff seemed less than forthcoming."

"Hmm, not sure." I'd be doing that in a heartbeat, if we had more manpower right now, but... "Let's keep that as a possible course of action. What–"

Voices from Barnes's desk area interrupted me. One of them was male. I didn't recognize it.

Bradley turned in that direction, as his sister stepped into the doorway. "Somebody's here who says he's Cissy's cousin," Barnes said.

"Oh, good lord," I muttered.

Sam snorted. "I wonder when her fairy godmother's gonna show up?"

Another voice, female, filtered into my office—one that I did recognize.

Kate!

"Um," I said, "I think she just did."

CHAPTER THIRTEEN

"I woke up this morning worrying about Cecilia," Kate said from the comfy chair that Sam had vacated. He now stood next to Bradley near the door, munching on his sandwich.

I looked longingly at my own, which was missing only two bites.

"What will happen now?" Kate continued. "Since she's remembered her identity, I'm not sure that she technically has to be in the hospital. But she's still pretty fragile."

"And there's the matter of the blood on her dress when she came in," Bradley said.

"Not to mention," Sam added, "that people keep showing up trying to claim her."

Kate's worried look morphed to downright alarm. "Who?"

"That guy you passed," I said. "I told Barnes to take him to an interview room and get him a coffee or something. He claims he's Cecilia's cousin."

I made eye contact with her. "You wanna observe while I talk to him? Give me your take."

Kate nodded.

Sam gestured toward my sandwich. "Why don't you eat that first? Give your brain some fuel to run on."

I grabbed it up, took a bite, then made a face. It was cold. I shrugged and ate it anyway.

"Can I observe too?" Sam said. "Things are kinda slow out my way this week."

"Sure."

Sam, Kate and Bradley crowded into the observation area next to the interview room. It was roughly the square footage of a broom closet, but long and skinny. More than a bit snug with all three of them in there.

Barnes had wanted to observe as well, but I'd pointed out that close quarters with others wasn't a good idea right now, with her cold.

The young man sitting at the interview table was not at all what I'd expected. I'd had an image in my mind of a stereotypical sleazy person—longish stringy hair, pockmarked oily skin, unkempt clothing.

Reality was a clean-cut, fair-skinned young man, about Cecilia's age, with short dark hair and wearing jeans, a gray tee shirt and a navy windbreaker. His boyish face would give Bradley considerable competition for handsomest man in the building.

Sorry, Sam, I thought. It wasn't that Sam was less handsome, but his were more rugged good looks.

I sat in the empty chair across from the man, my back to the one-way mirror. The video equipment would be running already, but the old-fashioned window gave a better view than the smaller video screen.

A can of cola was on the table, a few inches from the guy's left hand.

"I'm Chief Anderson," I said, "and you are?" He'd only given the watch sergeant the name *Johnny.*

"Johnny," he repeated now, giving me a weak smile.

"Last name?" I laid a pad of paper on the table and clicked my pen.

"Um, Smith."

"Okay, Mr. Smith. You saw our Jane Doe's picture in the newspaper, I take it?"

"Uh, online actually, on my phone."

Of course online, on the paper's website—young people didn't read physical newspapers these days. "And you recognized her?"

"Yeah. She's my cousin, Cissy."

"And how exactly are you related?" I asked.

"Um, whadaya mean?"

"I mean whose son are you? Which side of the family?"

He looked totally confused for a second. Then his face cleared and he smiled—a big mouthful of teeth, only a couple of them slightly crooked. "Oh, um, through Uncle Jake."

I glanced quickly over my shoulder and blinked twice, hoping Bradley was paying close attention.

Shifting back around, I asked, "And how are you related to Uncle Jake?"

Back to confusion on his face. "Um, he's my uncle."

I gave him a hard stare. Was this guy not too bright? "Your mother's brother or your father's?"

"Um, my father's?" He said it like a question—and he wasn't sure of the answer.

"And what is Jake's last name?"

"Um, Smith?"

I resisted the urge to shake my head. Definitely not the sharpest knife in the drawer. I changed tactics. "Are you and your cousin close?" I intentionally avoided saying her name.

"Um." He swallowed hard.

This guy sure said *um* a lot.

"Yeah, of course. We live with Uncle Jake."

"And how long have you lived with him?"

"Since I was twelve."

"What happened to your parents?"

"Jake said they died."

Hmm, no *uncle* this time.

"You don't remember it?"

He shook his head. "I don't really remember much from before twelve. Ja...uh, Uncle Jake said that was for the best. I was starting with a clean slate then."

"Did he tell you how your parents died?"

He shook his head again, more vigorously. "Look, when can I see Cissy? She must be terrified, all alone in jail."

I paused debating which to pursue first, the name or the jail comment. I went with the latter. "Why do you assume she's in jail?"

"Um, I don't know. I, uh..." He trailed off.

A soft knock and Bradley stuck his head in. I gestured for him to enter.

He approached the table and handed me a photo—of Cecilia. For a moment, I thought he'd misread my signal, then I spotted the other photo in his hand.

I didn't show the photo to Johnny. Of course he'd recognize it. He'd seen it online. "How tall is Cissy?" I asked.

"Five-eight," Johnny said. It was the first time his voice sounded confident.

"And how much does she weigh?"

"One-twenty."

I didn't have those details in front of me, but that sounded about right. But how did a male cousin know so confidently what she weighed?

"Is this her?" I turned the photo around and set it in front of him.

Relief brightened his face. He grabbed the photo up, and for a moment, I thought he might kiss it.

"Yes, yes, that's her. When can I see her?"

"In a little bit. She's fine. But she's in the hospital temporarily."

Johnny's expression reverted to confusion again, but before he could ask questions, I held out my hand to Bradley. He put the other photo in it. It was from Spencer's autopsy, a close up of the face, gray and lifeless.

I laid it on the table in front of Johnny. "Do you know this man?"

His face paled, and his lips curled downward. But he shook his head.

"Are you sure?"

He shook his head again, more vehemently, and closed his eyes.

"I think you do know him," I said more emphatically. "Is this Uncle Jake?"

His shoulders shook as his face clouded. He nodded slowly and let his head drop. "He's dead, isn't he?"

"I'm afraid so," I said, gentling my voice.

A soft sniffle. Then he raised his head and made eye contact. "Please, can I see Cissy now?"

"Soon. I'm sorry for your loss." I extended my hand.

He snatched his own hand back. He must have thought I was reaching for it.

"I was going to get rid of that soda can for you."

He grabbed the can. "It's not gone yet." He tipped it up and faked a sip.

I held my hand out.

And the sleazy guy I'd initially expected was suddenly looking at me. His eyes had gone hard, and his mouth curled up in a smirk. "I'll take it with me," he said, as he rose to his feet.

Bradley stiffened beside me, bracing himself.

But Johnny strode away from us, toward the door. "I'll be in touch," he said over his shoulder.

For a fleeting moment, I thought we'd be able to get fingerprints off the doorknob. Then I noticed the sleeve of his windbreaker—he'd let it slide down over his hand. And he was now turning the knob with the cloth covering his fingers.

Damn! That's got to be intentional.

Unfortunately, we had no grounds to detain him, but we hustled after him out into the hallway.

Barnes was exiting the bullpen. I gestured her over and whispered, "Follow him. Get that soda can when he dumps it."

The elevator bell dinged and we turned. Johnny was getting on it. He smiled and waved.

Barnes waited until the doors closed before racing toward the fire stairs.

Bradley and I darted across the hall to the floor-to-ceiling windows on the front of the building. We stood close to the glass, staring down at the sidewalk.

Seconds ticked by before Johnny exited and strolled off to his left. He still had the can in his hand.

Barnes wasn't far behind him, looking down at her phone in her hands as she walked.

Clever girl! I was quite sure she was actually watching her quarry carefully.

"Get somebody else out there," I said, "to help–"

I froze. The guy had suddenly lobbed the soda can out into the street, right in front of a bus.

He glanced back over his shoulder, and even from the third floor, I could make out the smirk on his face. He took off at a jog.

I looked back at Barnes and sucked in my breath. She was darting out into the road, hand up, trying to stop traffic. As she leaned down to snatch something off the ground, a taxi barely missed her head. She pivoted and ran back for the curb.

I put my hand over my pounding heart.

Meanwhile, another officer had exited the front of the building. He ran after Johnny, but the latter had disappeared among the pedestrians scattered along the sidewalk. The uniform kept running, though.

"Maybe he can still see him," Bradley said from beside me. I hadn't even noticed that he'd disappeared and then returned, I'd been so intent on willing Barnes to safety.

Now she raised the squashed soda can, holding it gingerly with two fingers, and grinned up at us.

"I'm gonna kill her," her brother muttered from beside me.

"You would've done the same thing," I said.

"Totally beside the point."

"Can you get that boy's DNA profile over to NCMEC?" Kate leaned forward in the visitor's chair, her eyes anxious.

I mentally deciphered the initials—National Center for Missing and Exploited Children. Out loud, I replied, "We've got to get the profile first." I picked up my desk phone's receiver and called Bert Deming.

"Yes, Chief," Bert said, "what can I do for you?"

"Officer Barnes brought you a soda can–"

"Yes, I got it. But I'm not sure we're gonna get any useful prints off of it, smashed up like it is."

"I'm more concerned about getting DNA from the saliva on it," I said. "Is there enough of a sample?"

"Yeah."

"What's the protocol to get priority at the FDLE lab for a DNA analysis?"

I expected him to say there wasn't any, that we waited our turn at the Florida Department of Law Enforcement's lab, like every other agency in this part of the state.

"Well, that's all changed now," he said instead. "Didn't you get the email from SAC Wilder?"

I vaguely remembered something from Dot Wilder. I sighed, trying to recall the details.

"Wait, lemme find it," Bert said. "Here it is. Quote, the FDLE's Jacksonville Regional Operations Center is proud to announce that we have acquired an approved Rapid DNA Device for our laboratory. This device can automatically produce a DNA profile in less than two hours. Understandably there will be a high demand for its use, so the protocols below will be instituted immediately, blah, blah."

The sound of Bert sucking in air. "The relevant protocol is, quote, 'DNA that will aid in an active investigation,' end quote, takes priority. DNA of a person who has been arrested is next. So it can be run through CODIS to see if the person is wanted for other crimes or has any aliases, et cetera. DNA that is needed for the prosecution of a case that has already been solved is next, and it has to go through a more rigorous process of being analyzed by a forensic scientist. As does any DNA collected from a crime scene, because it could be contaminated, or could contain DNA from multiple people."

"Such as the blood from that motel room," I said.

"Yes," Bert confirmed, "which is why that's taking so long. The email's signed Acting Special Agent in Charge Dorothy Wilder."

I made a note to touch base with Dot Wilder soon and discuss the lab's new toy in more detail.

"So," I asked, "where would DNA from a person of interest, who may or may not be related to a victim and/or to another person of interest, fall in there?"

"I could make a case for that being in aid of an investigation."

"Good. Get that sample from the can and take it to the lab yourself." I glanced up, made eye contact with Kate, who was sitting on the edge of her chair. "Oh, and how do we get a copy of the analysis over to NCMEC?"

"Uh." A pause, during which I suspected Bert was trying to figure out why such a request. "I'm not sure. If it's an arrestee, the DNA is automatically compared to DISC."

"What's that?" All these initials were giving me a headache.

"The DNA Index of Special Concern. It's a sub-index of CODIS, with DNA profiles from unsolved cases."

"Such as a child abduction?"

"Yeah. But I don't know if it would have the child's DNA, just any unidentified DNA from the crime scene. There's a special form to fill out to submit DNA to be entered in it, so not all agencies do that."

"Arrggh," I growled. I glanced at Kate again. "Just get the analysis and we'll send it to NCMEC ourselves."

"Okay, I'll see what I can do." Bert disconnected.

"He's gonna try to get a rush job on the DNA," I summarized for Kate.

Then I turned to my computer and plugged in a Google search for NCMEC. I began skimming the introductory paragraphs. My eye snagged on the date the organization was created—1984.

Three years after Meredith disappeared from that backyard.

CHAPTER FOURTEEN

"So, what are we going to do with Cecilia?" Kate asked, pulling me out of my reverie about Meredith.

I sighed. "We now have a connection between her and our homicide victim, which makes her a person of interest in that case and/or a possible witness. So if Dr. Moody feels he has to discharge her, I can make a case for taking her into protective custody. I'll have to research the laws on that here in Florida."

Damn, I thought, *if only I'd had a better orientation than the half-day of BS I'd received from my predecessor.* Although even if he'd been a better guide, that particular issue might not have come up.

This was an unusual situation, to say the least.

"I need to go to the conference room and add stuff to the murder board." I was about to add that Kate could go back to her folks' place and get on with her vacation. But she jumped up as if to follow me.

And I let her, feeling vaguely guilty. I shouldn't be screwing up her visit with her parents like this.

I looked back over my shoulder.

The guilt must have shown on my face because she pursed her lips and shook her head. "I'm a grown woman, and I'm invested in this now."

In the smaller conference room, I strode over to the murder board and was instantly aware of how gruesome the crime scene photos were.

I glanced Kate's way again. Other than avoiding looking directly at the goriest of the photos, she showed no signs of distress.

I reminded myself that she'd been in more than her share of violent situations through the years, usually ending up in those circumstances in an attempt to help her clients.

And this is why she's retired from doing psychotherapy. She tended to get too involved, to care too much.

I gestured for her to take a seat at the conference table, while I stood in front of the white board. There were three aliases after the victim's name, including Jack Smith.

I picked up a dry-erase marker and added *Uncle Jake.* Then I turned to Kate. "Our victim was a sleaze ball. He'd been arrested in Jacksonville in the past for making and distributing porn. Some of the videos that were confiscated have girls of dubious ages in them, one of whom might be Cecilia."

I made a mental note to check with Derek the Geek on the facial recognition results. Then thought, *no time like the present.* I took out my phone and texted Derek.

I turned back to the board and put a heading at the top of a blank area—*links between victim and Cecilia/Cissy Brown.* Under it, I wrote: *1. starred in his videos when 15?*

I pointed to the photo of the chair from the crime scene. "There were droplets of blood on the chair's legs and the outer edges of the back, but not in the middle, and Cissy had blood droplets on the front of her dress. We've speculated that someone sat in that chair and witnessed the murder."

I wrote: *2. Cissy could have been in the chair, witnessed murder?*

"But..." I turned back to Kate, "the blood type of the droplets on the chair and her dress are different from the victim's."

"Was the blood type the same on the chair and the dress?" Kate asked.

"Yes, but it was O positive, the most common type in the U.S. The victim's was AB positive, much less common."

My phone pinged. A reply from Derek. All three photos of the fifteen-year-old were the same girl.

I called him. "Are you sure?"

"Yeah, expressions may change but bone structure doesn't."

And our adult Cissy?"

"Same person. A bit thinner but again–"

"Bone structure. Got it. Thanks, Derek."

I repeated the absolute identification to Kate as I went back and erased the question mark after *starred in his videos when 15.*

My chest ached.

Kate pointed to the crime scene photo of the victim, John Spencer, naked and bloody in the bed. "I take it you all are assuming they were making a porn movie."

"Yes, and apparently one that included violence. Some of the fresh blood on the bed and on the wall behind it was O positive as well."

Kate's eyes searched the board. "No video equipment?"

"No, just a tripod and lights." I pointed to the photos of those. "No camera. And the place was wiped clean of fingerprints, except for two partials. They're not in the system."

Kate's eyes had gone wide. "That would've taken a lot of time, to wipe down the entire room."

"Yup. We're working under the assumption that there was another person in that room, besides Cecilia and the victim."

"You're pretty sure it was Cissy in the chair?"

I sighed. "I am now, after the interview with that kid this morning." I didn't point out that the other option was someone else in the chair and Cissy wielding the knife. But then her dress would've had more than droplets on it. And again, wrong blood type.

I ground my teeth in frustration. We had more pieces of the puzzle, but they were not fitting together very well.

I made another addition to the list. *3. Young man, calls himself Johnny Smith, says he's Cissy's cousin; identified 'Uncle Jake' from autopsy photo.*

"And they are both sketchy about their memories of their childhoods," Kate said. "They both could've been abducted by this Jake guy and brainwashed to forget their earlier lives."

I whirled around. "But how could he make them forget ten, fifteen years of their lives?"

She shrugged. "He's had plenty of time to work on them, tell them over and over what he wants them to believe. And we've seen how readily Cissy slides into a dissociated state. She would be more suggestible when like that."

She paused, took a deep breath, her face tight. "And there could have been some kernels of truth in what he told Johnny. Maybe he had been mischievous—most boys are, to some extent. And maybe his parents were neglectful, or at least preoccupied with busy lives...And frustrated with a prepubescent boy who was starting to talk back. Doesn't mean they didn't love him, but it would be easy enough, over time, for Jake to convince him they didn't."

"Did your son, Billy go through that phase?" He was now thirteen or fourteen, if I remembered correctly.

She rolled her eyes. "He's still in it." But her face brightened as she thought about her kids.

I smiled at her expression, even though I had no clue how parents could tolerate, much less continue to love teenagers. *I'll have to take her word for it.*

I turned back to add to the board, in parentheses under number three, *(both abducted by Jake?)* And my smile quickly faded, as my chest tightened.

My mind had flashed to Meredith. I began to push the thought aside, then froze.

How often did that happen? Thoughts of my cousin would surface and I'd routinely shove them away.

The lilac bush, the sound of the screen door slamming...

"Judith, are you okay?" Kate's voice, full of concern.

I realized I was swaying on my feet. "Yeah, I'm fine." I cleared my throat, forcing my eyes to focus on the white board in front of me.

A note next to the crime scene photos reminded me of another loose end. I texted Bert.

Blood and hairs from motel bathroom drain, and blood from under Jane Doe's fingernails, have any of them been tested yet for DNA?

We now knew she was Cecilia/Cissy Brown, but the case was still marked *Jane Doe.*

Bert's reply came right back. *All sent to lab, marked open investigation, late Monday. Nothing back yet.*

Did you compare the dark one to Jane Doe's hair under the microscope before you sent it off?

Yes. Could be a match. Same color and thickness. I didn't put it in my report because not big enough sample to be definitive.

And since the advent of DNA, microscopic matching of hairs was no longer considered state-of-the-art forensic science.

I blew out a sigh. It had been over two days since the evidence was sent to the FDLE lab. Their new Rapid DNA toy didn't sound as impressive now. Or was the demand just so great?

I added another item to the list of links between John Spencer and Cissy Brown. *4. Hair at crime scene could be hers.*

The conference room door popped open and Detective Cruthers's big frame filled the opening. "Chief, you're in here," he said in his deep, rumbling voice. "I was looking for you or Bradley, and when I couldn't find you, I figured I'd put this on the board a while."

He waved a photo in the air as he stepped farther into the room. "We've found the victim's car. It was parked on a side street and the PEO was about to ticket it for an expired meter, but when she called it in, the license plate number didn't match the vehicle description. That's when she remembered the BOLO for Spencer's car."

I took the photo from him. It was indeed a dark blue BMW, a medium-sized sedan. "What's happening with it?"

"I called the dynamic duo but only Ernie was in the lab. He said he'd get right over there and process it. The PEO is sitting on it in the meantime, but I thought I'd go over and check it out as well."

"Good. Tell the PEO 'good work' for me."

"Will do, Chief." Cruthers left the room, pulling the door closed behind him.

Kate chuckled. "You wanna translate a few things there. I know what a BOLO is but what's a PEO?"

"Parking Enforcement Officer." I found a spot on the board and inserted the photo. "The politically correct term for a meter maid."

"And the dynamic duo?"

I turned back toward Kate. "Oh, that's not police lingo. It's what we sometimes call the crime scene techs, Bert and Ernie."

She snickered.

And I smiled in spite of myself. "Please don't do that in front of anybody, though. I'm trying to get my people to show them more respect. They're excellent CSIs."

"Ah, I know what that is, thanks to the TV show."

"Yeah, but don't believe what you see on those shows. They're pretty unrealistic. CSIs do not actively participate in investigations, other than analyzing physical evidence."

She nodded. "Getting back to my question, what do we do with Cissy now?" She paused, looking a bit chagrined. "Sorry if I'm being pushy, but I can't just walk away from all this without knowing that she's getting the help she needs."

I resisted the urge to point out to Kate that she might be getting a wee bit too invested. Instead, I said, "Lemme call Dr. Moody and get his input."

But before I could place the call, the phone rang in my hand. I jerked some, then felt my heart rate accelerate at the name on the caller ID.

It was my cousin Paul. But he was working days this week, and personal calls were strictly forbidden while the dispatchers were on duty.

I answered the call.

"Cuz," his voice was low, a little breathless, "you might want to get over to the hospital. Your Jane Doe attacked that poor intern again and escaped. Again."

"Thanks." I disconnected and said to Kate, "Cissy may have just solved our dilemma. She's now committed another assault."

CHAPTER FIFTEEN

I'd plopped my portable light bubble on my car's roof and hit the button for the jury-rigged siren. Kate covered her ears.

As we raced toward the hospital, I instructed my Bluetooth to call the watch desk and had a shouted conversation with Sergeant Armstrong. I told him to put out a BOLO on Cecilia Brown and her male "cousin," Johnny Smith.

"The guy who was in here this morning?" the sarge yelled back.

"That's the one."

"You got it, Chief."

At the entrance to the locked ward, I was greeted by a rattled Officer Peters, wearing civvies—a chambray shirt and blue jeans. "I'm so sorry, Chief." She fell into step with me, waving a denim-clad arm in the air. "I needed to use the restroom, and that intern said he would stand guard for a few minutes. I checked on the girl, and she seemed to be napping." She ran a slender brown hand down her face, which had a distinct ashen undertone. "I left the door open so he could see her in there–"

I held up a hand, feeling bad because I was the one who had been short staffed and had sent her here without any backup or relief. But I was so pissed at Cissy I was afraid to say anything, knowing it would come out harsh. And Peters would assume my harsh tone was aimed at her.

I stood in the doorway of Cissy's room and let my eyes examine it. The bedding was rumpled but otherwise the tiny room was neat. Still...

"I want my CS guys to go over this room," I said to Moody, who was hovering behind me.

He opened his mouth.

"She's now been implicated in a homicide. And she didn't just bop this guy on the head today. This is a serious assault." I'd been told the intern had still been unconscious when they'd whisked him off to Neurology for a CAT scan.

Grim-faced, the doctor nodded.

I glanced up at a camera in the corner of the hallway. "Does that work?"

"Yes," Moody said. "But there aren't any in the rooms, for obvious reasons."

"I need to see the footage now."

I turned to Kate, standing off to one side. She nodded.

Moody took us to the security office where the head of security introduced himself. He was a big black man, mid-forties, shoulders like a linebacker, with a touch of silver sprinkled among tight black curls. He led us to a room with a computer, pulled an extra chair up beside his, and hit some keys. A grainy video began playing on the monitor.

He jumped up and gestured toward the two empty chairs. "I'll be in my office if you need anything else."

Kate and I watched the exchange between Peters and the skinny intern. Then she stuck her head inside Cissy's room and came out again, leaving the door open.

Peters walked away and the door drifted closed. The intern jumped up and knocked on it. It opened partway again.

Even with the grainy image, I could make out the come-hither look on Cissy's face as she talked to the unsuspecting intern, with only her head showing.

There was sound but it was even worse quality than the video, and they were keeping their voices low. I could only make out the words, "door open," in the first exchange. He was apparently reminding her that she was supposed to keep her door open unless she was changing her clothes.

"Oh, that's what I was doing," she said—I could barely hear it, but I could read her lips. She opened the door a little farther, revealing a naked leg and side of her body. "Changing my clothes," I lip-read.

My chest ached. This girl-woman had learned at an early age how to use her body to get what she wanted.

The intern, bless his heart, had jumped back, but she reached out and grabbed his wrist. She yanked him forward and then smashed the door into the side of his head, jamming it between the doorframe and the door.

Kate winced.

"That had to hurt like hell," I said.

The young man had crumpled in the doorway. Cissy stepped partway out the door, a white robe hastily wrapped around her. She held it closed with one hand while she grabbed the back of his belt and clumsily dragged him into her room. The door closed.

Three minutes ticked by. The door opened again and swung wide, revealing a body in the bed, covered with blankets as if it were someone sleeping.

"She's strong," Kate commented, "to be able to wrestle him into that bed."

I shrugged. "He's a lightweight, and she had some adrenaline going for her."

Cissy stepped from behind the door and looked up and down the hall. Then she sauntered out and headed toward the ward's exit. She was dressed in dark slacks and a light-colored loose-fitting blouse—clothes the hospital must have provided for her.

The image on the monitor jumped and we were observing from a different angle—a different camera, no doubt. Cissy was at the ward's exit, her back to us. A short pause and the door opened. She stepped out. The door swung closed, and the end of the hallway was empty.

"Seen enough?" I asked.

Kate nodded, her mouth a tight, thin line.

We exited the small room and found the security chief in his office. "I'm going to need the originals of those videos," I said, "and an affidavit that you removed them from the cameras."

He handed me a paper evidence bag, a signature scribbled on the outside. "Both sim cards are in there. And..." He handed over a sheet of paper, with the same signature scrawled across the bottom. "Used to be on the job."

"Here in Starling?" I asked.

"Yeah, but it weren't the friendliest of climates for a man of my persuasion. I retired the second I was eligible."

"By your persuasion, you mean?"

"African-American. What'd you think I meant?"

I didn't answer, just glanced sideways at Kate. She seemed absorbed in her own thoughts.

"Oh," he let out a hearty chuckle, "you're thinkin' of Dan Bradley. Nope, not of that persuasion. Heard he made lieutenant. Good on him."

I smiled. "I'll pass that on."

"Thanks. Tell Bradley that Sergeant Brookman says *hey*. I'd made it to watch sergeant before Black came on board. Then you might say my career stalled out."

I promised to convey his good wishes and thanked him for his help.

Dr. Moody met us outside the security offices. "Did you get what you needed?"

"Yes," I said. "Do you know if Cissy had any contact with anyone this morning?"

"I thought of that and asked the nurse. She said her brother called."

"Cissy doesn't have a brother," Kate said.

"You know that and I know that." Dr. Moody frowned. "But the nurse didn't. She let her talk to him."

I nodded. "Okay. Thanks for all your help, Doc. And there will be assault charges this time, no matter what the hospital wants to do."

His frown deepened, but he nodded as well.

We said our goodbyes, and Kate and I headed for my car. Once out of Moody's earshot, she said, "Those kids, they've never really had a chance..." She trailed off.

I blew out air. "I know."

<hr>

Once in the car, I called the sarge again and updated the BOLO to include what Cissy was wearing, and that she and her supposed cousin were persons of interest in a homicide as well as an assault.

Kate sighed beside me but said nothing.

Next I called Peters and told her to go home and get some rest. She apologized again for letting Cissy get away.

"Not your fault." My tone was still sharper than was ideal.

"I shouldn't have left my post," she said.

"Look, chalk it up as a learning experience and get some sleep." I disconnected and sighed again. *It was my fault, for not giving her enough resources.* But I wasn't about to admit to that out loud.

"Being head honcho isn't as easy as it looks," Kate commented.

I shot her a sideways glare as I started my car engine. Sometimes she was too observant.

But then I found myself confessing. "I didn't have any problem busting my people's chops in Baltimore County. By the time a detective made it to the homicide unit, they were already seasoned. If they screwed up and I came down on them, they knew they deserved it."

"But now–"

"Now," I interrupted with a growl, "I'm surrounded by way too many rookie cops and newbie detectives."

"So *now*," Kate said with a half smile, "you have to strike a balance between correcting them and encouraging them. Not an easy task."

I shot her another glance, this one begrudgingly grateful. "Yeah."

Halfway back to the municipal building, my phone rang. The dashboard screen said *Sheriff Taylor*.

I accepted the call. "Good morning, Sheriff," I said, with more cheer than I felt.

"Wish it was," the sheriff's voice came through the Bluetooth speaker. "Joe Brown has taken off."

"Why am I not surprised," I said.

A snort came through the line. "I went there last night. He wasn't there, and Cissy's mom, she was claiming the girl made the whole thing up."

Kate heaved a sigh from beside me.

"Stand by her man and all that jazz," the sheriff continued. "I told her to call me right away if he came home, and I put a deputy on the house. But somehow he snuck in, gathered up some stuff, and took off."

Kate leaned forward in the passenger seat. "Sheriff, where's the younger sister?"

A half-beat of silence. "At school, the mother said. But I'll check. Call ya later, Chief."

He disconnected, and Kate and I exchanged a look. Her face was kind of scrunched up, like she was trying not to cry.

A couple minutes ticked by. Then Kate said, "She's still fragile."

"She didn't seem all that fragile in that video." I immediately regretted the snappish tone. Softening it, I added, "My officers are trained in de-escalation techniques." Or at least most of them had already taken the FDLE training. "They won't use any more force than necessary."

I glanced over. Kate was frowning as she stared out the windshield.

"She's committed a crime now, and she's definitely connected to my homicide victim."

"I know," Kate said. "But *she's* been victimized for years."

I sighed, my throat tightening. "And taught to distrust the police and the system in general."

"The very people who could help her, if she gave them a chance." Kate's voice sounded a little choked up.

Was she thinking of her own teenage daughter? A daughter who had also been adopted by a stepfather. Edie's biological father had been killed before she was born.

But Skip had turned out to be the good guy that he had seemed to be. Cissy hadn't been so lucky.

Duh! Kate wasn't just becoming overly involved like she might with a client. It was more personal than that.

And did I just have a warm, fuzzy thought about Skip Canfield? The annoying P.I. who'd interfered in my cases more than once in Baltimore County. I resisted the urge to make a gagging noise as I pulled into the municipal building's parking lot.

I stopped beside Kate's car. "Call me when you find her," she said as she climbed out, her tone glum.

"Sure."

She stuck her head back inside the open doorway. "And try not to let it get to you."

"Ha," I snorted and pointed at her. "Pot, kettle, black."

She gave me a weak smile and closed the car door.

Once inside my office, I called my cousin Paul's cell phone, knowing it would go to voicemail since he was on duty.

Sure enough, a click and his voice announced, "This is Paul's phone. He's not around right now, so do your thing."

"Hey, call me when you're on break, okay?"

I was trying to focus on the daily incident reports, with little success, when he called back twenty minutes later.

"What's up, Cuz?"

"Thanks for the heads-up earlier," I said. "I would've gotten the word from my people, but it was good that I knew quickly."

"I figured it might be."

"Um, this case is reminding me..." I trailed off, debating how to approach the issue.

Dead silence on the other end.

"Do you know if your mom ever submitted any DNA to the Center for Missing and Exploited Children?"

"How would I know?" Paul snapped. "I was only eight."

I swallowed a sigh. This was what I feared the silence had meant. He was going straight to defensive anger.

"Paul, it wasn't your fault. We were only kids." I paused, recalling something I'd overheard my father say to my mother around that time. "And whoever it was, they had to have been watching for a while. They knew we often played out back."

"Yeah, well, why didn't they take you?" An angry shout.

I gasped. It felt like someone had slugged me in the chest.

"Oh my god, I'm sorry, Judith. I didn't mean that."

I struggled to catch my breath. "I know you didn't," I whispered.

"Please, forgive me."

"Already have." But that was a lie. His words were like a knife in my heart.

I shoved the feelings aside and said, "Look, this case is making me realize that Meredith could still be out there somewhere. If Aunt Jean didn't submit any DNA to NCMEC, we should get her to do that now. See if anything pops."

"Don't you dare stir Mom up!" Some of the anger was back in his voice.

"Paulie...Paul, if she's out there, she needs to know that we didn't abandon her—or whatever lies she was told by her abductor."

"And if she isn't out there, if she's dead..." His voice broke, and my stomach churned. "You will've gotten an old woman's hopes up and broken her heart all over again."

"Paul," I said, my throat tight, "why don't we start with your DNA and mine. If someone pops up as related to us, then..." I trailed off again.

A beat of silence. "Maybe. I guess."

"Lemme check with NCMEC and see how that works."

"Yeah, well, I gotta get back to work."

"I'll let you know what I find out."

He disconnected without saying goodbye.

Blinking hard to lubricate the stinging sensation in my eyes, I looked up the NCMEC number and placed the call.

CHAPTER SIXTEEN

At noon, Sam showed up with sandwiches from the deli for lunch. He'd brought one for Barnes as well.

She thanked him and eagerly unwrapped hers on her desk.

"Is that what I think it is?" I said.

"Veggie burger. I'm thinking about going vegan." She took a big bite.

I gave her an exaggerated grimace and led the way into my office. Once behind my desk I unwrapped my own sandwich and eyed the tomato and lettuce on top of the tuna salad.

Sam chuckled as he sat down in the comfy chair. "A small nod toward healthy."

"You forgot the cheese," I said.

"Nope. That stuff is full of fat and salt."

"Hmm, if I was into conspiracy theories, I'd think you and Barnes were ganging up on me." She was always bugging me to eat better.

Sam chuckled again and bit into his own sandwich, which was dripping with mayo and had orange corners of cheddar cheese sticking out of it.

"Ah, so you're saving me from myself, while you give yourself a heart attack."

He just grinned and chewed.

As I lifted my sandwich to my mouth, Barnes popped into the doorway. "They've got her. But the guy got away. Uniforms are bringing her in."

I nodded, put my food down and picked up my phone. I called Kate and gave her the news.

"I've been thinking," she said. "How would you feel about meeting with her in a conference room, you and me, instead of in your interrogation room?"

"Not great. For one thing, there's no recording equipment in there."

"We could record the audio on one of our phones."

"Why do you think that would be better?"

"I know you probably want to come down on her harder, now that she's actually committed a crime–"

"Yes," I interrupted, "that's exactly what I plan to do."

"But that will only get her to clam up. I think if we change the setting and try to get across to her that we want to help her, and her cousin for that matter, maybe she'll cooperate."

"Alleged cousin," I muttered, then sighed, debating with myself.

Part of me wanted to tell Kate that we appreciated her help but we'd take it from here.

Something told me that might damage our friendship.

Damn! But what could it hurt, trying it her way?

"Okay. How soon can you be here?"

"Twenty minutes. I'm on my way."

I shook my head as I hung up the phone. Well, at least I had time to eat.

I glanced down at my sandwich and was reminded that I'd never heard back from Mr. B at the deli.

I picked up the phone again.

———◦———

Mr. B had apologized for not getting back to me and had promised to look up the credit card slip right away.

But I hadn't heard from him by the time Kate arrived. Sam had finished his lunch and left by then.

Barnes informed me that she'd turned the murder board around in the conference room so it faced the wall. "Do you want me to bring Cissy in there?"

"No, I'll get her." I had an idea. Gesturing for Kate to join me, we headed to the holding cells.

"I'm so sorry," I quickly said to Cissy as we approached. "They shouldn't have put you in here. I just have some more questions for you."

I didn't cuff her but I did hang onto her upper arm. Playing good cop did not include giving her a chance to get away again.

I settled her and Kate in the conference room and asked if they wanted anything to eat or drink.

Cissy gave me a sharp look and shook her head.

"Are you sure?" I asked. "It's pretty warm out there today." Indeed, we were now in full-blown Florida spring, hitting the low eighties most days, but the high humidity had not kicked in yet.

She shook her head again.

I walked around the murder board and removed a photo of our victim, the one that was the least gruesome. Then I sat at the end of the table rather than across from the young woman. Kate had taken a seat one down from her on the same side. Not crowding her but sending the message that she was, literally, on her side.

"Cissy," Kate began, "the Chief could really use your help. We think you might know something, maybe without even realizing that you know it, that could help solve a tragic crime."

"Before you said you didn't know him," I said, "but now that your memory has come back some..." I turned the photo face up and slid it over in front of the young woman.

She looked down and gasped. "Johnny said he was dead, but I wasn't sure if I should believe him."

Hmm, interesting. I filed the disbelief concept away for later exploration and said in a gentle voice, "He's Uncle Jake, isn't he?"

She nodded.

"Did you live with him?" I asked.

She started to nod again, then grimaced. "Well, I guess you'd call it that. We stayed in different motel rooms most of the time. Sometimes we slept in the car."

"And what did you all do for money and food?"

"Oh, we ate at diners mostly, or sometimes got fast food and took it to the motels with us. But I wasn't allowed to eat too much, had to watch my figure."

All this was said in a matter-of-fact tone of voice. And it was interesting that she'd picked the last part of my question to answer first.

"And how did Uncle Jake pay for all that?" I asked again.

She met my gaze, her eyes wide. "With the money from the videos we made." The same matter-of-fact voice.

She looked and sounded innocent enough, but was it feigned innocence?

I was struggling to resist the urge to become tougher with her.

Kate leaned forward. "Was Jake always with you?"

"No," Cissy said. "Sometimes he left us in a motel room for as much as a day or two, told us not to budge. Johnny went out once and Jake was so mad when he found out. Sometimes he left us to sleep in the car while he went somewhere. He never said where and we weren't allowed to question him."

I had a funny feeling that Jake wasn't always "living" with them. He was probably making good money off the videos and either had a place somewhere, or was staying at nicer hotels himself.

Also, some of those absences might have been when he was arrested, but he would've made bail each time, within a day or two at most. And the solicitation charges, those that weren't dropped, most likely wouldn't have involved jail time, not if the judge assumed he was just a poor schmuck looking for sex, not a porn video producer.

"Did you ever drive anywhere," I asked, "while you had the car to yourselves?"

Cissy shook her head rather vehemently. "No, he said we weren't old enough to drive, not responsible enough. We never learned."

"But you drove the intern's car the other day."

"Yeah, but only to get away from the hospital." She shuddered. "I pulled into that lot when I almost hit a woman walking her dog."

So it was unlikely that she'd driven Spencer's car into Starling Monday morning. She had probably walked from the motel, maybe after wandering around for a while.

My chest ached.

At what point had her brain decided to push all memory of what had happened, all memory of who she *was*, out of conscious awareness?

I shook my head slightly, forcing my thoughts back to the car. Johnny could've driven it into town, or someone else could've stolen it, while that desk clerk was napping. We might never know since it had been wiped of prints, except for a few smudges and partials.

Kate was looking at me, her expression grim. I recalled the word she'd used earlier—*brainwashed*.

Yes, this John Spencer, aka *Uncle* Jake had thoroughly brainwashed these kids, so much so that they were afraid to disobey him even when he wasn't there. The ache in my chest intensified.

I quietly pulled in a deep breath. *Okay, time to get down to what happened at that motel.*

"Sunday night," I said, "you all were in a room at the Beachview Inn–"

"We were?"

"We think so, Cissy," Kate spoke up. "They found some hair in the bathroom drain. You may have taken a shower there?"

"Oh, okay. I don't remember that." Her forehead furrowed. "But I kinda remember Jake pulling the car into that motel's parking lot. We'd been there before..."

I nodded. "Can you tell us what happened that night?"

Her face clouded. "Uncle Jake's movies were getting mean."

When she didn't elaborate, Kate said in a soft voice, "Mean how, Cissy?"

"Before, it was just sex. Me and him or me and Johnny. Sometimes a three-way. Maybe some spanking, and occasionally we'd pretend it was a rape. But then I'd stop fighting once things got going and acted like I loved it."

I struggled to keep my face impassive. *Great.* Jake was feeding into every rapist's fantasy, that women actually liked it.

"But lately?" Kate prompted.

"He began using a knife. He'd pretend he was going to slit my throat. I didn't have to act scared. I wasn't sure how far he'd go." Her voice was a bit agitated now, and her eyes were glassy.

I was careful not to move or make a sound, not wanting to break the spell.

"One time he acted like he was going to cut my boob off." She cringed in her chair. "That's when Johnny suggested we pick up hookers to do the rough stuff with. He pointed out that we didn't want to have wounds and scars on my skin, especially in the ones where I was supposed to be a virgin."

I dared not look at Kate.

"So we started doing that," Cissy continued, "but then Uncle Jake got worse and worse. He almost killed a woman in Tallahassee."

I made a mental note to contact Tallahassee's police and see if they had an open assault case with a prostitute victim.

"What happened the other night?" Kate asked, her voice still gentle.

Cissy shook her head. "Jake brought a prostitute to the room, and some guy was standing outside, like he was a guard or something. Jake said we were gonna begin with a threesome so I got undressed. I put my dress over the chair so it wouldn't get messed up. It's..." she lowered her gaze to her blouse. "It *was* the only clothing I had."

Now Kate and I did exchange a glance. That solved the mystery of the chair—the dress had been draped over it.

The poor girl's only clothing.

I ground my teeth. If John Spencer weren't already dead, I might've killed him myself.

The young woman was shaking her head again. "That's the last thing I remember until I was walking into the building here. No." She sat up straighter. "That's not true. I remember asking someone where the Chief of Police would be. They told me the police station was on the third floor of this building."

"Who's they?" I asked.

She shrugged. "Some guy. He seemed nice."

I nodded and moved on. "Where was Johnny while all this was happening the other night?"

"Oh, he wasn't back yet."

"Back from where?"

"Tallahassee. He told Jake he was hungry so we pulled into this convenience store lot. Jake gave him some money, and Johnny went inside. He'd whispered to me, though, that he was really gonna use the money in the pay phone there, to anonymously call the cops and let them know where the woman was, the one Jake hurt." She shuddered. "But then he tried to shoplift a candy bar—I guess to cover for the fact he'd used the money to make the call. He got caught."

I was amazed they had found a pay phone, although they did still exist in mini-marts and such in poorer neighborhoods where not everyone could afford cell phones.

Wait! If Johnny didn't have a cell phone how did he call the hospital, pretending to be Cissy's brother?

"Jake just left him there?" Kate was asking.

The girl actually smirked. "He knew Johnny could get out of it. He's talked his way out of worse situations."

Jake had taught these kids well how to be con artists and petty thieves, as well as porn stars. And Johnny had willingly come back to Jake when he could've turned him in, or at least taken off on his own.

Talk about Stockholm Syndrome.

And Cissy seemed almost proud of Johnny's wile. What happened to the no stealing/being beholden rules she'd spouted before? Did they only apply to herself, not to others?

"Tell me more about Johnny," I said. "When did you first meet him?"

Cissy's brow wrinkled. "I don't remember. He's just always been there..."

"With you and Jake?" Kate clarified.

Cissy nodded.

"How is he related to Jake?" I asked.

"He's his nephew."

"But whose son is he?" I nudged. "Jake's sister's or brother's? Or his nephew by marriage?"

Cissy rubbed the bridge of her nose. Kate shot me a look that I took to mean I was pushing too hard.

But I really wanted to get all I could out of this young woman. Who knew what detail might unlock the puzzle of what exactly happened in that motel room. Not to mention who Johnny really was, if Kate's theory was correct and he had been kidnapped.

But I could try a different tactic. "Johnny said his parents are dead," I said, softening my voice. "Do you know how they died?"

Cissy shook her head. "That's what Jake told him to say, if anybody asked. His parents really gave Johnny to Jake."

"What do you mean?" Kate asked, her voice a little strangled.

"He was a bad kid, always getting in trouble, so his parents didn't want to deal with him anymore, and they gave him to Jake." Cissy's tone was matter-of-fact, her body language relaxed, as if she hadn't just said something horrific.

Why would anyone tell a child that? Even if it were true.

But I didn't want to believe that it was true.

I glanced Kate's way. Her eyes were an icy gray, her lips pressed into a grim line. Something told me she had heard of worse things parents had done to their kids, in her line of work through the years.

Believe it, Anderson. It could be true.

Kate ran a hand down her face, leaving a neutral expression behind. "When did Jake tell Johnny all that?"

"All the time, when we were younger." Again, the matter-of-fact tone. "He'd remind Johnny that if he didn't do what he was told, Jake might give him away as well."

This time I avoided looking Kate's way. If we made eye contact, I suspected neither of us would be able to hide our horror.

Cissy turned in my direction. "What's going to happen to me now," she asked in a child-like voice, "without Uncle Jake or Johnny?"

Kate glanced at me. Her eyes said loud and clear, *see what I mean, still fragile.*

More like helpless. These kids might be great petty criminals but they had no clue about how to live in the world of law-abiding citizens.

CHAPTER SEVENTEEN

I'd been concerned that Cissy might freak out when I told her she was still under arrest for assaulting the intern. But she actually seemed relieved.

"Do I get dinner?" she asked, a bit timidly.

"Of course," I said and gave her a genuine smile. "And tomorrow, I'm going to talk to the ASA and request that you be given community service in lieu of jail time for the assault. That is assuming that intern has no long-term injuries from what you did."

She dropped her gaze. "I'm sorry I did that. He's a nice guy."

Then her head jerked up. "But if I'm not in jail, where will I live?" Her voice was panicky.

Kate reached out and patted her arm. "We'll work something out. You won't be on your own."

"But if you have community service to do," I said, "that means you have to stay in town here until it's completed. If you take off, you'll be arrested and sent to jail."

She nodded.

Maybe I'll ask Bill Walker to look in on her a couple of times tonight...to check that she's coping okay in the holding cell.

"What would you like for dinner?" I found myself asking.

Sheez Louise, I am turning soft. Been hanging out with Kate too much.

The latter was grinning at me.

I resisted the urge to stick my tongue out at her, as Cissy answered, "Mac and cheese?"

At four-thirty, I got ready to go to the deli, to get Cissy a double serving of what Mr. B billed as the best macaroni and cheese in northern Florida. Not being an expert on all things mac and cheese, I couldn't say if he was right about it being the "best," but it was pretty darn good.

As had become my habit, I paused to extract my Glock from my locked desk drawer. Ever since a gang had tried to take over the entire city a few weeks back, I wasn't sure that even a simple errand to the deli across the street would remain "simple."

I tucked the gun in its holster at the small of my back, made sure the tail of my jacket covered it, and headed out.

I was in luck. Mr. B had just made a fresh batch of mac and cheese, and he had the credit card slip for the mysterious Sara S. "I was about to send Becky over with it," he said.

"No problem. Thanks." I glanced at it and my stomach tensed. *Damn!* No name on it, only a scribbled signature at the bottom.

I hurried back to 3MB and handed the mac and cheese off to the watch sergeant to deliver to the holding cell. Then I gave the credit card slip to Barnes. "Do your research thing with that and see what you can find out."

She out-did herself. Within a half hour, she not only had the woman's last name but also an address.

"How'd you get them to fork over the address without a warrant?" I asked.

She smirked at me.

"Never mind. I'm not sure I want to know. Come on. Let's see if this Sara Sanders is home."

But our luck ran out at that point.

The apartment was the upper level of a white Cracker-style house in a quiet suburban neighborhood. Somehow I doubted she brought her johns here. Indeed, I doubted she thought of them as johns, more likely they were "clients" in her mind.

Ringing the bell on the frame of the side door—with *21A* stenciled above it, in dark blue to match the house's shutters—got no response. I nodded and Barnes rang it again.

A plump woman of a certain age, with hair dyed so black it was almost purple, came around the front corner of the house. She wore a multi-colored flowered house dress and pink flip-flops. "Can I help you?"

Standing in the driveway, we introduced ourselves and established that she was the homeowner and Sara's landlady. But she hadn't seen her in several days.

"Think for a moment, please," I said. "When exactly was the last time you saw her?"

She tilted her head. "It was early evening on Sunday, around sixish. She was going out, all dolled up, and she waved. I was gettin' my mail." She gestured toward the mailbox out at the curb. "I'd forgotten to get it on Saturday."

"Was she on foot?" I asked.

"No, an Uber picked her up. That's mostly how she gets around."

"And you haven't seen her since, ma'am?" Barnes asked.

"No, but I'm sure she's been around. She's very quiet, works from home. I barely ever hear a peep out of her."

The woman's face became pinched. "Is she in some kinda trouble?"

"Not with us," I said, "but there's a possibility she may be in danger from someone. We need to find her." The first part of that was a lie; she might very well be a murder suspect. And the second part—well it was mostly speculation. *If* Sara was the other party in that motel room, and *if* she was there against her will, as in the guy at the door was that pimp Misty had mentioned, then she might be in danger.

"Um, do you know what she does for a living?" Barnes asked.

"She said she had one of those, whadda ya call it, teleport jobs?"

"Telecommute?" I asked.

"Yeah, that's it. She worked from home, on her computer."

Barnes and I exchanged a glance.

"How about her social life," I said. "Does she entertain much?"

A head shake. "No, but she goes out a lot, almost every evenin'. I have a rule, no overnight visitors without prior permission. I told her it would be okay if she had a regular fella, ya know... But she said, no, she preferred to go out. And she said somethin' kinda odd—'my home is my haven.'" The landlady made air quotes.

"Can we see her apartment?" I asked. "We might be able to find some hint about where she is."

The woman frowned. "I'm not sure I'm comfortable with that."

"We'll only look around, I promise. We won't touch anything." I paused. "I'm really quite concerned for her safety."

The landlady's expression defined the concept of *conflicted*, but finally she nodded and pulled a set of keys out of the pocket of her house dress.

She unlocked the door and led the way up the stairs, calling out, "Sara, are you home, dear?"

At the top of the steps was another door. The landlady hesitated again, and I made a show of putting my hands in my pants pockets. Barnes followed suit.

It was a bit of a risk. We didn't know exactly what was on the other side of that door, but my gut said Sara was long gone.

The landlady unlocked the door.

"Let us go in first, ma'am," I said, "just in case."

She stepped back and let me go through the doorway.

My eyes went wide. The place was a wreck. My hand flew to the Glock under my jacket.

I glanced over my shoulder. "Stay out there, ma'am," I ordered.

She opened her mouth, perhaps to protest, but, once Barnes was through the doorway, I closed the door in her face.

We both drew our guns and quietly cleared the rooms. The apartment was empty, except for the disturbed furnishings.

Said furnishings were high end, heavy oak tables scattered about, some upended, leather sofa and loveseat—in far better conditioned than my old sofa—and expensive drapes bracketing a large window air conditioner in the living room. The AC was currently off and the room was stuffy.

Lamps and magazines were flung about, and a couple of potted plants had been upended on the plush white carpet.

A gasp from behind us. I whirled around.

The landlady had apparently gotten tired of waiting and had opened the door.

"I'm assuming Sara's a better housekeeper than this," I said.

"Oh my lord, yes." Dismay in her voice as her head swiveled, taking in the mess.

I didn't tell her that the kitchen was in even worse shape. Everything from the cabinets and fridge had been dumped on the floor.

"Was somebody pissed," Barnes said quietly from beside me, "or were they searching for something?"

"I'd say some of both," I whispered back.

"Bedroom window's open," she told me.

A clanking sound from that direction. "Fire escape," she yelled, and we both bolted for the bedroom doorway.

But by the time I got to the open window, a tall man was halfway across the sandy backyard. He wore blue jeans and a dark hoodie, and a big pistol was silhouetted in his hand.

"Damn!" Barnes said from behind me. "I looked out there and could've sworn no one..." She trailed off and followed me out the window and down the rattling metal stairs.

I was fifteen feet from the guy when he reached the back chain-link fence. He jumped halfway up it, reminding me of Spiderman, and scrambled to the top. As he teetered there, he looked back.

My steps faltered. He was ugly to the point of being grotesque—his cheeks gaunt and pock-marked, his nose bent in two places, and a nasty scar from one temple to his chin.

But no sign of the gun in his hands. He must've pocketed it.

I reached the bottom of the fence and grabbed for his foot. He yanked it away and dropped to the other side of the fence, then took off.

I tried to insert the toe of my low-heeled pumps into a dia-mond-shaped link. It wouldn't fit. I grabbed the links toward the top of the six-foot fence, and pulled up, but without a foothold, I couldn't get up far enough to get over, and the top edges of the metal mesh would've torn up my clothes, and maybe my flesh, if I'd tried.

I swore under my breath. In my younger years, I would've vaulted the fence as easily as he had.

Barnes was suddenly beside me and making a go at the fence. She managed to get over it but slowly, encumbered as she was by the things attached to her duty belt.

"Careful. He's armed," I yelled as she dropped to the other side and ran after him.

I mentally said a quick prayer for her safety as I pulled out my phone and jogged back to the house. I called the watch desk and requested backup, although I held out little hope that we would find the intruder.

The landlady was standing on the small stoop outside the entrance to Sara's apartment.

I gestured for her to step aside. "I need to look around some more. Do you think you can tell if anything is missing?"

"Maybe." She followed me back up the stairs.

She went through the swinging door into the kitchen. A sharp gasp. After a moment, she came back out, her face puckered.

Silently, she walked past me and into the bedroom. Another few moments passed.

"Mrs. Chief," she called out.

I swallowed a chuckle and went into the bedroom.

The landlady stood next to the closet. It held mostly empty hangers. "He took her fancy clothes and jewelry." She pointed to a jewelry armoire, its drawers hanging open, also close to empty.

I stepped over and examined both closet and armoire carefully. There were a couple of casual blouses hanging in the back of the former and a few stray pieces of costume jewelry in the latter. I suspected Sara had cleared out both, rather than the intruder.

He certainly hadn't been carrying any women's clothing.

"Did she have luggage?" I asked.

The landlady nodded. "Yeah, two fancy suitcases." She gestured toward the bare closet floor, indicating that was where they were normally stored.

Barnes bustled into the room. "Sorry, Chief. I lost him."

"He had too much of a head start," I said as I walked over to the still open window. I leaned out and examined the fire escape more carefully. A small metal landing, about ten feet long, led to the top of the steep metal steps.

"I did look out there," Barnes said from behind me, disgust at herself in her voice.

"He could've been plastered against the wall beside the window."

"I should've stuck my head out."

I pulled my own head back in. "And you'd be dead now."

She paled a little, and I was reminded that she was still a rookie.

"We'll talk about it later." I led the way back to the living room.

"Do you have any idea where Sara may have gone?" I asked the landlady.

She shook her head. "But I do have her cell phone number. Do you want me to call it?"

"No," I said quickly. I didn't want to give Sara any warning that we were on her trail. "But can you give it to me?" It might be different from the one Misty had given us, which Derek had not been able to trace.

She nodded and pulled an iPhone out of the pocket of her house dress. "It's a new number."

Yes!

"She's only had it for a couple of weeks," the landlady continued. "She said not to give it to anybody, but since you're the police." She turned her phone toward us.

Barnes hastily jotted down the number on its screen. She pulled out her own cell phone and spoke quietly in it. She was giving the number to Derek.

"I'd like to take a few of these magazines," I said, waving a hand in the direction of a pile of them on the floor. Then I pointed to a framed photo beside it, the glass smashed. "And that photo. That's Sara, correct?"

She nodded again.

"And I'm going to send my forensic people out to go over the apartment, so it will be off-limits for a day or two," I added, handing her my card. "If Sara comes back, call me right away."

"Sure thing, Mrs. Chief." The landlady gave me a small salute.

One end of Barnes's mouth quirked up. I hid a smile, relieved she was recovering her equilibrium so quickly.

I'd instructed the uniforms the sarge had sent as backup to canvas the neighborhood, asking if anyone had seen a butt-ugly stranger.

"Should we phrase it that way, Chief?" one of them asked, with a poorly disguised grin.

I scowled at him, thinking, *You've been hanging around Sergeant Armstrong too much.* Armstrong tended to be a tad irreverent.

I called for a BOLO on the ugly guy and left one officer to guard Sara's apartment until Bert and Ernie were done with it.

Halfway back to 3MB, Barnes's phone buzzed. "Text from Derek. That phone is a burner, and it last pinged off a cell tower near the Amtrak station in Jacksonville, Monday at eight in the morning."

I sighed. "Guess that's our next stop."

"Uh, Chief. I hate to tell you this but you don't look so great. Maybe you're coming down with what I had?"

I had to admit, now that the adrenaline rush was gone, exhaustion was setting in. I hoped Barnes was wrong, that it wasn't her cold germs working on my system, but only lack of sleep, thanks to last night's nightmare.

"I can follow up with Amtrak," she said, "and take the magazines to Bert and Ernie's lab."

I thought for a moment. No Sam tonight. He'd jinxed himself by saying out loud that things were slow out in the county. This afternoon, two ski-masked idiots had held up a convenience store and then a fast food place. They were still at large and it was all hands on deck at the Clover County Sheriff's Department.

It would be good, though, to have a quiet evening followed by an early bedtime. And I really did want to give Barnes more responsibility, now that we were hiring a departmental clerk who would take many of the tedious tasks off her plate.

"Okay, I'll drop you in the parking lot. Call me if you find anything interesting."

We were almost to 3MB, slowed some by rush-hour traffic, when my phone rang. *Sheriff Taylor* came up on my dashboard screen. Wishing it was *Sheriff Sam* instead, I punched the button to accept the call.

"Hey, Sheriff. What can I do for you?"

A heavy sigh. "Wanted to give y'all a heads up. Mrs. Brown reported her younger daughter missing just now. She never came home from school and none of her friends know where she is."

I stifled my own sigh. "You think she's with her stepfather?"

"Most likely." A pause. "She's fifteen now, by the way. And she was nine when Cissy ran a...um, disappeared."

My stomach tensed as the implication sank in. Nine—one year shy of the age Cissy was when the stepfather started abusing her.

I shook my head, trying to get my tired brain to focus. "Description of the girl?"

"Five-five, slender, dark hair and eyes. Pretty." His voice had gone a bit gravelly. "Like her sister."

"Okay, I'll add that info to the BOLO we have out on Brown here, but..." I trailed off.

"But he and the girl could be anywhere by now," the sheriff said, his tone now forlorn.

"Was he a friend?" I asked, trying to sound sympathetic.

Another sigh. "More like a friendly acquaintance, but it sure is disappointin' when someone you thought was a good un turns out not to be."

"So true," I said. "My condolences." Maybe that was a stupid thing to say, but it felt right.

"Thanks, Chief. I'll keep ya posted."

"Likewise."

CHAPTER EIGHTEEN

A faint ringing sound in the distance jerked me awake. I sat up.

I was on my old black leather sofa, wrapped in my comfy terrycloth robe. Some sitcom was on the TV, the characters babbling away. I had no clue who they were.

I got a whiff of myself as I leaned down to grab my laptop case. I needed to take a shower before bed.

My personal phone rang again. I fished it out of the leather case and answered without checking the screen.

"Hi, Judith," a woman's voice. "Hope this isn't too late to be calling."

Still a little disoriented, I wondered if this was a telemarketer, or a politician. It was an election year.

"How have you been, dear?"

Of course, Aunt Jean!

"I'm good. How are you?"

"Okay. Nothing to complain about, except old age." A low chuckle.

"I'm beginning to be able to relate."

"Nah, you're still a spring chicken."

I laughed. "More like a late summer/early fall chicken. What's up?"

My aunt was trying her best to sound cheerful, but she wouldn't normally be calling at nine-fifty at night.

"Um, have you talked to Paulie lately?"

"Yes, just today."

"Is he okay?"

I hesitated a second, recalling the touchy topic of that conversation. "Yes, seemed to be."

At least he was okay physically. I wasn't so sure about mentally.

"I've been calling him for three days now, and he hasn't returned my call."

My stomach tensed. That was not like Paul. But I made an excuse for him. "Uh, he's pretty busy with his new job."

"I know, but we talk almost every day. He promised we would when he told me he was moving down there."

For a second, I was actually glad I was an orphan. No parental obligations. Then guilt tightened my chest. What I would give to have my mother with me again.

"Well, maybe that's become harder than he thought it would be," I said out loud. "His schedule varies sometimes."

"He was the one who suggested it. Are you sure he's okay...I mean, it's that time of year."

I wanted to play dumb and say, *What time of year?*

But I didn't.

Memories flooded back. The yard, the lilac bush, the screen door slamming.

A hollow pit opened in my stomach and my throat closed.

I must've made some kind of sound because my aunt asked, "What is it, Judith? What aren't you telling me?"

"Um, I think he's taking it harder than usual this year." I caught myself about to say that a current case was stirring up memories for both of us. She might ask what case, and she didn't need the thought in her head that Meredith could've ended up like Cissy.

"Did he say something?" Aunt Jean asked.

"Um, yeah. He didn't mean it, though."

"What did he say?" Her voice had shifted to her no-nonsense Mom tone.

"Oh, I said something about the guy must've been watching for an opportunity, and he said something stupid like it should've been me." I faked a laugh.

Silence for a beat. "I thought I'd gotten that nonsense out of his head."

"What nonsense?" I asked.

"He thought the guy was stalking you, since it was your yard. But for some reason, he took Meredith instead."

"What?" I screeched. "My yard? No it wasn't, it was yours. I remember the lilac bush. That's where I was hiding."

"Not that day. Your mother was babysitting for me. I had a doctor's appointment. The follow-up visit after my final round of chemo. I found out I was cancer-free, and then–" She broke off with a choked sob.

"Look, we don't need to talk about this," I quickly said, even though I was dying to ask questions. How could it have been my yard? The lilac bush was in Aunt Jean's yard.

Another sob, cut short. "No, we do. Perhaps we've been quiet about it for too long."

"The lilac bush?" My own voice was choked.

"That was your favorite place to hide when you all played in my yard. But that day, you were at your own house. Your mother said she went inside to answer the phone, but nobody was there. And when she came out, you were all gone. She waited a bit, thinking whoever was 'it' would flush the other two out soon. But then you crawled out from under the hedge and Paulie swung down from a branch in the locust tree."

The locust tree. Yes, it was in my backyard. We called it the money tree, because its small, oval leaves looked kind of like coins. We had even used them as currency when we'd played store.

I sniffled and swiped at my cheek. The back of my hand came away wet.

"Your father blamed your mother," Aunt Jean was say-ing, "even though I didn't. That became his excuse to drink even more, and to eventually start beating her, like our father beat us."

I closed my eyes, trying to digest that info. A vise tight-ened around my chest, making it hard to breathe.

And that was the answer to another mystery—why my Aunt Jean had sided with her sister-in-law instead of with her own brother when my parents split up.

"Are you there, Judith?"

"Yeah. Um, one of the things that upset Paul was me talk-ing about how the guy must've been watching the yard."

"Yes, that was your father's speculation at the time, and the police thought so too. That he'd probably been watch-ing the yard for a while, waiting for his chance." Jean's voice was hoarse but she wasn't crying now. Indeed, there was a hard edge to her tone.

A short wave of relief, followed by the vise tightening again. Was this what survivor's guilt felt like?

"Your father kept yelling at your mom that she should've been paying closer attention when you played out there, that she should've noticed something."

It was the kind of irrational thing people think and say when something bad happens. The what-ifs. But Mom must've already been thinking the same things. She didn't need Dad yelling at her.

"Your mother was never the same after that," Aunt Jean said, her voice now mournful.

"Aunt Jean, did you ever give your DNA to the Center for Missing and Exploited Children?"

A long silence. "No, I didn't know you could do that."

"Not that you should," I quickly said, "know that, I mean. They didn't even exist until three years after Meredith…" I trailed off, then sucked in air. "And it wasn't until ten years ago that they began trying to find kids with the parents' DNA."

"I can do better than my own DNA," Aunt Jean said. "I still have Meredith's hairbrush. Where is this lab anyway?"

"I don't know but I'll find out," I said, excited now. "Wrap the hairbrush in tissue paper and put it in a box. I'll make arrangements to get it sent by courier. But we should send in your DNA as well. Hair DNA degrades over time."

"I'll get one of those DNA kits meant to establish paternity," she said. "Just let me know where to send it."

"Good." I paused. Now that I was in cop mode, more questions came to mind. "Did my mother remember seeing anything, maybe something she didn't think was important at the time?"

"No, and she wracked her brain."

"How about the neighborhood. Was there anyone there that took an interest in us kids?"

"No. The police explored all that back then."

"Yes, but we know more now than they did then. In the early eighties, they would've been focusing on someone who was obviously odd. Now we know..." I trailed off again, realizing where I was going with that. Now we knew child molesters didn't always look like the monsters that they were.

But Aunt Jean didn't need to hear that either.

"I'm going to research the land records," I said, "and find out who owned houses around there at the time."

"That sounds like a lot of work."

"Yeah, I'll have to fit it in when I can. But in the meantime, NCMEC can do their thing with the DNA."

I paused, then said, as gently as I could, "Aunt Jean, the first thing they'll do is search for a match with any unidentified bodies."

"I know, Judith. I already thought of that. Even if she's gone, I...I need to know."

"One more question. Did Paul see or hear anything from up in that tree?"

"He heard a yelp, cut short. He thought Meredith had found you, so he stayed hidden."

And he's no doubt been beating himself up for that ever since.

"Okay, I'll send you the info about the courier and such." I paused, took a deep breath. "I love you, Aunt Jean."

My throat hurt as I realized I'd never told her that before.

"I love you too, sweetheart. Good night."

I disconnected, dropped the phone in my lap, and sank back into the sofa cushions.

"Oh my God," I said out loud.

After another restless night, I was at my desk indulging in a third cup of caffeine and searching arrest records on my computer. I was anxious to track down the man who'd broken into Sara Sanders's apartment.

Assuming he was connected to the pimp who'd been trying to force Sara to work for him, I had used the search terms, *male* and *prostitution*. But that had gotten me too many young male prostitutes. I'd narrowed the search by age, over thirty. Still it was a long tedious process. If only I could use the word *ugly*, but I doubted any arresting officer would use that word in his or her report, no matter how fitting.

Barnes stuck her head in my door. "Good morning."

"Where have you been?" I asked, trying to keep the grumpy out of my voice.

Her cheerful expression evaporated. "I had to sign my new lease this morning. I thought I told you yesterday."

"Sorry. You did. I just forgot. Any joy at the train station last night?"

"Not much." She leaned against the doorjamb. "The evening ticket folks didn't recognize Sara's picture. But the supervisor got me in touch with the local captain of the Amtrak police, who said they'd search the records for Monday morning and let me know if they found anything."

"What else is around the area that could provide her with transportation?"

"A couple of car rental places," she said, "including one of those that rents older cars pretty cheap. They aren't always scrupulous at checking IDs. My new friend at her credit card company said there haven't been any Uber charges since Sunday night, but she did take out a large cash advance at an ATM near the train station."

"She could've taken a cab to the airport and paid cash, then used a different credit card to purchase a ticket."

"Or cash. She took out $500, the ATM's limit. Or she could've melted away into the crowded city of Jacksonville."

"I doubt that. She'd want to get far away from this pimp who's trying to force her into his stable. Check the airlines."

"Got it." Barnes left my office.

I went back to my search. And fifteen minutes later, I hit pay dirt. I printed out two copies of the mug shot and the arrest report for pandering and accessory to felony pimping. He'd been picked up in Jacksonville in a sting operation in 2019, and the prostitutes who were arrested with him had said at the time that he worked for their pimp.

But they refused to name the pimp. And Mr. Ugly, whose real name was Marvin Nielson, was later released when the women resisted testifying against him.

I took the printout to Barnes's desk.

She grinned up at me. "Amtrak's head cop just called me. Sara Sanders caught the nine o'clock train Monday morning to Tallahassee."

"Alright. Things may be starting to break our way with this case." I handed one set of printouts to her. "Here's our fleet-footed intruder. Get a BOLO out on him. Suspected breaking and entering, for now."

"You got it, Chief." Barnes's phone rang and she grabbed the receiver. "Chief Anderson's office...Actually, she's standing right here."

She handed me the phone, saying, "It's Bert."

"What've you got?" I asked my crime tech.

"Fingerprints on the magazines," Bert's voice was excited, "they matched the partials we found in the motel bathroom, but not the unidentified ones in the car."

"Thanks, Bert." I repeated the news to Barnes.

She smiled, but then grimaced. "Proves she was there at some point but does that mean she's the killer?"

"Good question. She could've left before the murder."

"Or been there another time. But then who moved the car?"

"It still could've been her," I said. "The prints in the car could be from someone else. Maybe another hooker that Spencer brought in to make his sleazy movies."

Eyeing the stacks of paperwork on her desk, I changed the subject. "How's the search for a new departmental clerk going?"

"We've had a few applications but I haven't had time to check them out."

"Try to make time today, Gloria." I used her first name quite intentionally. "The sooner we have someone on board, the more time you will have for more interesting things."

I glanced at my watch. "Speaking of soon, I'm going to take Cissy to her arraignment in a little while."

Barnes's forehead furrowed. "You don't usually go to those yourself."

"Yes, but I want to keep track of her. I'm going to try for protective custody, but the judge may not go for that." I shook my head. "But I think it's dangerous for her to be roaming around loose, especially now that her stepfather is on the move. Not to mention a killer may be looking for her if she witnessed Spencer's murder."

"My new place has two bedrooms. She could stay with me for a while."

"And put you in danger as well." My stomach churned at the thought.

She rolled her eyes, not bothering to point out that she was a sworn police officer. "It's third floor, only one way in or out. Easy to guard with one uniform when I'm not home."

"Or even when you are. You gotta sleep sometime." I stopped, thought for a moment. It was a good solution, and I needed to stop being a mother hen where Barnes was concerned.

She'd come dangerously close to dying a couple of times in the last few months, but had been lucky. I was afraid, however, that she'd eventually run out of luck.

I sighed. "When are you moving in?"

"This evening. I don't have all that much stuff. Cissy can have my bed. I've got a sleeping bag."

"Okay. Get that BOLO going and set up some interviews with clerk applicants for next week, then go home early and get yourself moved."

"Thanks, boss." Her grin was back.

I managed a weak smile back, but my gut was saying that Cissy staying with her was a bad idea.

CHAPTER NINETEEN

Wait! I started to call Barnes back into my office.

Then I saw her note on my desk, with the Tallahassee Chief of Police's name and private line number.

I smiled and placed the call on my cell phone, as I headed for the holding area. I was definitely getting to know my colleagues in the region with this case.

The state capital's chief said he would put the word out with his people that the young woman in my BOLO, Sara Sanders, was possibly in the Tallahassee area. And he'd let me know if they came up with any leads on her whereabouts.

"Thanks, Chief," I said as I arrived in the front of Cissy's cell.

"No problem. Welcome to Florida," he replied, and we disconnected.

"It's time for your arraignment," I told Cissy.

She grimaced. "Do I need a lawyer?"

I unlocked the cell door. "You can request one today, but you'll be asked to enter a plea. You can change it later." I gestured for her to turn around.

Handcuffs in place, I led her out of the cell. "Would you like some fresh air? We can walk." I wanted more time to chat with her than the short car ride would afford.

"That would be good but it's kinda embarrassing..." she trailed off and gestured with her head over her shoulder, indicating her cuffed hands.

If she thought I would take them off, she had another thought coming. Instead, I removed my own pantsuit jacket and draped it over her shoulders. It hung down to her knuckles in the back.

Once we were out on the sidewalk and headed toward the courthouse a block away, I said, "I'm going to recommend you be released on your own recognizance *if* you are willing to go into protective custody."

Her steps slowed as she gave me a startled look. "Why?"

"Why protective custody?"

"No, why would you help me after all the trouble I've been?"

I paused, gathering my thoughts. "Because I don't think you are a bad person. And that part of Sunday night that you still don't remember, I think you may have witnessed something you shouldn't have, and you may be in danger."

I resisted the urge to tell her I thought she'd been exploited by her stepfather and her "Uncle Jake." Kate had warned me that Cissy might not see it that way, that she'd been trained to view their behavior and her life as normal. Or at least as an acceptable lifestyle.

I stifled a shudder and continued, "My assistant, Gloria Barnes has offered to let you stay with her until we get this all sorted out, and there will be an officer guarding you. If you behave, I'll talk to the ASA about community service in lieu of jail time, okay?"

"Yes. Oh, thank you, Chief." She stopped walking and turned toward me, her eyes shiny. "If I wasn't cuffed, I'd hug you. You've been so nice to me."

I was just as glad she was cuffed. And not only because of my aversion to hugs.

I was pretty sure her reaction was at least partly an act.

———◦———

The arraignment had gone smoothly, once I'd gotten the prosecutor aside and explained the convoluted situation. Cissy and I headed back to the municipal building, minus the handcuffs.

She glanced sideways at me. "That guy, Bill...is he single?"

My shoulders tensed. *Oh shit!*

"Yes," I said out loud.

"Hmm," she said.

I clenched my teeth to keep from telling her to leave Bill Walker alone.

He was a grown man after all, and mature beyond his thirty-some years.

But he had a good heart. Would he see through Cissy's maneuvering?

And why am I assuming she plans to manipulate him?

I glanced her way. She had a small smile on her face.

My stomach clenched. *Maybe I should warn Bill.*

I spent the rest of our silent stroll back to 3MB trying to figure out how to phrase such a warning.

I sat Cissy down in the small waiting area near the watch desk, where Sergeant Armstrong could keep an eye on her, and told her to wait for Barnes.

Barnes's desk was deserted. I took that to mean she was busy moving into her new apartment. I texted, asking that she let me know when she was ready to receive her houseguest.

My attempt to wade through that morning's incident reports was interrupted by a soft knock on the frame of my open door.

Bradley said, "While we're waiting for some action from that BOLO on Sara Sanders, I thought I'd interview Ms. Hopkins from Accounting. Wanna sit in?"

"No, but I'll observe." I rose from my chair. "What did you tell her?"

"I sent a uniform upstairs asking her to come down and help us sort out some confusion over the mileage vouchers."

I wasn't sure that giving her a warning about the topic of the conversation was the best tactic, but Bradley was a seasoned interrogator. I wasn't about to interfere.

We fell into step with each other, headed for the interview rooms. "She seemed kind of shy when I spoke with her," I said. "Two of us might be too overwhelming."

Bradley nodded. "Shy is my assessment of her as well."

I went into the observation area and Bradley entered the interview room. "Sorry about having to bring you in here, Clara," he said, waving a hand in the air to encompass the room. "The conference rooms were both in use."

"That's okay," she said, her voice soft. She ducked her head but gave the one-way mirror, which hid my presence, an intense glance.

Did she suspect someone was observing?

Bradley plopped a folder on the table and sat down across from her. She eyed the metal ring welded to the table, to which we cuffed detainees.

Her cheeks flushed as she pulled her own hands—not cuffed, for now at least—off the table and lowered them to her lap. Her gaze darted around the room.

Oh yes, she knows what's coming.

"I'm going to record this," Bradley said, "just for form's sake, so there's no confusion later. Is that okay?"

She nodded, but her eyes did the ping-pong routine around the room again.

Bradley stated for the recording who was present and why. Then he pretended to consult the folder in front of him. "Officer Barnes tells me that there's a separate bank account for the mileage payouts, and you send her a check each month.

Then she divvies up those funds to the detectives, based on the vouchers we submitted."

Clara stared at him.

"Is that correct?" he prompted.

"Uh, yeah," she said, her tone wary.

"And the accounting records show that you write that check out to..." He scanned down the page in front of him with his finger, as if he were looking for something, but I suspected it was mostly for effect. "Ah, here it is, the 'Police Department Mileage Reimbursement Fund.'"

"Well, um, yeah."

Bradley pulled some papers out of the folder. He made a show of sorting through them and laid two of them in front of her.

"So, I was wondering if you could clear this up for me." He pointed to one of the pages. "This is my copy of the last voucher I submitted, before I was assigned a department vehicle. And this," he pointed to the other sheet, "is the voucher from accounting's files."

He paused, let her read the numbers. "It's two and a half times the amount of miles I submitted."

She sat back. "Oh, well, that's for the bonuses."

"And what bonuses would that be?"

"Um, you know, to you detectives, to reward you for hustling."

"I see. And who distributes these bonuses?"

"Umm..." She squirmed a little in her chair. "Uh, it used to be Chief Black." Her eyes darted around the room again. "I guess it's Chief Anderson now."

Bradley nodded. "And how does this whole bonus system work exactly? It looks like the check you issue goes into an account at Cirrus Bank and then another check is issued from that account, for a much smaller amount."

He slid another paper over in front of her. I assumed it was a copy of one of the checks Barnes had received. What he wasn't telling Clara was that we already knew, from the records Cirrus Bank had provided, that she, Clara, had set up the account there and she was the only authorized signature on it.

"Well, um, yeah," she said. "I guess the chief likes to let the bonus money accumulate some."

Hmm, then why is the current balance in the account only a couple hundred dollars?

"How did this all get set up originally?" Bradley asked.

She visibly relaxed some, her shoulders sagging from the release of tension.

Does she actually believe she's on safe ground now?

"Chief Black asked me to handle the vouchers that way," she said. "At first, he was just increasing the number of miles by about ten percent. It varied some, depending on the detective. He said that was because some of y'all worked harder than others. He had me give *him* the extra amounts."

That jived with the bank records. A check made out to *Cash* had been drawn against the account each month.

"He'd hold off until mid-month," Clara continued, "then give out the bonuses. He said that way it helped y'all to have enough gas money to get through the month."

Shit, she believed that bull hockey. I was really glad I wasn't in the room with them. I would've blown things by scowling at her.

But I loved watching Bradley work. His interview style matched his personality, laid back and unflappable.

"And that made sense to you?' he asked now, as if he were only making conversation.

"Well, sorta." She leaned forward, her expression earnest. "I asked him, early on, if all that was really okay. He said the mayor had approved it. And a couple of days later, the mayor happened to be in accounting and he came over to my desk and said that the chief's arrangement for the detectives' travel fund was authorized by him."

"Mayor Daniels?" Bradley asked with a slight lift of his eyebrows.

"No, no. The one before him. Mayor Johnson."

Chief Black's brother-in-law! Excitement bubbled in my chest. We'd suspected he was in on some of the corruption but hadn't found any proof. Hopefully, we could get this girl to testify.

"He said it was a way to give the detectives a little more pocket money, without having to get approval for pay raises from the City Council."

"Who said?" Bradley asked. "The mayor?"

"No, Chief Black."

"You said it started out as about ten percent above the real mileage figure. How'd it get so high?" He tapped the copies of his vouchers.

She squirmed again and looked away. "It crept up gradually. At first, you all would bring your vouchers to me and then the chief would stop by and alter them. But after a while, he said not to even bother looking at them. He'd bring me the real figures. He'd come upstairs with a fistful of vouchers, and he'd take the ones y'all had submitted and tear them up."

"And you thought that was okay?"

His tone had still been mild, but her face began to pucker. Tears leaked from her eyes. "Not really," she said, barely above a whisper. "But I'd already been going along with it, and you know how the chief is. He's so big, and he has that booming voice and he kinda..." She trailed off.

"Sucks all the air outta the room," Bradley finished for her.

She nodded, more tears flowing. "I suspected it was wrong, but I didn't know what to do."

"But you kept doing it after Chief Black retired."

She nodded again, swiped at her cheeks with the back of one hand. "He said to keep sending the one check to the chief's office downstairs but send the other one, made out to cash, to his home. I told him I wasn't comfortable doing that, and he—" she choked off, looked away.

Bradley sat quietly, giving her time.

"He, uh, said I was already in too deep." She turned back toward Bradley. "And if he got in trouble for just trying to give his men some extra cash, then I would get in trouble too."

The bubbles of excitement had fizzled out, replaced by a dull ache in my chest. This young woman couldn't be more than late twenties. And John Black probably hadn't thought twice about dragging her down with him.

Bradley sat forward, brought his face closer to hers. "I hate to have to tell you this, Clara, but I never saw a penny of that extra money. And I'll bet none of the other detectives did either. Black was lining his own pockets."

She nodded yet again and sniffled. "I kinda suspected that when he made me keep it up after his retirement."

Bradley grabbed the box of tissues on one end of the table and slid it in front of her.

She gave him a feeble smile and took a couple. She blew her nose, then said, "Now what?"

"Now I write up what you told me and you sign it."

"But I'll be incriminating myself."

He nodded slightly. "I think the chief will want to talk to you about that."

A look of sheer terror crossed her face.

"Chief *Anderson*," Bradley quickly said and rose from his chair.

The terror faded, but she still nervously bit her lower lip.

I sat at my desk, but instead of getting back to the incident reports, I was staring into space.

I'd told Clara Hopkins that I couldn't guarantee anything, but I would try to get her a light sentence—maybe only probation since she had no priors—for her role in the fraud. *If* she helped us gather evidence against Black and his brother-in-law.

I'd referred to the former top cop as *Mr.* Black, no longer willing to share the title of Chief with him.

Clara was to continue as if nothing had happened, and if contacted by Black act as if everything was fine.

It was the eighteenth of March, so we had almost two weeks to figure out how to gather that evidence when he brought her the fake vouchers on the first of the month.

I'd called Dot Wilder at FDLE and asked about Black's bank accounts. "We've frozen all of them," Dot had told me. "Except one joint checking account with his wife. It didn't have any suspicious deposits in it. None of the other accounts were in the name of the police department or this 'Police Department Mileage Reimbursement Fund.'"

Bradley was now trying to track down any other accounts the former chief might have.

My thoughts were interrupted when my phone rang. Caller ID read *Tallahassee PD*. My heart rate kicked up a notch as I answered.

After the annoying pleasantries were dispensed with, the Tallahassee chief of police said, "We've got your gal."

"That was fast," I said.

"One of our detectives has a CI who's a call girl. She was happy to turn in the new competition in town."

"Okay, I'll arrange for someone to come get her, but in the meantime, could we set up a Zoom interview? Time is somewhat of the essence here." I still was not happy about Barnes taking Cissy into her home. I felt for the girl, but she hadn't exactly proven herself to be trustworthy.

"I think that can be arranged," the Tallahassee CoP said. "Say, at three?"

"Great."

"I'll send you the link."

"Wait, Chief," I said. "I know this is below your pay grade, but could you point me in the right direction to check on a shoplifting case in your city, at a convenience store around the middle of the month?" Didn't hurt to check Cissy's story about why Johnny hadn't been with them Sunday night.

"Hang on. I'll do a quick computer search." The clacking of keyboard keys.

"Perp might've given the name Johnny Smith," I said, "although that could be an alias."

"Here we go," the Tallahassee chief said. "Happened at two-ten last Saturday morning. Officer responded to a shoplifting call, but the store owner opted not to press charges. The kid gave some story about being homeless and hungry. Officer wrote it up, but he had to let the kid go. And yes, he gave his name as Johnny Smith."

"But he wasn't processed?"

"Correct," he said.

"About what time was Johnny cut loose?" I asked, masking my disappointment. No arrest meant no fingerprints were taken.

"Report doesn't say but I assume right then."

Which gave Johnny from early Saturday morning to make his way to Starling. He probably hitchhiked.

But why did Spencer keep moving around? Was it to avoid detection, or to find fresh faces for his disgusting videos? Maybe some of both. And maybe because he had with him a missing child, now an adult.

I flashed to something Johnny had said, that he had no memory of his childhood before age twelve.

Maybe two *missing children, now adults.* If they'd gotten comfortable in a community somewhere, Cissy and/or Johnny might have blabbed to a neighbor about their history, or lack thereof.

A throat clearing. "Anything else, Chief Anderson?"

"Um, yes. Do you also have a report of a prostitute being assaulted with a knife that night?"

"Hang on." More keys clacking. "Yeah, that's correct. She damn near died. But how'd you know that?"

I mentally gave Johnny kudos for daring to make that call. He most likely saved the woman's life. To the chief, I said, "You may find that the tip about the woman was called in from that same convenience store's pay phone."

"Holy hell! We didn't make that connection."

"Why would you? Your department is huge. The detective on the assault case wouldn't review every beat cop's report."

"Yes, but my chief of patrol should've caught it."

I felt sorry for the patrol chief, but anything more I said in his defense probably wouldn't help. "I think all of this is related to my homicide here in Starling," I said. "And if it is, you may be able to put that assault case in the solved column."

I paused. "But let me talk to Ms. Sanders first before I fill you in, if that's okay?"

"Uh, I guess," he said. "But tell me this much, who do you think assaulted the woman?"

"My homicide victim."

CHAPTER TWENTY

The Tallahassee chief opened the Zoom meeting, then he bowed out. "I'll let you explain yourself to Chief Anderson, Ms. Sanders." His face disappeared, replaced by a black square with *Tallahassee PD* in the middle of it.

I wondered if he was still recording the meeting. I had no problem with that. I certainly was.

Sara Sanders was a voluptuous blonde with fair skin and a hint of freckles. Faint yellowish spots around one eye verified Misty's story about her black eye.

I read Sara her rights and asked if she understood them. She nodded.

"You have to say it out loud, Ms. Sanders."

"Yes, I understand."

"Do you want a lawyer at this time?"

She hesitated, then said, "No, I got nothing to hide."

Before I could say anything, she blurted, "But I don't understand why you got me arrested. I didn't do anything wrong."

"We have reason to believe," I began, "that you were in a room at the Beachview Inn last Sunday night, March thirteenth. Your prints were found there."

Her face paled even further. "Um, yeah, I was there, for a while."

"And were you aware that John Spencer was murdered in that room sometime that night or early the next morning?"

She froze for a second. "But it was self-defense."

A zing of adrenaline shot through me at that confession. "Well, that claim might have held up, Ms. Sanders, if you hadn't left the scene."

"I repeat, *I* didn't do anything wrong."

"Okay, well, the murder aside, there's failure to report a crime, obstruction of justice and evidence tampering, since you wiped down the room."

"I didn't do that. It was the other woman."

"Who did what? Wiped down the room?"

"Yes."

I intentionally let out a soft sigh. "Why don't you start at the beginning and tell me exactly what happened?"

She gave me a wary look. "I was taken there against my will."

"By the ugly dude employed by the pimp who's been harassing you." I made it a statement, not a question. I wanted her to believe I already knew the whole story, just wanted to hear her version. She'd stick closer to the truth that way.

"Where and how did he get his hands on you?" I asked.

She shuddered. "I was going to see one of my regulars. He—the ugly dude as you called him—grabbed me as I was about to ring my client's bell at the apartment house entrance. He dragged me into an alley and jabbed me with something." She paused, gulped some air. "Next thing I knew I was naked and tied to a bed in that motel room."

When she didn't continue, I nudged, "And then?"

"There was this fat guy there. He already had his shirt off. He was really hairy, except on top of his head. There, he was bald."

John Spencer, our murder victim, although less and less was I willing to think of him as a *victim*.

"The ugly guy told him to go ahead and hurt me if he wanted, but not to kill me, or mar my face. His boss wanted me back. He went out the door, but I saw his shadow outside the window. He was gone later though."

I nodded, encouraging her to keep talking.

"There was this other woman there. She was young—tall and thin, and totally naked, but she was kinda spacy. The fat guy dropped his pants and climbed onto the bed. He, um...he took out a knife. And while he was...raping me, he began cutting on my arms." Her face twisted and she slapped a hand over her mouth.

I thought I heard a strangled sob.

Then she swallowed hard and lowered her hand. Maybe she'd been about to vomit.

"I screamed at first, but he threatened to cut my throat if I didn't quiet down." She shivered. "After that I was cussing and sobbing, and begging him to stop. But he just kept grinning at me."

I was feeling a little queasy now myself. I made a mental note to ask her later for her blood type—I was betting it would be O positive. But I didn't want to interrupt the flow of her story.

She rubbed her hands over the outside of her upper arms. "It turned out the cuts weren't deep but they hurt like hell."

She paused, sucked in air. "He, um, gestured for the other woman to join us and he got up. She pretended to be my Lesbian lover. She cleaned the cuts with a damp cloth, and kissed them. I tried to stop crying." Sara made a slight gagging sound. "To pretend it was all okay, hoping they would let me go after..."

What kind of sick movie was he making, I thought, then wondered if he would've divided it into several videos.

"The woman got up off the bed after a while," Sara was saying. "She picked up the knife. I guess it had fallen to the floor. I was so scared, I thought she was gonna kill me."

Another deep breath. "Then the fat guy jumped on top of me. I was bracing for him to start cutting on me again, or worse. But–" She stopped abruptly.

"But what?"

She glanced away, swallowed hard. And when she turned back to face me, her eyes had gone hard. "That woman, she stabbed him."

Sara had shown me the abrasions on her wrists from being restrained and the thin, scabbed-over cuts on the inside of one of her arms. I grit my teeth, while trying to maintain a neutral expression. The bastard had picked one of the most sensitive areas.

The wounds supported her claims, but I wasn't sure I believed all of her story.

Nonetheless, as soon as the interview was concluded, I went out to the watch desk to collect Cissy. I had quite a few new questions for her.

But she was gone.

Before I could open my mouth, Sergeant Armstrong said, "Barnes came and got her."

Damn, she was supposed to text me. "How long ago?"

"About an hour."

"Thanks, Sarge." I bolted for the fire stairs, fumbling my phone out of my pocket. I hit the speed dial number for Barnes as I ran down the steps. It went straight to voicemail.

Wait! She'd lost her phone.

I paused on a landing long enough to find the contact labeled *Barnes temp phone.*

It too went to voicemail.

Double damn! I left a message. "Gloria, be careful around Cissy. Sara Sanders just accused her of killing Spencer."

My stomach hollowed out as I realized I didn't have Barnes's new address.

A quick debate. I opted not to go back upstairs.

Instead, I ran out to my car, hoping she would call me back before I got too far. Or I might be able to find her another way.

I started the engine and instructed my Bluetooth to text Bradley. *Do you have your sister's new address?*

I swung my car out of the parking lot, headed toward her old place. She'd said the new one wasn't far from there—her main motive for moving was the new place allowed pets.

Would she have given her new address to HR yet?

My phone pinged. A mechanical female voice read Bradley's return text out loud, "Sure do. 29 Maple Street, Apartment B30."

I plugged the address into my GPS, then called Kate. I filled her in on the gist of the interview with Sara. "I'm on my way to my assistant's apartment. She offered to take Cissy in, but that was before we knew she's a killer."

"You still don't *know* she's a killer," Kate said, her voice firm. "She's only been *accused* of it, and by someone who also has a good motive."

An extra jolt of adrenaline zinged through my system, but I didn't have time to argue with Kate.

"Well, I'm about to confront her. If you want in on that conversation, better get over here."

"Yes, I want in on that conversation. I'm on my way."

I gave her the address. "Got it," she said. "*Please*, wait for me."

"Can't guarantee that." In total cop mode, I disconnected without saying goodbye. Then wished I hadn't. My chest tightened. I didn't want to lose my friendship with Kate...

I shook my head to clear it as I entered an apartment complex of three buildings. On the hunch that the middle one would be B, I headed for it.

My phone rang and the dashboard screen read *Bert Deming*.

I debated whether or not to answer, but I hit the button. "Make it quick, Bert. I'm in the middle of something."

"DNA came back on that kid, and the Center for Missing Children found a match."

"Wait, what? We already know who she is."

"Not her. The guy. He disappeared in a shopping mall when he was eleven."

CHAPTER TWENTY-ONE

"The kid's name is James Theodore Franks, Jr.," Bert continued. "Went by Teddy. He was with some friends in the food court, hanging out while his parents were shopping. The boys went up to the various kiosks to get food, and Teddy never came back to the table."

I climbed out of my car, switching the call to my actual phone. "Where was this?"

"Vermont, nine years ago. Oh, and the NCMEC sent his fingerprints. I checked them against the ones in Spencer's car. They're close to a match. Except again, the ones in the car have some straight lines across them."

"So Spenser tried to obscure both kids' prints," I speculated.

Bert didn't respond. He tended to stick to concrete evidence.

After a beat, he said, "I'm pretty sure Teddy, aka Johnny, was in that car at some point."

I had no doubt of that now, based on what Cissy had told us about them practically living out of that car. And he was probably the person who'd driven it into town. "Thanks, Bert."

I pocketed my phone as I reached the main door of the apartment building. There was a key swipe gadget, but when I pulled on the door's handle, it opened. Either the key reader was broken, or it was only activated at night.

Inside, I went up two flights of stairs to a small landing with three doors, marked B30, B31 and B32. My hand on my Glock under my jacket's tail, I knocked on 30's door.

Barnes answered the door in civvies—sweats and a pink tee shirt, with *Yeah, I hit like a girl. What of it?* printed on it. Her eyes widen some at the sight of me.

Then she glanced down at her shirt front. "My brother gave this to me for Christmas last—"

"Everything okay?" I interrupted, in a low voice.

"Yes. Why wouldn't it be?"

"You didn't answer your phone."

"Oh, sorry. It's in the bedroom. No pockets in these sweats." She patted her hips and stepped back to let me into the apartment.

"And no gun either, but you let me in without checking the peephole?" My voice was much harsher than I'd intended.

Barnes blinked twice, her expression confused. "The peephole's too high. I didn't notice before I moved in. And I thought you were the pizza guy." She sounded a little hurt, but this was not the time to worry about her feelings.

I walked past her without answering. Cissy sat on an overstuffed green sofa. Cardboard boxes were piled around the room. Two of them were acting as end tables, each holding a glass of red wine.

I gestured toward the empty end of the sofa. "May I?"

Barnes's eyes widened a bit again, but she nodded. "Of course. Would you like some wine?"

"Still on duty," I whispered.

Her eyebrows went up, then another nod.

I'd never been in Barnes's old place, but I didn't have time to take in my surroundings all that much. I settled in the corner of the sofa, half turned toward Cissy.

Barnes sank to the floor, cross-legged, next to the box with her glass of wine.

"Cissy," I began, "I think we've found the other woman who was in that motel room with you." I paused, let that soak in. "Have you had any more details of that night come back?"

She shook her head. "Not really."

I resisted the urge to ask her what that meant and stayed quiet. One of the hardest things in interrogations for me, *not* talking.

"I remember there was blood flying around," she said, "and I looked over at my dress, to make sure it was out of the line of fire."

Hmm... That fit with what she'd said earlier, that they'd done the cutting stuff before.

I waited silently, but Cissy didn't add anything.

Finally, I prompted, "The other woman is named Sara. She says you pretended to be her lover, for the camera."

She nodded. "That sounds right. Jake often made videos of me with other women. He said guys thought that was hot."

"But do you remember it from that night?"

She shook her head again.

I was debating if I should haul her back to 3MB and an interview room with recording equipment. But she was answering my questions. Best not to disrupt that. I pulled out my phone instead. "Do you mind if I record this, so you don't have to repeat it all later."

Her eyes grew a bit wary. "Um, I guess not."

I set the phone to record, and put it on the cushion between us. "So, you said that was not unusual, to be videotaped while being with other women. But you don't remember it last Sunday night in the motel, the night that the man you call Uncle Jake was killed?"

She nodded.

I nudged the phone, and she said, "Yes, that's right."

A sharp rap on the door. Barnes popped up and headed for it.

I cleared my throat. Johnny was still out there somewhere. Although how would he know where Cissy was? I didn't even have Barnes's new address until a few minutes ago.

Barnes glanced my way, got the message, and stood on her tiptoes to look out the peephole. "Dark curly hair, so I'm guessing female. Some gray in it."

"It's Kate Huntington."

Barnes nodded and opened the door, invited Kate in.

"That was fast," I said to her.

"I was already coming this way," Kate said. "My mom had a doctor's appointment in Jacksonville so I dropped her off and was going to stop in to check on things." She turned toward Cissy. "So, how are you?"

The young woman smiled. "I'm good. Gloria and I are roomies now."

I wasn't sure how I'd break it to both of them that the roomies arrangement was going to be short-lived.

Barnes had wandered off. Now she returned with a chrome and vinyl kitchen chair. She set it down and gestured for Kate to take it. Then she sank to the floor again, this time well out of reach of her wineglass. I suspected she'd figured out that she was back on duty now too.

"Cissy, do you have a phone?" I asked.

Her face brightened. "Yeah, I do now."

"How did you get it?" I was keeping my voice as gentle as possible, not wanting to spook her. I felt like I was trying to communicate with a curious but skittish deer.

"Johnny slipped it to me, as we were leaving the police building earlier. He walked past without looking at me and put the phone in my hand."

Out of the corner of my eye, I saw Barnes stiffen. Obviously, she'd missed that little exchange.

"Did you call him?" I asked.

"Um, no..." Her eyes were full-blown wary now.

She's lying.

Heart racing, I rose and power-walked to the door, slipped the safety chain in place.

Kate was following all this, her head swiveling back and forth, but she hadn't said a word.

I sat back down and turned to Cissy again. "Tell me more about Sunday night. What else did you or Jake do with Sara?"

Cissy blinked but didn't say anything.

"Do you remember holding the knife?" I nudged.

She closed her eyes and scrunched up her face. After a beat, she said, "I think so. I remember it was all slippery, hard to hold onto."

I glanced toward Kate and was startled to see that she was glaring at me.

"Cissy," she said, "just tell us what you actually remember, not what you think we want to hear, okay?"

Cissy opened her eyes and nodded.

"Can you recall what you were thinking or feeling," Kate asked, "while you were holding the knife?"

Her face scrunched up again, and a tear leaked out of one eye. "I felt sick to my stomach. I didn't want..." A small sob escaped. She grit her teeth. "I didn't want to hurt people anymore."

"And what did you do with the knife?" I asked.

"I, uh, I think I pushed it against something."

"The handle or the blade?" I demanded.

Kate was glaring at me again. I made myself ignore her, keeping my eyes on Cissy, who began shaking her head, more and more vehemently.

"I don't know," she half shouted. Then she burst into tears and buried her face in her hands.

The next thing I knew Kate was on the sofa between us, almost pushing me off the edge. And she was blocking my view of Cissy's face.

Damn it, Kate!

I jumped up and took Kate's abandoned chair. She had her arms around the sobbing girl.

I leaned forward. "Cissy, did you stab Jake?" I couldn't see my phone. I hoped it was still recording and Kate wasn't sitting directly on it.

"I don't know," Cissy wailed.

Kate's expression was full-blown stink-eye now.

I pointed at her. "You and I need to talk," I hissed softly.

It wasn't ideal breaking off the interrogation at that moment, but it would give Cissy a couple of minutes to calm down.

Kate stood and I took her arm, practically dragging her across the room. My stomach was roiling. I was going to lose her as a friend. But I couldn't let her keep this up.

We turned to face each other. I let go of her arm and whispered, "Kate, you can't interfere like that."

"Judith," she hissed back in a low voice, "you can't ask her leading questions like that."

"Of course I can."

"No, you can't."

I took a deep breath. "Look, I know you feel protective of her, like she's your client, but–"

"I'm not trying to protect her, you idiot," she spat out. "I'm trying to protect *you*—from yourself."

I froze, my stomach hollowing out. "But you asked her leading questions yesterday, about taking a shower." My voice sounded whiny in my own ears, like a child defending herself against a parent's anger.

That's messed up.

Kate sucked in her own deep breath. "I did, but we were already pretty sure that *had* happened. And it was a fairly innocuous thing, something to use to maybe trigger her memories of the rest of what happened."

I glared at her, somehow still feeling like a chastised child.

"That's *not* the same thing," she said, "as pushing her on what she did with the knife. She's not a normal suspect, and you can't continue this way. Not if you want any of this to stand up in court."

"What do you mean?"

Kate heaved a sigh. "When someone has an intact memory and knows what did and did not happen, you can ask all the leading questions you want, I know that. Skip has told me that the police can even legally lie about certain things in an interrogation. But Cissy doesn't remember what happened consciously, so anything you say acts as a suggestion and contaminates her memories."

"Damn!"

She shook her head. "Not only won't it hold up as evidence, but now you can't trust if something she says she *does* remember is an actual memory—or something her mind has made up based on those suggestions."

Shit! "But Sara says she stabbed the guy."

"And what makes Sara such a reliable witness?" Kate snapped.

I opened my mouth. A muffled sound behind me. I whirled around.

But there was nothing there, only a short hallway and two open doorways, leading to bedrooms.

Another sound, then a crash, and Barnes ran past me. I took off, pulling out my Glock. But when I reached the bedroom doorway, I reholstered my gun.

Barnes had already collared the intruder, literally. I almost laughed out loud. She had him by the scruff of his jacket's neck, with one of his arms twisted behind him.

It was Johnny. Or Teddy...

Oh crap, we're not starting that name game again. He stays Johnny, for now.

Cissy had indeed called him, and given him the address of her new place. Either that or he'd used the GPS in the phone to track her.

The room held only a rolled sleeping bag by one wall and a small bookcase under the window. The crashing sound had been a lamp hitting the floor as Johnny climbed through the window from the fire escape.

I tossed Barnes my cuffs.

"Stop squirming or you're gonna dislocate your shoulder," she told him as she clicked the cuffs on one and then the other of his wrists. "You're under arrest for illegal entry." She quickly patted him down and marched him past me.

I followed down the hall, trying and failing to wipe the grin from my face.

But it vanished when I saw what was going on in the living room.

Cissy had an arm looped around Kate's neck, with a cell phone in that hand.

I recognized the pale pink cover. It was the one Barnes had lost several days ago.

And in Cissy's other hand was another of Barnes's possessions—her service weapon.

CHAPTER TWENTY-TWO

"Let Johnny go," Cissy barked.

Barnes and I froze. She let go of Johnny's arm.

He jogged over to Cissy, his cuffed hands throwing him a little off balance. "Come on," he said in a gruff voice. "Let's get out of here."

For a second, Cissy's expression was conflicted. Then it hardened and she nodded.

Johnny trotted out the door and she began to follow, using Kate as a shield.

Not that she needed one. I didn't dare try to pull my own gun. Her finger was on the trigger of the pistol she had aimed at us. And her hand was shaking.

"Let Kate go, Cissy," I called out. "You don't want a kidnapping charge hanging over your head, do you?"

At the open doorway, Cissy shoved Kate forward. She stumbled and fell onto a box, and Cissy took off.

I dropped to one knee beside Kate. "You okay?"

She nodded, her eyes wide.

I pulled my Glock and started to stand.

Kate grabbed my arm. "Be careful."

"Always."

Barnes ran past me, a small revolver now in her hand. Her backup piece.

On the landing there was no sign of Cissy, Johnny or Barnes. The building's outer door slammed below me. I raced down the two flights of stairs.

Outside, Barnes was running around the far corner of the building. I bolted over to that corner and peered around it. Barnes was standing in the middle of a back parking lot, her head swiveling as she looked around.

And she had a gun in each hand.

"She glanced back at me. "They're gone. Where the hell did they go?"

She held up one of the guns. "I found this in the grass beside the building." It was her service weapon.

I blew out air. Maybe Cissy had dropped it accidentally, but I suspected she'd left it on purpose.

Heaven forbid she steals something, while escaping from the police.

"How'd he move so fast with cuffs on?" Barnes asked as we headed back toward her apartment.

"They seem to have lots of practice running from cops," I said. "And he'll be out of the cuffs soon enough."

Barnes raised her eyebrows.

"They've both starred in bondage porn videos. They know their way around handcuffs. How the hell did she get your gun?" My voice was a bit terse. I decided I was okay with that.

Her cheeks flamed as she started up the stairs ahead of me. "I put it in my lock box on the mantel."

I vaguely remembered there being a fireplace in the living room. *In Florida? Why?*

"I'd turned my back to her," Barnes continued, her voice strained—she knew she'd made a rookie mistake. "I thought she couldn't see me drop the key into an empty vase, also on the mantel."

I opted not to chastise her. She was already beating herself up.

Kate was waiting by the open apartment door. "I take it they got away."

I nodded, having trouble meeting her gaze. I tried to swallow the lump that had suddenly formed in my throat.

She glanced at her watch. "Look, I gotta go pick up Mom. I'll call you later, okay?" She slipped past me and went down the stairs, headed for her car.

I watched her go, my stomach queasy. *Oh well, it was a nice friendship while it lasted.*

My internal attempt to make light of it failed. My chest was tight. I opened my mouth to suck in air, as my mind flashed to the dead woman on the floor.

A teenager's voice inside my head, *Don't let anyone get too close.*

Barnes appeared beside me on the landing. She was now wearing her uniform, but her hair was still down. "Kate doesn't seem to be all that fazed by her brief stint as a hostage."

I cleared my throat. "Sadly, she's no stranger to violence. And in her younger days, she could kick ass."

"Sounds like she has some stories to tell," Barnes said as she handed me my cell phone from the sofa.

"Oh yeah. Come on, apparently our workday isn't over."

———

I'd called and told the sarge to put out a BOLO—again—on Cissy and Johnny.

This is getting embarrassing.

When we arrived at 3MB, Sergeant Armstrong advised me that the uniform we'd sent earlier to fetch Sara Sanders had made good time. They were on their way back.

"And Sheriff Pierson's in your office," Armstrong added, with a twinkle in his eye.

I hid a smile. Sam had texted me on the way here. He'd caught his armed robbers and wanted to take me to dinner to celebrate.

At least somebody's having a good day.

"I can't leave yet," I told him, as I entered my office. "We've had some complications." I gave him a succinct summary of the events at Barnes's apartment, leaving out my argument with Kate. My eyes burned suddenly and my throat tightened.

I shook my head to clear it.

"You want me to call out for pizza then?" Sam asked.

"Barnes has one already. She'd ordered one for her and Cissy's dinner. The delivery guy arrived as we were climbing into our cars. Thank heavens he wasn't more prompt or he might've been caught up in the craziness."

As if on cue, Barnes came through my open office door and deposited a pizza box in the middle of my desk. She'd stop at our little vending/coffee area to get paper plates and napkins. And somewhere along the way, she'd found time to put her long dark hair up in its usual bun.

The pizza was plain cheese and no longer all that hot, but I could've eaten the box at that point. I couldn't recall if I'd ever eaten lunch.

"Cissy insisted on just cheese," Barnes said. "Because, quote, 'I have to watch my weight.'" Her attempt to mimic Cissy's accent failed. She added, "I resisted the urge to point out that she wasn't making porn movies anymore."

My stomach did an uncomfortable flip as I realized she might very well end up a prostitute though, especially if we couldn't find her again.

I put down my half-eaten piece of pizza and booted up my computer, looking for Bert's report. "As Kate had suspected," I said, "Johnny was taken as a child as well. He was eleven." I filled them in on the details of how Cissy's companion had been kidnapped.

"So he's an innocent too," Sam said, his tone mournful.

"Yeah, who's been taught to be a petty thief and porn star." I grabbed the pizza box and stood. "Let's go to the conference room and add things to the board."

At least then I might feel like I was accomplishing something.

They followed me, plates in hand, out of the bullpen and down the hall. "Don't start without me," Barnes said and veered off toward the vending machines.

Once in the conference room, I used the time she was gone to erase some question marks.

"We now know for sure that Sara was the third person in that motel room," I was saying as Barnes came in, carrying a can of cola and her paper plate. "And guess whose prints match the ones in the car." I wrote *Johnny* next to the car photo and added a question mark.

Barnes pulled two more cans of cola out of her pants pockets, and I almost smiled. She placed one by my plate and passed the other to Sam.

"So maybe Johnny arrived sooner than he claimed," she said, "and he moved the car."

"And here's another tidbit," I said. "Johnny didn't have a cell phone in Tallahassee. He had to make an excuse to go into the convenience store to use their pay phone. But later he does have access to a phone since he called the hospital."

"He could've found another pay phone," Sam said.

I grimaced. "Maybe, or the victim had a phone in his car, and it is now in Johnny's possession."

"There were no phones registered in Spencer's name," Barnes said, "so it would have to be a burner."

I pointed a finger at Barnes. "Get Derek to see if he can track any of those calls, including any today to or from your lost phone."

She made a face. "Which is now in Cissy's possession."

Sam snorted softly. "Musical phones."

Barnes put down her slice of pizza and pulled out her own disposable to call Derek.

Sam popped the top of his soda. "Not a very nutritious dinner, but..." he muttered and took a long swig, his Adam's apple bobbing in his throat.

I looked at him, an odd mixture of anger and love filling my chest. At the same time, my stomach hollowed out.

What the hell is that all about?

I shook my head—now was not the time to be sorting out my feelings. Turning back to the white board, I moved Sara's photo over to a blank area and succinctly added the key elements of her version of the events in that motel room.

Then I moved to another blank area, put Johnny's name at the top—with a slash and *Teddy Franks* after it. Under that, I wrote *1. Identified as missing child, Vermont, 9 yrs ago.* Then *2. B&E Barnes's apt, fled with Cissy,* and *3. Had Barnes's phone; gave it to Cissy.*

I debated whether to put anything about Cissy's temporary possession of Barnes's gun up there. Did I want to embarrass my assistant further? I decided to wait on that for now.

I also left out the interference from our psychological consultant and our resulting hissing match. Again embarrassing, among other things. I should've figured out that I couldn't use the same questioning tactics with an amnesiac as I would with other suspects.

But I'd never dealt with—what did Kate call it...*dissociative fugue*—before.

All too often, in this new position of chief, I was encountering issues beyond my background as a homicide investigator. I wasn't as prepared for this job as I, or my superiors here, had thought I would be.

But, I reminded myself, *they didn't hire me strictly for my policing skills.* Mayor Hayes, back when he was still the city council chair, had admitted to me that they'd hired me mainly because of my reputation for integrity. They'd wanted someone who could and would clean up a corrupt police department.

Speaking of which...

I turned and glanced at the conference room door, making sure it was closed. "We've got something else going on right now too," I told Sam. I filled him and Barnes in on the interrogation of Clara Hopkins from Accounting.

Sam's face had a weird expression on it when I'd finished. "Are you done here? Wanna take a ride with me to John Black's house?"

Realization dawned, and my stomach did an unpleasant flip. If I hadn't had so much going on, I would've seen the risk sooner.

Sam had jumped up. We both bolted for the door.

Barnes's mouth was hanging open as I ran past her, but I didn't take the time to fill her in on our suspicions.

And it looked like those suspicions were correct.

John Black had been the Chief of Police of Starling, but he lived with his wife in Clover County, their two kids long since grown and out of the house. The windows of that house were now dark in the gathering dusk, and the usually immaculate lawn and flower gardens were a little unkempt.

We rang the doorbell, knowing there would be no response. Then we walked slowly around the house. Most of the curtains were drawn but we found a crack between the ones in the dining room.

Enough light filtered down from a skylight to allow us to make out the furniture. There were no objects on the mahogany table or the matching sideboard against one wall, and a couple of the latter's drawers were hanging open.

I squinted trying to make out what was beyond the glass in the china cabinet across the room. It was all darkness. Was it empty?

Damn, why didn't I see this coming?

I shook my head. Beating myself up wasn't helpful. Out loud, I said, "Black's wife drives a minivan, doesn't she?"

"Yup," Sam said, his tone sour. "Pulling up a moving truck for the furniture would've been too obvious, but no doubt they stuffed everything small and valuable in that van."

I turned toward him. "He kept submitting the fake mileage vouchers after he retired, and even after he was arrested–"

"To build up an escape fund," Sam finished my sentence, "since all his accounts were frozen." He shook his head. "Pretty risky, actually downright crazy."

I shrugged. "What did he have to lose? He was already facing several decades in prison, and he's in his sixties." I paused, my shoulders sagging. "And he's pulled it off, so far at least."

He sighed. "I'll put out the BOLO, nationwide. You call Dot Wilder and tell her the bad news. She likes you. She's less likely to yell at you for losing her crook."

"Grrr," I grumbled. "*We* didn't lose him. That judge agreed to house arrest, against everyone's advice."

Sam sighed again. "I'll also get a search warrant to look through the house. You wanna bet me on whether his ankle bracelet is somewhere inside there?"

"Nope. Not taking that bet." I pulled out my phone.

CHAPTER
TWENTY-THREE

Dot Wilder did not take the news well that Black had flown the coop. But she wasn't angry with me or Sam. Indeed, she sounded remorseful. "I should've put someone on his house. I knew you and the sheriff didn't have the resources to do that."

"For most people, the ankle monitor would've been sufficient," I pointed out, as I reached my car. Sam waved from where he was leaning against his cruiser, his own phone to his ear.

"Yes, but Black's got a lot of contacts in his good ole boy network."

"I can't believe he got more money out of the city." I climbed into the driver's seat. "Even after he was arrested. That takes..." I hesitated, trying to think of a diplomatic way of saying it.

"Balls the size of Kansas," Dot said.

I laughed, despite the gravity of the situation. "Yeah."

I decided to take advantage of Dot feeling bad. "Speaking of limited resources, would you be pissed if I offered Wellbourne a job here...Permanently, I mean."

A couple of silent seconds ticked by.

I sat in my car, resisting the temptation to mention my ulterior motive. Yes, Wellbourne had the makings of a great detective, but she was also female and Black. And I was determined to diversify the male-dominated, mostly lily-white department I'd inherited.

"No, yes," Dot finally said. "I mean, no, I won't be pissed. Yes, make the offer. I think she'd be happier there."

I suppressed a chuckle. If I was getting soft, I was no worse than this woman, who'd managed to make it to regional director in the FDLE.

"And here's a promise." Dot's voice had turned grim. "I *will* track that bastard Black down."

It was now after eight, but I wanted to interrogate Sara Sanders again, this time in person, before calling it a night. With Barnes in the observation area, I entered the interview room and sat down across from the prisoner.

The Tallahassee PD's computer camera hadn't done Sara justice. In person, Sara was beautiful—smooth, creamy complexion, wavy blonde hair cascading down her back, big blue eyes and a voluptuous body. She wore skinny jeans, wedge-heeled sandals and a red loose-fitting, long-sleeved sweater.

As instructed, the uniform who'd brought her into the room had removed her handcuffs. Her well-manicured fingers were laced together on the table in front of her.

I repeated the Miranda warning and confirmed that she understood her rights. Then I said, "First, let me reassure you that we have identified the man who abducted you, and we are searching for him. He will be charged with kidnapping, assault, and anything else I can come up with to throw at him."

I paused. "And we're looking into who he works for, to do what we can there."

"Protect and serve," she said with a wry smile.

"That is our goal." I leaned slightly forward. "Now, *you* are charged with failure to report a crime and obstruction of justice. Whether or not I throw anything else at you will depend on how cooperative you are. And if you're really, really helpful, I may drop the obstruction charge."

"Where do you want me to begin?"

"How about with how and why you became a call girl? And by the way, I'm not going to arrest you for that, since I have no proof, but I am curious."

She sucked in air and heaved out a sigh. "That is a rather long, boring story. The short version is I went to a party with a friend in college. She introduced me to a guy who said I could get all the, quote, 'dates' I wanted, *and* get paid quite well for just going out and having fun."

"And that's *all* you do?" I asked with my own wry smile.

"No, but that's where my honorarium scale starts."

"Wow, never heard it called *that* before. And what honorarium do you expect for, say, only partying with someone?"

"Arm candy starts at $500 an hour. Additional perks are, of course, more than that."

"And I suppose you screen your customers carefully."

"Oh, yes, quite carefully. But I prefer to call them *clients*, or to their faces, *companions*."

"And are those the services—arm candy plus perks—that this pimp in Jacksonville, Mr. Ugly's boss, wants you to provide?"

She smiled again, a bit more fully. "Mr. Ugly. I like that. Yes, only here in Starling, not Jacksonville. And I doubt he'd be doing the careful screening."

So this pimp wasn't only trying to add to his stable. He was trying to fill the void left by the escort service and trafficking ring we'd busted last fall.

I managed to maintain a neutral expression, even though a lump of dread was forming in my stomach. "And when you wouldn't comply," I said, "he figured he'd try to break you."

Her face clouded. "Yes, I believe that was the idea. I'm pretty sure that set-up in the motel was prearranged. The fat guy was told by Mr. Ugly," a ghost of the smile again, "that he could cut me enough to make me scream but not to leave serious scarring. And nothing on the face," she shifted in her seat, "or certain other parts of my body."

I nodded. "May I see some of the cuts?"

She shoved up the sleeves of her sweater.

I worked hard to keep from wincing. The insides of her arms, from elbow to wrist, were marred by long angry red welts, some with scabs, a couple still sporting butterfly bandages. They looked far worse than they had in the Zoom video.

"How'd you get them treated?"

"At a doc-in-a-box in Tallahassee. I told the nurse there that I'd broken up a fight between my cat and my neighbor's."

"But how did you take care of them before you got to the walk-in clinic?"

"That motel might be sleazy but they're generous with towels. They were thin but clean. I wrapped one around each arm. I'd worn a long-sleeved dress. I put that on and managed to get the sleeves over the towels. I probably looked like the Pillsbury dough boy but they helped keep the towels snug against the wounds, to stop the bleeding."

"Okay, walk me through all that, step-by-step."

Something flickered in her eyes. Anxiety?

"The other girl...Cissy you called her...she cut me loose. I grabbed my dress and ran into the bathroom. I, um, took a shower, and wrapped the towels around my arms like I said. Then I peeked out of the bathroom door."

She paused and gave a dramatic shudder. Perhaps a little too dramatic.

"Fat guy was on the bed, with the knife sticking out of him, and the girl, Cissy, she was wiping down the room, muttering, 'No prints. No prints.'"

"Wait, back up some. How did you get away from Fat Guy? His name was John Spencer, by the way. When Cissy was cutting you loose, what was he doing?"

"Oh, um..." Her gaze darted around the room a couple of times. "He was passed out, lying on top of me. I think maybe she knocked him out with something."

I nodded like I believed her, which I didn't. Though she'd likely been telling the truth about the shower and the towels. The rest of the story had several discrepancies.

"I had to shove him off of me," Sara was saying, "after she cut me loose."

"Okay, then what happened, when you came out of the bathroom?"

"He, uh, had a knife sticking out of his side at that point. I assumed Cissy had stabbed him. Mr. Ugly was gone, thank heavens, so I left." She sat back, as if I should accept that as the end of the story.

"Okay, but how did Cissy get my business card?"

"Business card?" She blinked. "Oh yeah, I gave it to her. The way Misty acted, I thought it was like a get-out-of-jail-free card. And I hadn't done anything wrong, so I figured the girl needed it more than I did."

I pursed my lips. "And you weren't planning on sticking around Starling anyway at that point."

Sara ducked her head but didn't reply.

"So, tell me how you got from that motel to Jacksonville, without a phone or any money?"

No answer but another flicker in her eyes. Definitely anxiety, this time.

"Did you take Spencer's car?"

She blinked again. "Um, car? What car?"

It didn't ring true.

I said, "There was no wallet or phone on Spencer or in the room."

Ignoring that information, she said, "I walked."

Like hell you did!

"I don't think so. It's a good twenty miles to Jacksonville."

She turned her head to the side and licked her lips. "I, um, found his keys in the pocket of his pants. I looked through his car and found a couple of prepaid phones. I took one and called an Uber driver I know. I'm one of his regulars. He took me home, off the clock."

Hmm, and the other phone, we're assuming, ended up in Johnny's possession.

Out loud, I asked, "There was no wallet in his pants or his car?"

She glanced sideways at me. "Yes. In the glove box. I left it there, along with the car keys. I'm not a thief."

"Okay... We have your own burner phone pinging off a tower in Jacksonville, near the train station, early the next morning. And you withdrew $500 from an ATM near there."

She seemed to hesitate, then said, "When Mr. Ugly grabbed me, my purse went flying. My Uber friend took me back to my client's apartment building, and we found it under a bush beside the sidewalk."

"So you went home and packed, and your Uber friend drove you to the train station in Jax."

She nodded, chewing on her lower lip. It was now swollen some, and her eyes were red-rimmed. But she was still drop-dead gorgeous.

I squashed an unprofessional spurt of envy.

"He's quite a friend," I said.

She sat up straighter. "It's not what you think. He's a good guy. I offered him money for his time and gas, but he wouldn't take it."

"Who'd you call from your own phone?" I asked.

She shook her head. "No one. I turned it on to use the banking app to move some money around. So I could get to it easier later."

I tapped my fingers on the table. "Okay, let's go back to the motel for a minute. The knife was sticking out of Spencer's, aka Fat Guy's body when you came out of the bathroom. Did you notice how many stab wounds there were?"

"Um, no." More chewing on her lip.

"How much blood was there?"

"I don't know," she said, her tone annoyed on the surface but anxious as hell underneath. "Some around him, and some sprayed on the walls."

"On the walls, big smears or like a mist of droplets?"

"Droplets." She gave another shudder. This one looked genuine. "When he was cutting on me, he would intentionally flick the knife toward the wall, and then film it."

A chill ran through me. He was one sicko. But I kept my expression neutral.

"That reminds me, the camera, where was it?"

She hung her head and sighed. "There were two of them, one on a tripod and one he held, off and on. I took them. I didn't want those videos getting out there on the internet."

"And you took his phone." A statement, not a question.

She nodded without raising her head. "In case he'd recorded anything with it."

"What did you do with them?"

"Tossed them in the river, along with the cell phone I took from the car."

Damn the Sofki River. It was a great trash can for criminals.

"Why didn't you take the car?"

Her head came up and her cheeks paled. "It smelled like Fat Guy. It made me gag. I just wanted to get away from there."

"Understandable, but you could've called 911 anonymously on that burner phone."

"I was only focused on getting out of town, before Mr. Ugly realized I was gone and reported that back to his boss."

"Makes sense." I paused for effect. She seemed to be on a roll with the truth, for a change. I wondered if she would continue along that course. "Back to the knife. Did you take that too?"

She shook her head.

"I don't believe Cissy stabbed him," I said. Actually, I *was* willing to believe it now, after she'd pulled a gun on me.

But I wanted to see what Sara would say. I leaned forward again. "Remember I said if you cooperated..." I trailed off, then added, "My guess is that whatever you did, it would be considered self defense."

She sighed. "Okay, um, Cissy cut one wrist loose, and pressed the knife into my hand. He was on top of me. I, uh, couldn't get him off."

"He wasn't unconscious though," I said. "Cissy hadn't knocked him out."

She sighed again and shook her head. "No, he was... raping me, grunting like a pig. I don't think he'd even realized she had cut that wrist loose and left the room. I..." She trailed off and leaned back, hugging herself.

"I stabbed him. He yelled and rolled off of me." She stopped, sucked in air. "By the time I got myself cut free of the bed, Cissy was out of the bathroom, her hair wet. She put on her dress and then started wiping fingerprints."

She gestured as if she could see a bed in front of her. "He was lying there, but he was still breathing. I wanted to run out the door naked. But I made myself go take a shower, to clean the wounds mostly, and get his filth off of me." She scrunched her face up in disgust. "The rest of what I told you is the truth."

Hmm, that didn't quite add up. She stabbed him once, while he was on top of her, and that was enough to incapacitate him? And she was sure enough that he wasn't going to come around that she took a shower? Not likely...

"You only stabbed him *once?*"

"Yeah." She ducked her head.

I cleared my throat, gave her a hard stare.

Her eyes flicked toward me, then down again. "Um, it might have been twice, in his side. But I swear he was still alive. He started groaning as I was going out the door."

"So you just left and didn't call the police or an ambulance. You left him to die. That's second-degree murder."

Her eyes went wide and her mouth dropped open. Stark terror crossed her face. "No! I mean, Cissy was there. She could've called for help."

"True, but *you* didn't."

In reality, I wasn't at all sure what the ASA might charge her with, since—if her account was true—the stabbing could be seen as self defense, and yes, Cissy was still there to render aid.

Another thing didn't add up, though. There were three knife wounds, two to the side—that part jived with Sara's story. But what about the third one?

The ME had said in the autopsy report that one of the wounds to his side was shallow, probably the first, somewhat hesitant thrust. The other one to his side was deeper and collapsed his lung.

That could indeed render him immobile, but wouldn't kill him right away, the report had said. The ME believed that the wound in the chest, which went through his heart, was from a third thrust. And it was the fatal blow.

The question was whether Sara was lying and she'd landed all three. Or did the third one come from someone else?

Maybe Cissy...

CHAPTER TWENTY-FOUR

I instructed Barnes to take Sara back to her holding cell, and I headed for my office.

Noises drew my attention to the watch desk. A woman was standing in front of it, her shoulders heaving as she sobbed.

The evening watch commander, Sergeant Johnson stood behind his desk, looking helpless.

I strode toward the scene.

"Please, please, just tell me where my daughter is," the woman wailed. "Where's my Cissy?"

"I'm sorry, ma'am," the sarge said. "Um, we don't know where she is."

The woman was crying so hard she was half hunched over.

I quickly took in the cotton dress, bare legs and loafers. "Ma'am," I said. "Can I see some ID?"

"I already checked," Johnson said. "Her driver's license says she's Audrey Brown, from Alabama." He picked up the handles of an open black purse that was sitting on his desk. "It's clean," he said to me out of the side of his mouth, meaning no weapons.

He tried to hand the bag to its owner, but she was still hunched over, sobbing.

I held out my hand for the purse. "Ma'am, please come with me."

She jerked upright. "Who the hell are you? Some social worker?"

"I'm the Chief of Police. If you'll come to my office with me, I'll explain what's going on."

She looked me up and down. "*You're* the Chief of Police? Yeah, right."

"She is, ma'am," Johnson injected. "Chief Judith Anderson."

"Ma'am," I said, "please come with me." I gestured with my free hand toward the entrance to the bullpen, while handing her the purse with the other.

She took the purse but shook her head. "I'm not going anywhere until you tell me where my daughter is."

I blew out a small sigh. "We are currently searching for her."

"But I thought you had her," the woman protested.

"We did. She was arraigned and released on her own recognizance, but then she helped someone else escape police custody and took off with him."

"What? That's crazy. *My* daughter would not break the law."

Any residual doubts about her identity faded. This was the woman who taught Cissy not to steal or "be beholden." Unfortunately, other life events had intervened since those lessons had been learned.

"Ma'am," I said, a bit more firmly. "It's a very long story. Please come to my office so I can tell you what's happening more privately."

The woman blinked, looked around, and seemed to realize she was in an open area with various personnel walking by and staring. She nodded.

I ushered her to my office and got her settled in the comfy visitor's chair.

Barnes appeared in my doorway.

"Ma'am, would you like something to drink?" I asked. "Coffee, water, a soda?"

"Um, water, I guess."

Barnes disappeared, and I left the door open so she could bring in the cup of water she was fetching.

The bullpen was mostly deserted anyway. Only one detective—Cruthers—sat at his desk along the back wall, typing a report.

I gave Cissy's mother an abridged rundown of all that had happened. At one point, Barnes returned and slipped a cup of water in front of her on the desk. She retreated, but left the door open.

I knew she was hovering nearby, one part curious and one part ready to assist if needed.

"You're telling me that my daughter has all these charges against her," Mrs. Brown said, "and she's goin' to jail?"

"I'm trying to avoid that if I can. I see Cissy as more a victim in all this than a perpetrator. Most of what she's done is only what she's been taught to do."

The woman stiffened in her chair. "I never taught her none of that."

"No, no, that's not what I meant. Uh, I thought Sheriff Taylor filled you in."

She stared at me for a moment, brown eyes wide above high cheekbones. I could see where Cissy got her good looks, but her mother was a worn-down version of her.

Then Mrs. Brown raised her hands partway in front of her. I thought for a second that she was going to start praying. But she dropped her face into her hands and moaned.

"I was hopin' he'd gotten it all wrong," she sobbed out, "that Cissy would tell me..." She trailed off and cried into her hands.

Barnes slipped into my office with a box of tissues. I nodded and she left them on the desk. Then she leaned against the doorjamb, her notepad discreetly nested in her palm.

"What did you hope Cissy would tell you, Mrs. Brown?" I asked.

She lifted her head and sniffled. Noticing the tissues, she grabbed one and wiped her cheeks. Then she made eye contact with me. "That she'd gone of her own accord, like we'd all assumed. And then met up with this Jake fella later."

That was actually a possible scenario. We hadn't yet filled in the blanks of how Cissy had ended up with Jake.

"What did the sheriff say?" I asked, my voice low and gentle.

She shook her head slightly. "That my husband..." she choked a little on the word. "that maybe he'd sold her to this Jake."

I caught my jaw before it dropped, but Barnes wasn't so quick. She gave me a startled look.

"He got the phone records for our home phone," the woman said, "from back when Cissy disappeared. There were several calls to a number that he said was a prepaid disposable phone. He traced that phone to its seller. It was bought with cash in the next town over, along with five other phones. But it had been too long. No one at that store remembered the buyer."

She paused. "The sheriff said maybe it was this Jake fella."

Kudos to the sheriff for some good police work. But how likely was it that Jake still had those same burner phones all these years later? If he was their purchaser in the first place.

If it did go down that way. There was no proof that the phone calls were about Cissy. There were a half dozen ways Cissy could've ended up with Jake. I had little doubt, though, that Joe Brown had a hand in his stepdaughter's disappearance.

But why was Sheriff Taylor telling the wife all this? To jolt her into believing her husband really was a slime ball?

Maybe.

"Miz Chief," Cissy's mother said, interrupting my thoughts. "Please, please, find my girl. She's all I got left."

I wanted to reassure her that we'd find her younger child too, and her no-good husband, but that was a long shot at this point.

Instead, I said, "We're doing the best we can, ma'am."

———◆———

I sat at my desk, staring into space.

Barnes had left with Audrey Brown, with instructions to help her get a hotel room. Barnes had wanted to take her home with her.

"And how well did that work out last time?" I'd said, my tone acerbic. "Stop taking in strays, at least the two-legged kind."

Barnes had frowned, but then nodded. I'd told her to go on home afterwards.

Now I was trying to decide if there was anything else I could do tonight, or should I just go home myself.

It was after ten, kind of late to call Sheriff Taylor. And what would we discuss anyway?

We didn't have any of Spencer's burner phones in our possession. Maybe after we caught Johnny—*if* we caught Johnny—and if he had one of Spencer's phones, we'd be able to link Spencer to Cissy's stepfather.

Wait, maybe that Uber driver could give us the number of the burner phone Sara used to call him. I made a note on the pad on my desk to follow up on that tomorrow, then placed both hands on my desk top to push myself to a stand.

A rapping sound and I jerked.

"Sorry, I didn't mean to startle you." Sam was standing in my doorway, smiling at me. "Do you realize you're the only one still here?"

I wiggled my fingers for him to come in and sat back down. "So, what are you doing here?"

"I went to your apartment but you weren't there. I figured you were still here. And before you ask why didn't I call," he held up his cell phone, "it ran out of juice."

He plopped down in the comfy chair. "That's how long this day has been. And I left my charger at home."

"So, what'd you find at Black's house?"

"As predicted, the ankle monitor. In the master bedroom on the floor. But we didn't find much else. He and his wife cleaned out anything of value, plus most of their clothes."

"Where do you think he went?"

He shrugged. "Maybe the Caymans. I'm guessing he has some offshore bank accounts that the FDLE didn't find."

"Well, he's Dot Wilder's problem now," I said with a sigh.

Sam stood up, and even though the bullpen was completely empty, he walked around my office, closing the copper blinds that turned it from a fish bowl into a cozy den.

I knew what was coming and I wasn't sure how I felt about it. I'd been mad at him earlier, or was I mad about something else? I couldn't remember. It *had* been a long day and an even longer evening.

He walked over to my chair and took my hand, pulling me to my feet.

"I'm sorry," he said, as we stood inches apart.

"About what?"

"Whatever I did earlier to piss you off."

I shook my head. "What if you didn't do anything wrong? Why are you automatically apologizing?" I loved that this man was so easygoing. No way he could put up with me otherwise. But this bordered on being wimpy.

He gave me a lopsided grin. "Even if I did nothing wrong, I'm sorry it pissed you off, whatever it was. You know, like I regret it, but don't necessarily feel guilty about it."

He paused, leaned in and kissed my nose.

I pulled back some and faked a chuckle, as I tried my damnedest to figure out what I'd been mad about earlier. "I think you've been hanging around Kate too much lately. That sounds like the kind of psychobabble she says."

He grinned again. "Psychobabble or not, I like her. I see why you're friends."

A short but sharp pain in my chest. *Are we still friends?*

Wait, am I mad at Kate, not Sam? Or at myself, for even trying to balance so many relationships—when I know I'm crappy at them?

"Anyway," Sam was saying, "I regret that *something* pissed you off, because I would much rather you be happy."

He pulled me closer and wrapped his arms around me. A gentle hug, offering solace, for both of us, at the end of a very long day.

I stiffened slightly, then willed myself to relax, putting my cheek against his khaki shirt front.

But my mind flashed to Meredith, and that sunny afternoon. And it dawned on me...when had I ever been truly happy?

Not since that day, in the hours before she was snatched.

I'd had happy moments—graduating from the police academy, closing big cases, making love with Sam. But prolonged happiness required that one be content.

My chest tightened. True contentment didn't stand a chance...

Not with the memory of that day lurking behind a thin curtain in my mind.

CHAPTER TWENTY-FIVE

Saturday morning, I was dragging and couldn't figure out why. I'd gotten a decent night's sleep. Only one bad dream—my dead mother, again admonishing me to find Meredith. But I'd gotten back to sleep readily enough.

Yet this morning, I was tired and couldn't drum up the motivation for my usual workout.

I went for a run on the riverwalk instead, but thoughts of Kate kept intruding—was that friendship gone for good? My chest felt hollow.

I cut the run short and went home to shower, and then to the office, hoping to distract myself with the perpetual paperwork.

At my desk at 3MB, I braced myself. First, I needed to get a potentially difficult conversation out of the way. I called the cell number Sheriff Taylor had given me.

After an exchange of good mornings, he said, "No signs of Brown returning to town here. I swung by their place this morning. The house is all closed up, like nobody's there at all. And no hits on our BOLO yet."

I didn't bother to fill him in on where Mrs. Brown was. Not yet.

"Did you learn anything else about him?" I asked, oh so innocently.

"As a matter of fact, we got his laptop from the house."

I sat forward in my chair, ready to offer the services of Derek the Geek.

But the sheriff said, "Had my tech guy look at it."

Ah, apparently they had their own geek. I shouldn't underestimate his small-town staff.

"Well, he's my fourteen-year-old nephew," the sheriff said, "but he's a genius with computers."

I swallowed a snort. "Lemme guess, he found porn sites."

"Oh yeah. But even more interestin' were some old emails. Brown thought he'd deleted them, but my nephew knew how to find 'em. Going back to six years ago, when..." he paused, probably building suspense, but I already knew what was coming, "he *sold* Cissy to some guy whose email address starts with misterporn."

I pretended to be surprised, then said, "When did you find this out?"

A pause. "Um, yesterday afternoon."

"With all due respect, Sheriff, why didn't you get this info to me sooner?"

A longer pause, then the sound of air being blown out. "Honestly, I, uh... Look, I thought of Joe Brown as a friend. I was just a deputy when all this happened back then. And he seemed real broken up 'bout Cissy takin' off. We used to meet on Fridays after work and get a couple a beers. And he'd get all maudlin after a bit, goin' on about how he loved that girl like his own."

My mind flashed to Kate and how trying to work together again seemed to have destroyed our budding friendship.

"It's rough," I said, "when the job intersects with our personal lives."

"Yes, and that happens all too often in a small town," the sheriff said. "My cousin's in my drunk tank as we speak. Anyway, I'm sorry I didn't tell ya sooner...I guess I needed a little time, ya know, to get used to the idea."

I made what I hoped was a sympathetic noise. "Well, thanks for filling me in."

And now I couldn't tell him about Mrs. Brown showing up late yesterday, not without admitting that I'd already known he suspected her husband had sold Cissy. A touch of guilt tightened my chest.

I ignored it and signed off with the sheriff, promising to let him know if Joe Brown made another appearance in Starling. I hung up the phone and sighed.

At least now Taylor was aggressively pursuing evidence against Brown. A woman scorned had nothing on a law enforcement officer who's been made to feel like a fool.

Did Cissy know, on some level at least, that her stepfather had trafficked her to an abuser? What a great way for him to make sure she never slipped and told someone she'd witnessed her friend's death—sell her to a pervert who would take her to another state.

My gut twisted. I had a strong suspicion that Brown would show up in Starling. He'd want to silence the person whose testimony could put him in prison for a very long time.

Then another thought hit me. Had he already silenced the younger daughter, whom he'd most likely also been abusing?

Was there another grave now, in those woods where Cissy and Kristen had once played?

I called the weekend watch sergeant and told him to bring in extra uniforms to patrol the streets.

To hell with the overtime budget.

"I want that girl found," I said. "*Today.* And remind everyone that she's more a victim than a perp. I don't want her hurt if it can be helped."

"Got it, Chief," the sarge said and disconnected.

I was hanging up my desk phone's receiver when Kate appeared in my doorway. My mouth fell open before I could catch myself.

"I figured you'd be in today," she said. "My mom had another appointment this morning, on this side of Jacksonville, so I thought I'd stop by."

Stop by why? Cissy was gone.

The worrisome thought crossed my mind that Kate's mother sure was having a lot of medical appointments lately, and on a Saturday morning yet. Was something wrong with her?

Kate leaned forward. "Um, I wanted to apologize."

Apologize for what? I was the one who'd been obnoxious.

I opened my mouth, but Barnes appeared in my open doorway, in uniform.

"What are you doing here?" I blurted out. So much for a peaceful morning, catching up on paperwork.

"Interview with a potential clerk." She waved a hand in the air, as if shooing away that topic. "An officer just spotted Cissy, and that guy Johnny, going into a motel."

I jumped up. "Where?"

"The Beachview Inn."

"Why the hell would they go back there?"

At the same moment, Kate said, "I'm going with." She'd also risen from her chair.

I spun toward her. A tumble of emotions cascaded through my chest and into my stomach, turning the latter queasy—surprise, worry, annoyance, anger. And relief.

Were we still friends? How long would that last if I said no?

My mind flashed to an image of her husband—six-four, two-fifty and all muscle. And yet he was an easygoing guy, until something threatened his wife or family. Then he was known to fly into a rage.

My stomach flip-flopped. I swallowed hard, shook my head, but my mouth said, "You stay in the car."

She nodded, although I wasn't sure if that was acquiescence or only acknowledgment of my words.

There wasn't time to hash that out now, however. I took off for the front hall and the fire stairs at their other end. Kate was right on my heels, with Barnes behind her.

The three of us piled into my compact car and I pulled my makeshift light bubble from under my seat. I jammed it on the roof—it had a strong magnet base that would keep it there—and hit the button for my siren.

Kate's body was tense as she leaned forward in the passenger seat, tugging against her seatbelt. It didn't seem like the right moment to finish our conversation about who was apologizing to whom. Especially since we'd have to yell over the siren. And Barnes was in the backseat.

The latter was on her phone, requesting backup.

"Nobody goes in until I get there," I yelled over my shoulder.

"To answer your question," Kate said in a loud voice, "familiarity."

Ah, my question why the Beachview...

"And/or Johnny knows that clerk," I added, "the one who Spencer had in his pocket. And could get him to keep it quiet that they were there."

"I take it then," Barnes yelled from the backseat, "we won't be stopping at the office for the room number."

I turned off the siren when we were a couple of miles from the old motel. In the parking lot, a police cruiser sat idling near the office, sirens and lights off. I could make out a silhouette in the driver's seat.

I pulled up behind the cruiser. Barnes was already opening her door before I came to a full stop, and Officer Thompson was climbing out of his car.

I spotted Johnny in front of a room, halfway down the length of the motel. "Get back in!" I yelled and hit the accelerator.

Belatedly, I glanced over to make sure I hadn't dumped my assistant onto the pavement. I squealed to a stop in front of that room.

We all clambered out of the car.

"Back in there," I barked, pointing at Kate and then at the passenger door, still hanging open.

She stopped moving but showed no sign of returning to the car.

I shook my head and hustled to join Barnes beside the motel room door. Thompson jogged toward us. I gestured for him to stay back for now.

Barnes raised a foot and mimicked kicking, her eyebrows raised as a question mark.

I held up a finger, then gingerly tried the knob. It didn't budge.

A quiver of anxiety in my chest. We didn't have a warrant. But we did have cause to believe two fugitives were in that room.

Noises behind the door. Was there a back window they could be climbing out of?

Screw this!

I made a circling motion with my hand. Thompson got the message and took off around the end of the building.

"Police. Don't move," I yelled. "We're coming in."

I gestured to Barnes. She shifted in front of the door and raised her foot. I prayed the door was as flimsy as it looked.

It was. And Barnes's heavy oxford was a sufficient battering ram.

The door popped open. "Police," I yelled again, "Don't move."

Barnes pulled her gun and darted through the door, going right. Glock in hand, I went left.

But the young people were standing beside the bed, hands in the air. Cissy's eyes were wide with fright and shiny with tears.

We all froze for a moment.

Then Cissy looked right at me and said, "I remembered the rest of it...of what happened that night."

Cissy was sitting on the bed, with Johnny in the only chair in the room. Both had been instructed to keep their hands where we could see them.

Barnes stood by the open door, her gun holstered but her hand resting on the butt.

I stood at the end of the bed, my gun arm hanging along my side, finger outside the Glock's trigger guard. But I wasn't ready to holster it yet.

"Tell me," I said.

"The first part, that's the same... Feeling disgusted and thinking I'd take a shower." Cissy paused and sucked in air. It came out on a shudder. "Then I saw the knife on the floor and I picked it up. I cut the woman's wrist loose and pushed the knife handle into her hand. I think I had some thought like, 'at least she can defend herself now.'"

She shook her head slightly. "There's a bit of a blank spot still. Next thing I remember, I'm in the shower, washing away the blood. I cleaned up the bathroom, went out and put my dress on, and started wiping all the surfaces we might've touched. Jake always made us do that, wipe everything down." She paused, her eyes glazing over.

"Where was Jake at that point?" I asked, to pull her out of whatever altered state her mind was trying to slip into.

She shook her head again. "He was lying on the bed. At first, I thought he'd fallen asleep."

"And Sara, the other woman?"

"She'd gone in the bathroom. Came out after a while with her clothes on. She handed me a card and said something like,

'You'll probably need this more than me.' I just stuck it in my skirt pocket."

The pools in her eyes overflowed, tears trickling down her cheeks. "That's when I saw the knife and all the blood on the mattress under Jake." She let out a half sob.

Was she *crying* for the man who'd used her for years?

Actually, I could use Kate's help about now. I glanced toward the open doorway. But for once she'd listened and was staying outside. I didn't want to stop Cissy to go get her, though. If I interrupted the flow, the girl might clam up.

Cissy gulped in air. "I don't remember leaving the room. I walked around for a long time. Then I saw a sign that said *Police*, and an arrow. I guess, at some point, I'd looked at the card, because I remember thinking, 'If I'm the police chief, I should go there.'"

Movement out of the corner of my eye. My head whirled toward the doorway.

There, as if I'd conjured her up, stood Kate, a grim expression on her face.

My skin tingled. Something was off.

Barnes stumbled forward, almost falling into Johnny's lap.

Did Kate shove her? Why would she do that?

Then the awkward cant of Kate's head registered. A muscular arm circled her neck, holding it that way.

She jerked forward, and I saw the man behind her—salt and pepper hair and a rugged face—above Kate's head.

I recognized the face. The bogus first sheriff, Cissy's stepfather.

But before I could raise my gun arm, he growled, "Drop it or she's dead."

———◇———

This guy was no hardened criminal, that's for sure.

When he'd ordered me to drop my gun, I'd done so—on the end of the bed. Then I'd taken an exaggerated sideways step away from it.

Didn't he realize I was still within lunging distance of it?

Although I'd need a second or two to get it and aim. And I couldn't do much with Kate's body shielding him. I'd wait for my opening.

"You too," Brown ordered, waving his pistol toward Barnes.

After a nod from me, she carefully removed her service weapon with two fingers and also tossed it on the bed.

Where the hell is Thompson? Was he still out back, oblivious to the fact that we were being held at gunpoint?

Somewhere along the way, Johnny and Cissy had both stood up. Again, they were side by side next to the bed. He seemed to be trying to shoo her behind him.

But she was frozen in place, staring. "Daddy?"

The man grinned. "Yes, baby, it's me."

Her face had brightened, but her mouth was still frowning.

"Come over here." He gestured with his gun hand. "You and me and your sister, we're gonna take a nice trip."

"Don't move, Cissy," I ordered, praying our backup would get here soon.

Brown glared at me as he kicked the door closed behind him. It slammed, then bounced back open a few inches, the latch plate torn from the frame by Barnes's earlier kick.

Movement in my peripheral vision again. I caught myself before turning my head, glanced sideways instead. A teen girl's face, peeking up from the bottom of the window.

Relief washed through me. The sister was alive.

"I told you to come here," Brown ordered.

"Cissy," my voice was sharp, "I'm quite sure he plans to hurt you, like he did your friend Kristen."

Both stepdaughter and stepfather turned their faces toward me, confusion on the first, rage filling the second.

Then Brown glared at Cissy. "I told you never to tell no one."

She was shaking her head vehemently. "I didn't, Daddy, I swear."

"She probably doesn't remember telling us," Kate said. "She was in a fugue state."

"Shut the fuck up," Brown yelled, tightening his arm around her neck.

My stomach heaved. I had to do something soon or someone was going to get hurt, or worse. Hardened criminal he may not be, but he was a desperate one.

De-escalate... de-escalate...

"Look, you don't want to be shooting any cops here," I said, in what I hoped was a soothing voice. "You know the manhunt will be relentless, until they find you. You just want to get away clean, right?"

Brown was gaping at me, his mouth slightly open.

A high voice from outside the room, the words indistinct. Was it the younger girl? Or Wellbourne? I glanced at the window again without turning my head. The face had disappeared.

I held out a hand in a placating gesture. "We can't let you take the girls. But we'll let *you* go if you release the woman." I couldn't say Kate's name. I was afraid I'd choke up.

And I didn't want him to know "the woman" meant something to me.

Brown's expression turned sly. "Nope, the girls come with me, and so does this lady. Our guarantee that you won't follow. I hear sirens or spot a cop car and she dies." He tightened his grip on Kate's neck again, and she gasped for air.

He started backing toward the door. "Come on, Cissy. Your sister's waiting."

I glanced at the window again. The girl was gone. Instead Wellbourne's light brown, freckled face was looking right at me. Her out-of-control spirals of red-brown curls never looked so beautiful.

But I'd allowed my eyes to linger too long. Joe Brown turned partway toward the window, dragging Kate with him and recklessly swinging his gun around.

I was about to pounce on my Glock, when Cissy took a step forward.

"I'll go, Daddy." Her voice shook. "Please, please, don't hurt anyone else."

"No!" Johnny's voice, and something whizzed past my ear.

A gunshot roared.

CHAPTER TWENTY-SIX

I grabbed my Glock from the bed and brought my shoulder up under Brown's gun arm.

Yelping, he let go of Kate and stumbled backward. She staggered to the side.

His gun slid from his hand as he hunched over, his other arm wrapped across his middle like he was in pain. Had Kate elbowed him?

The door crashed in, and Bradley and two uniforms stormed into the room. Brown crumpled on top of his pistol.

A quick glance at Kate. She'd landed on her butt on the carpet, but nodded that she was okay.

Barnes had also grabbed up her weapon and had it trained on Brown. But he hadn't moved.

His own pistol drawn, Bradley grabbed the man's shoulder and tugged. Brown flopped over in a pool of blood, a knife sticking out of his side.

That's what whizzed past my ear.

Bradley scooped up the gun.

Brown's hands were wrapped around the knife's handle. "Take it out," he groaned.

"No!" I yelled. "That will make it bleed worse."

Bradley uncurled Brown's bloody fingers from the knife and cuffed him in front. "Paramedics are right behind us," he huffed out. Then he shed his jacket and ripped off his shirt to stuff around the knife, trying to stem the flow of blood.

I turned back to Kate. She was struggling to her feet. "Check Cissy."

Both the young woman and Johnny had disappeared below the edge of the bed. I scrambled around it to find Cissy kneeling next to him. Johnny lay on his back, his shirtfront bright red, a hole in his chest pulsing blood.

I grabbed the sheet off the bed. It was gray and threadbare. Praying it was clean, I wadded it up and jammed it against Johnny's wound. "Hang in there. You're gonna be okay."

I wasn't at all sure I believed that. The bullet hole was close to his heart.

But he wasn't paying attention to me. His eyes were on Cissy. She held his hand, tears streaming down her face.

He glanced my way, then back at her. "I did it. Don't blame Cissy." His voice was strained. "Jake was passed out. I saw the knife and..." he coughed and blood trickled from the corner of his mouth, "...figured this was our chance...to get away..."

A fist closed around my heart. "Shh, shh, don't talk," I said in a soothing voice. But my stomach was churning. The hole in his chest wasn't the only issue. The kid was bleeding internally.

"I stabbed him..." Johnny's voice was barely a whisper now.

"Shh, don't say anymore," I repeated. "An ambulance is on the way." I vowed silently to get this kid the best lawyer in town.

He looked up at Cissy, a goofy smile on his face. "I love you."

"Stop lying to protect me," she said, kissing his hand. "It's okay. I remembered. That other woman stabbed him."

I knew he wasn't lying, though. But I couldn't bring myself to tell Cissy that Sara hadn't dealt the fatal blow, Johnny had.

And then it didn't matter.

Johnny's eyes lost their light and his muscles went limp.

"Wait!" Wellbourne's voice from the door.

Confusion for a second—who was she yelling at? Then a young teen raced into the room.

"Cissy!" She leapt over her stepfather's legs, threw herself at Cissy. And they were hugging each other tight, laughing and crying at the same time.

A weak smile tugged at my mouth. At least Audrey Brown would be getting both her little girls back.

My gaze drifted to Johnny's blank face, and my throat tightened. I hadn't had a chance to tell him that his parents had loved him, had missed him every day—as I missed Meredith.

A vise closed around my chest. Someone was sobbing.

Kate's arm slipped across my shaking shoulders, and I realized with horror that the sobbing was coming from me.

I swallowed hard and ducked my head so the uniforms wouldn't see my wet cheeks.

CHAPTER
TWENTY-SEVEN

It was Sunday, but I was at my desk anyway, to tie up loose ends from the Spencer homicide case and catch up on the paperwork that had backed up some over the last week.

I had ordered that Sara Sanders be booked for failure to report a felony but not for obstruction of justice, since she had cooperated, more or less. And I'd called the Assistant State Attorney's office, hoping no one would be in. The ASA and I tended to rub each other the wrong way.

My wish was granted, and I'd left a voicemail letting her know that Sara had assaulted Spencer but it could well be considered self-defense, and perhaps in light of all that had happened, the failure to report could be knocked down to a misdemeanor.

I knew I'd get a return call on Monday, reminding me that it was the ASA's office that determined charges, not the police. But the ASA was ultimately a fair woman. She would probably show Sara some mercy.

I'd also approved the rotation of officers assigned to guard Joseph Brown in the hospital, where he was recovering from his knife wound.

Unfortunately, Officer Thompson was in the hospital as well, with a concussion. Cissy's sister had told us that "Daddy" had asked her to distract the police officer. She'd done so by pretending she was lost, then watched in horror as her stepfather came up from behind and knocked Thompson out with the butt of his gun.

On TV, people wake up and act like everything is fine a few minutes after such a blow. In real life, if the person's hit hard enough to knock them out, there's often brain damage, quite possibly permanent.

Thompson had regained consciousness after a few minutes, but he was far from okay. The most his doctors would say was they were guardedly optimistic. So another assault of a police officer charge had been added to our long list of charges against Brown.

And we weren't the only ones with such a list. When I'd called Sheriff Taylor last night to give him the news that Brown was in custody, he'd indicated he would be requesting immediate extradition.

That argument—who would get first crack at Brown—I was more than happy to leave to the ASA. Either way, it was unlikely he would ever see the light of day outside of prison walls.

Now, I should be tackling the backed-up paperwork.

But instead, I was staring into space, thinking about Meredith.

Or rather, thinking about the fact that I *always* thought about her, every single day. For a fleeting moment, at least, before shoving the thought aside. Those thoughts were so woven into the fabric of my life, I'd stopped noticing them years ago.

My personal phone pinged. I picked it up from my desk. A text from Kate.

Is this a good time to talk?

I glanced at the incident report awaiting my review on my computer. *Oh yes, this is a great time to talk!* Anything to delay the paperwork.

I picked up the phone and tapped the icon to call her.

"Hey there," she said, sounding a bit breathless, "I'm packing to fly home later today, but I wanted to touch base before I go."

Not being sure what the polite response was to that, I kept quiet.

"So, how are you doing?" Kate asked.

Okay, that question I could handle. "I'm good. How about you?"

"Not bad, all things considered. Although that's a little more excitement than I'm used to these days. But I slept well last night, knowing Cissy was back with her family."

Wish I could say the same, I thought. I'd had a couple of nightmares last night, including one in which Aunt Jean and my dead mother had ganged up on me.

"I talked to Cissy's mom," I said, "before they left last night, and pointed out that she would need counseling, as will the younger girl. She seemed to get it."

"Good." A pause. "If only Johnny could've had the same outcome." Kate's voice was now mournful.

I sighed. "In his case, though, he'd be facing a murder charge."

"Wouldn't all that Jake had done to him, wouldn't that be mitigating circumstances?"

"Yes," I said, "and the charge may very well have been knocked down to second degree, or maybe even manslaughter. But Jake wasn't an immediate threat. Johnny could've just walked away."

Coulda, woulda, shoulda. My Aunt Jean's voice in my head.

Would I have done anything differently than Johnny had, if I'd been in that position? Probably not. I'd want to make sure the monster couldn't come after me.

"You're positive then," Kate said, "that he was telling the truth, that he was Jake's killer?"

"That's the most likely scenario. The knife he threw at Joe Brown, it was the murder weapon. A switchblade, with a six-inch blade. It had traces of dried blood on it—Jake's aka Spencer's type, AB positive. DNA will likely confirm it's his."

I made a mental note to talk to Barnes about checking people's socks when she frisked them. I suspected that was where Johnny had been carrying the knife. Or he might have hidden it somewhere, so he wouldn't get caught with it on him.

And I needed to talk to the mayor and city council. If they wouldn't give my department its own building, we at least needed to reconfigure the entrance to the third floor to make it more secure.

Why hadn't John Black done more to protect his people from potential threats? I made a scoffing noise as I answered my own question—because he was best buddies with the low-lifes.

"Judith, you there?"

"Oh sorry, I got distracted. Um, we also found Spencer's credit cards, some cash, and a disposable cell phone in Johnny's pockets. We believe he drove Spencer's car into town, took the wallet and the phone and then walked to 3MB, looking for Cissy."

"I think he really was in love with her," Kate said. "Otherwise, he would've taken off."

"Yeah...Hey, I have a question for you," I said.

"Shoot."

"Johnny seemed shocked, even wept some, when I showed him Spencer's, aka Uncle Jake's autopsy picture. Was he faking all that? It seemed sincere at the time."

"It probably was. He'd been with Jake for a decade. In a weird way, they would've bonded as a family unit."

"Stockholm Syndrome."

"Yes, but there's more to it than that. Humans need to belong. And if they can't belong in a group or with someone who is healthy, they'll bond to people who are unhealthy, just so they can belong."

"Like gangs," I said. "That's a big part of the appeal to poor kids with dysfunctional families."

"Exactly. But that didn't change the fact that Jake was abusing and controlling them. Johnny wanted to protect Cissy, get her away from all that."

"He was likely afraid of how far Jake might eventually go with that knife. It sounded like Jake was escalating."

"Yes," Kate agreed. "But even so, Johnny would've mourned the loss of the attachment, the sense of family, he'd had with him."

"Makes sense, I guess."

I wondered what would've happened if Cissy hadn't developed amnesia—if she didn't have my business card, hadn't found her way to the police station. Johnny would have found her, hiding somewhere. Or maybe she would've stayed at the motel, so programmed to being controlled that she would wait for someone to come and take over.

I imagined her sitting in that straight-back chair, a dazed look on her face. Only my brain decided to substitute Meredith's face for Cissy's. My heart squeezed.

And a strangled noise managed to escape my lips.

"Judith, you okay?"

"Yes...um, is Skip still taking new cases?"

"Well, the PI agency is, but he only works certain ones. Why?"

"I think I'd like to hire him, but I'd want *him* to work it, if he's willing." I thought about his partner and her husband. "Or Rose and Mac. Nobody else."

A beat of silence, then she asked, "What do you want them to do?"

"Uh, do you have plenty of time right now?"

"Sure, no problem. I take it you have a long story to tell."

"Yeah." I took a deep breath. "I want them to find my cousin, Paul's sister."

AUTHOR'S NOTES

If you enjoyed this book, please take a moment to leave a short review on the book retailer of your choice. Reviews help with sales and sales keep the stories coming. You can readily find the links to these retailers at the *misterio press* bookstore (https://misteriopress.com/bookstore/).

This is Book 5 in this series; Book 1 is *Lethal Assumptions*, and Book 4 (the one just prior to this one) is *Felony Murder*. The next installment, Book 6, will hopefully be out in late winter/early spring, 2025. It is tentatively titled *Founders, Keep Her* (excerpt below).

This book was proofread by multiple sets of eyes, but proofreaders are human. If you noticed any errors, please email me at kass@kassandralamb.com so I can have them corrected.

Heck, email me anyway. I love hearing from readers!

And you may want to sign up for my newsletter at http s://kassandralamb.com to get a heads up about new releases, plus special offers and bonuses for subscribers. You will receive a free novelette, *The Tell-Tale Bark*, the prequel to the Marcia Banks and Buddy cozy series, AND a free novella, *Sweet Sanctuary*, the prequel to my Kate Huntington Mysteries. The C.o.P. on the Scene Mysteries are a spinoff from this series. Judith is a secondary character in that series, first showing up in Book 4, and playing a more extensive role in most of the books after that.

Also, *misterio press* has a readers' group on Facebook (https ://www.facebook.com/groups/misteriopressmysteries) where we chat with readers and also offer giveaways, contests and other goodies. Please stop by and check it out!

Let me spread around some gratitude here, and then I have some interesting background info for you. First, a huge thank you to my sister authors at *misterio press*, Shannon Esposito and Kirsten Weiss, who helped me polish this story with their great feedback and proofreading. And an extra thank you to Shannon, the co-founder of *misterio*, who is also now writing police procedurals. As always, we prop each other up and keep each other going on this sometimes twisted journey!

Also much gratitude always to editor Marcy Kennedy, from whom I have learned so much about writing, and to Melinda VanLone who continues to make my internal visions for book covers become eye-catching realities. And last but never least, love and gratitude to my husband who does my final proof-reads. Any mistakes you may have noticed are not his fault. I have a tendency to keep tweaking and monkeying with things, and I sometimes introduce new typos after his work is done.

I hope fans of my Kate Huntington series enjoyed her contributions to Judith's investigation. I felt quite nostalgic as I wrote the parts that included her. If you haven't read that series yet, you can find the first book, *Multiple Motives* on most ebook retailers for only 99 cents.

As Kate says, dissociative fugue is a very real and very rare psychological disorder. I have only seen one case of it, in a student. The story Kate tells is based on my real experience with that student, with some details changed to protect anonymity.

This kind of amnesia, for one's entire previous life and one's own identity even, presents a very different kind of mystery to the law enforcement personnel and mental health professionals who try to help. They must painstakingly piece together not only where the person came from but who they might be.

Fortunately, in many of these rare cases, the person spontaneously recalls their identity and history, but they then are often amnesiac for everything that happened while they were in the fugue state.

This was the case with my student. She had no idea where she had gone nor what she had done during the two months she was absent from her normal life. Often times that information is never retrieved.

It is a disorder that fascinates mental health professionals (but of course is quite distressing for those who suffer from it). And I thought it would be interesting to make it the focal point of a fictional plot.

The subplots in this story, I'm afraid, did not develop quite as smoothly as the main plot. I hope you are not too frustrated with the fact that they aren't totally tied up at the end of this book. I do intend to continue the saga of the former police chief's flight from accountability in the next story.

The other subplot, regarding Judith's abducted cousin, sprang forth from my brain mid-book. I love when that happens, but it can also be a little disconcerting. Here I thought I knew this hard-nosed (but a bit gooey on the inside) cop, and then this tidbit of her history reveals itself.

The search for Meredith will definitely continue in the next book, and while progress will be made, Judith, Paul, and Aunt Jean may or may not find out what ultimately happened to her until some future book.

Actually, the seed for this subplot idea was planted by an article I read recently, describing the reunion of an abducted child with her biological parents fifty years after she was taken!

But we will have to wait and see the outcome for Meredith.

Ironically, long before that subplot idea was hatched, I had already planned the basic plot of my next C.o.P. on the Scene mystery—the disappearance of a two-year-old on Founders' Day in Starling, Florida.

The National Center for Missing and Exploited Children has just this past month—October, 2024—celebrated its 40th anniversary. (Their hotline number is 1-800-THE-LOST.) This organization has found over 400,000 missing children during the last four decades. And with new DNA technology, they will be able to help even more families who have suffered the ultimate nightmare, a child gone missing.

And speaking of new technology, there are indeed new Rapid DNA devices that have automated many aspects of DNA analysis and can produce results in a couple of hours. Slowly but surely, law enforcement agencies around the country are acquiring these devices, which are often game changers in their efforts to solve crimes.

I have no clue if the FDLE labs around Florida have these devices yet, but hey, this is fiction, so I can bequeath one upon the Jacksonville regional office. Also, please note that Dot Wilder is not the real-life Special Agent in Charge of that FDLE office. She is a fictional character.

Please stay tuned for my next story in the C.o.P. on the Scene Mysteries. Here's a short excerpt:

~~

CHAPTER ONE

I do not normally wish my life away. But today I was wishing it was tomorrow...the day *after* Founders Day.

The annual celebration of the incorporation of the City of Starling, Florida had been described by one of my officers as "a second Fourth of July, only with even more drunk and disorderlies."

And domestic violence calls, when some of those drunks went home and got disorderly with their families. And lost children. So far we had reconnected three minors—two girls and a boy, ranging from ages four to ten—with their parents.

I pulled at the neck of my uniform shirt. Mid-August in Florida was not the best time to be decked out in one's dress blues. But I'd ordered everyone, even my detectives, to wear their uniforms, to make our presence as obvious as possible. Hopefully to avoid problems, and also to make it easier for folks with problems to spot us in the crowd.

The sun was now setting, but it seemed to be getting hotter, or at least muggier. Dusk settling over the city meant that the parade of boats was about to start—the final fanfare of the celebration when local boat owners sailed slowly along the Sofki River, their boats alight with decorations, mostly patriotic displays of flags and eagles.

Now, the city's entire population of eleven thousand souls, plus several hundred tourists, was crowding onto the river-walk to watch the flotilla. I keyed my radio. "Armstrong, Bradley, make sure your people are watching for pickpockets."

An ear-splitting scream temporarily silenced the noisy crowd. Then the sea of people parted as a frantic woman surged toward me, dragging a two-seater baby stroller behind her.

"Officer, you've got to help me. My little girl is gone!"

———◦———

My radio crackled with static. "Divers are on their way." Bradley's voice.

I turned away from the mother I'd been trying to both console and interview. "Can they even search in the dark?" I whispered into the radio.

"They say yes. They have lights, but it will be slow going."

I turned back, and said for the umpteenth time, "We're going to find her." But I wasn't as confident as I hoped I sounded.

This wasn't the same as the other kids, who had presented themselves to an officer when they'd realized they were sepa-rated from their parents.

This was a two-year-old. She'd pulled loose from her mother's hand and shoved through the legs in front of her, moving toward the riverwalk's railing.

The mother had called after her and had tried to follow, but people were slow to move aside to let her double-wide stroller through. Only when she'd screamed had they realized she wasn't just trying for a better view.

"My God," the woman sobbed now. "You can't know what it's like, to have to choose between your kids. I couldn't leave the baby..." She trailed off and cried harder.

No, I couldn't know, because I'd never had kids, but... "Of course you couldn't," I murmured.

Why the hell did you let her out of the stroller? I thought.

I spotted Jenny Coleman pushing her way through the crowd and breathed out a sigh. She was a social worker and the head of Children and Family Services for this area. She would take the mother off my hands, before I slipped and said some of my not-so-understanding thoughts out loud.

I introduced the two women and Mrs. Brailoch practically collapsed into Jenny's arms. "She insisted on walking. She hates the stroller," she sobbed out.

I rolled my eyes behind her back, and Jenny pursed her lips. "Come on," she said in a soothing voice. "Let's get you and the baby out of this chaos."

Good idea! The nine-month-old had been crying for the last ten minutes, picking up on his mother's tension. But she had barely noticed.

I took a deep breath and decided I should cut her a break. Indeed, I had no idea what she was going through, or why she'd made the choices she'd made. And where the hell was her husband? It was a Saturday, so he shouldn't be at work...but maybe he was. Not everybody worked nine to five, Monday through Friday. All I'd gotten out of the mom was that he was an accountant.

I pulled out my phone and texted Jenny. See if you can find out where the father is.

The phone pinged in my hand. But it wasn't Jenny responding. It was a text from my assistant.

Chief, found something you need to see.

As I approached, I immediately noticed that Officer Gloria Barnes was not her usual neat self. Her uniform was rumpled after a day of herding pedestrians, and several tufts of dark hair had pulled loose from her bun and hung in frizzy clumps around her face.

The expression on that face was the grimmest I'd ever seen on her as she pointed to something on the railing of the riverwalk. We were about a hundred yards south of the spot where the little girl's mother had lost track of her.

And there, perched on the top of the railing, was a teddy bear. The pink sunglasses the mother had said little Ashley was wearing were balanced on his nose.

———◇———

ABOUT THE AUTHOR

Kassandra Lamb has never been able to decide which she loves more, psychology or writing. In college, she realized that writers need a day job in order to eat, so she studied psychology. After a career as a psychotherapist and college professor, she is now retired and can pursue her passion for writing.

She spends most of her time in an alternate universe with her characters. The portal to that universe, aka her computer, is located in Florida, where her husband and dog catch occasional glimpses of her.

Kass has completed the ten-book, traditional mystery series, The Kate Huntington Mysteries (set in her native Maryland, about a psychotherapist/amateur sleuth), plus four Kate on Vacation novellas (with the same main characters). She is also the author of the thirteen-book Marcia Banks and Buddy cozy mystery series, about a service dog trainer and her sidekick and mentor dog, Buddy, set in north central Florida.

And she has started a new series of police procedurals, with Lieutenant Judith Anderson from the Kate Huntington series as the main character in the C.o.P. on the Scene Mysteries (four books out with more to come). Judith moves to northern Florida to become the Chief of Police of a small city, and just eight days on the job, she finds herself one step behind a serial killer.

To read and see more about Kassandra and her books, please go to https://kassandralamb.com. Once there, be sure to sign up for the newsletter to get a heads up about new releases, plus special offers and bonuses for subscribers (and free stories).

Kass's e-mail is kass@kassandralamb.com and she loves hearing from readers! She's also on Facebook and Goodreads, and she blogs about psychological topics and other random things at https://misteriopress.com.

Kassandra also writes romantic suspense under the pen name of Jessica Dale.

~~

Please check out these other great *misterio press* series:

Karma's A Bitch: Pet Psychic Mysteries
by Shannon Esposito

Multiple Motives: Kate Huntington Mysteries
by Kassandra Lamb

The Metaphysical Detective: Riga Hayworth
Paranormal Mysteries
by Kirsten Weiss

Dangerous and Unseemly: Concordia Wells
Historical Mysteries
by K.B. Owen

Murder, Honey: Carol Sabala Mysteries
by Vinnie Hansen

Payback: Unintended Consequences Romantic Suspense
by Jessica Dale

Full Mortality: Nikki Latrelle Mysteries
by Sasscer Hill

Buried in the Dark: Frankie O'Farrell Mysteries
by Shannon Esposito

Her Little Secret: Detective Mila Harlow Mysteries
by Shannon Esposito

To Kill A Labrador: Marcia Banks and Buddy
Cozy Mysteries
by Kassandra Lamb

Lethal Assumptions: C.o.P. on the Scene Mysteries
by Kassandra Lamb
Never Sleep: Chronicles of a Lady Detective
Historical Mysteries
by K.B. Owen
Bound: Witches of Doyle Cozy Mysteries
by Kirsten Weiss
At Wits' End: Doyle Cozy Mysteries
by Kirsten Weiss
Steeped In Murder: Tea and Tarot Mysteries
by Kirsten Weiss
The Perfectly Proper Paranormal Museum
Mysteries
by Kirsten Weiss
Big Shot: The Big Murder Mysteries
by Kirsten Weiss
Steam and Sensibility: Sensibility Grey
Steampunk Mysteries
by Kirsten Weiss
Maui Widow Waltz: Islands of Aloha Mysteries
by JoAnn Bassett
Plus even more great mysteries/thrillers in the *misterio press* bookstore.

Made in United States
North Haven, CT
24 November 2024

60853474R00143